Austin suddenly felt like he'd just been kicked in the gut.

He'd been too long on the cynical frontier. He couldn't remember the last time he'd met someone so trusting, so lacking in guile. "Do you have any idea how beautiful you are, Emily Kendall?" he asked softly. "What a face and figure like yours can do to a man's insides?"

Emily hunched the jacket closer around her shoulders. Austin's words were making her feel all topsy-turvy inside. "I'll have to ask you to stop talking like that, Mr. Matthews. I'm sure it's highly improper." Her voice dropped to a bare whisper.

Austin's last breath had stopped dead in his throat. She looked small, enveloped in his coat. Her lips, full and the color of wild chokecherries, trembled slightly. "I'll show you something that's improper," he said huskily, reaching out for her....

Dear Reader,

This month brings you *The Sorceress*, by popular author Claire Delacroix, an intriguing medieval tale of dreams and magic. It's the prequel to the author's *Romance of the Rose*, the first of the Rose series.

And from Merline Lovelace comes the next book in her Destiny's Women trilogy, *Siren's Call*, the story of an Athenian sea captain and the Spartan widow he claims as his captive. And when Rafe Sugarman returns home to Mississippi, he finds peace in the arms of Serena Quinn, in *The Sugarman*, by author Mary McBride.

And last but not least, our fourth title this month is *Brides for Sale* by Ana Seymour, a rollicking Western where a woman arrives in Seattle with high hopes for a respectable marriage and ends up falling for the town's most notorious bachelor.

As always, Harlequin strives to bring our readers the finest stories and the most memorable characters. We hope you enjoy them.

Sincerely,

Tracy Farrell

Senior Editor
Harlequin Historical

Please address questions and book requests to:
Harlequin Reader Service
U.S.: 3010 Walden Ave., P.O. Box 1325, Buffalo, NY 14269
Canadian: P.O. Box 609, Fort Erie, Ont. L2A 5X3

ANA SEYMOUR

BRIDES for Sale

Harlequin Books

TORONTO • NEW YORK • LONDON
AMSTERDAM • PARIS • SYDNEY • HAMBURG
STOCKHOLM • ATHENS • TOKYO • MILAN
MADRID • WARSAW • BUDAPEST • AUCKLAND

ISBN 0-373-28838-7

BRIDES FOR SALE

Books by Ana Seymour

Harlequin Historicals

The Bandit's Bride #116
Angel of the Lake #173
Brides for Sale #238

ANA SEYMOUR

has been a Western fan since her childhood—the glory days of the shoot-'em-up movie matinees and television programs. She has followed the course of the Western myth in books and films ever since, and says she was delighted when the cowboys started going off into the sunset with their ladies rather than their horses. A native Minnesotan, Ana tries to share her love of history with her two teenage daughters.

"For there is no friend like a sister...."

This one's for you, Barbara Jane

Prologue

Seattle, Washington Territory—1864

Austin Matthews stepped out into the chilly October night and slammed the Occidental Hotel's ornate door behind him. He cleared the wooden sidewalk in one long, angry stride, then stopped to take a deep breath. The end of the cheroot in his mouth was ground into a shapeless mass. He threw it to the ground in disgust.

"Damn Mercer for a priggish bastard!" Austin said under his breath. He had been too upset to notice the woman sitting on the iron bench in back of him, and flinched when she addressed him.

"The meeting didn't go well, I take it." The woman's voice was almost as low as a man's. It vibrated in the night air like the low purr of a cougar.

Austin turned. Flo was in the shadows, but her voice was unmistakable. And even in the dark he could recognize her bright red hair. His angry features relaxed a bit. "Have you been waiting for me all this time?" he asked her.

Florence McNeil stood up gracefully. She stepped out of the blackness of the hotel porch and down into the street. She was an extraordinarily tall woman, her eyes on a level with Austin's. In the dim moonlight, her expression was grave. "I've a lot at stake, too, lovey," she said, taking his arm.

The tense muscles of his arm eased under her gentle grip. "It's not as if I believe the man can do what he says." Austin started walking up the street, slowing his natural pace in deference to Flo's ever-pinching shoes. "But the idiots are lined up in there like shantyboys on payday, all of them aching to throw away three hundred dollars for one of Asa Mercer's untouched belles."

"Three hundred dollars!" Flo's deep voice rose a full octave.

Austin's scowl was replaced with his much more customary grin. "Three hundred dollars. A cheap price for an unsullied, New England-bred bride, according to Mr. Mercer. Blue bloods, all, he's in there telling them. And they're lapping it up like hound dogs at a leaky still."

Flo met Austin's restored good humor with her own generous smile. "They *are* idiots," she agreed. "Of course, when you've got ten men for every woman, the market gets a bit pricey."

"Hell, at our place they can get as many women as they want for three dollars apiece."

"They can get a *woman*, Austin, but not a *wife*," Flo corrected him gently.

"Same thing."

Flo sighed. It had taken her a long time to stop her heart from overworking itself every time Austin Matthews came near. It still did a little sideways leap every now and then when he dressed that gorgeous ex-logger's body of his in those fancy duds he'd brought back from San Francisco. But it had taken her brain less than a day's acquaintance to realize that this was one man who was not the settling down kind. Not marriage, not love, not even consistency.

Austin Matthews was more than generous when sharing his considerable expertise and well-honed body with the ladies of his choosing. But when it came to commitment, he was the most hardcase miser she'd ever met.

"Well, it can't hurt business *that* much," Flo said soothingly. "Saturday nights I have to turn 'em away. A few dozen brides isn't going to make much difference to a town growing as fast as this one."

"The man claims he's bringing back five hundred of them—a whole shipload of sour-faced old maids just itchin' to start in a-naggin' at the good men of Seattle." Austin's grimace didn't quite disguise the handsome features of his face.

Flo reached up one gloved hand to brush a lock of chestnut hair from his forehead. "Now, Austin honey," she said, "if they're as bad as you say, our place will be busier than ever."

Austin's irrepressible humor rose once more to the surface. "I guess you're right. Just 'cause a man's got himself hitched doesn't mean he can't eat a little grass over the fence now and then."

Flo shook her head. "You're a bad man, Austin Matthews," she said with mock reproof.

Austin threw back his head and laughed. Florence McNeil had never been to Scotland, but her voice carried the soft burr of the land of her ancestors, and Austin found it could soothe him out of the thorniest mood. Flo's hair had probably been legitimately red at some point in her life. Now, of course, it was a flaming beacon that could be seen from blocks away. Definitely not a color the good Lord had ever incorporated into any living thing. But Flo's level head and shrewd business sense more than made up for her flamboyant appearance. Though it had been Austin's money that had started the Golden Lady, he readily admitted that it had been Flo's management that had made it prosper. It was now one of the top establishments in Seattle's increasingly notorious Skid Road district.

They walked in silence for a few moments, the lights of the commercial district giving way to faint glows from behind the oil-paper windows of Seattle's hastily built residences. Occasionally a brighter light shone from behind real glass, but curtains were rare. Most amenities had not yet arrived in the fast-growing port and logging town.

"How's he planning to find five hundred women?" Flo asked at last.

"Mercer says there's just a whole passel of ladies back East looking for a man. It appears the war's darn near wiped out the local crop."

Flo nodded soberly. The Civil War that had savaged the eastern half of the nation for three and a half bloody years had not really touched the folks out West, but there was hardly a person who didn't have kin back home who had suffered the loss of a loved one. "Well, they'll surely have their pick out here." She shot her companion a sly look. "Maybe you should consider buyin' yourself one, Austin. Three hundred dollars is practically pocket change for you."

Austin stopped suddenly and swung Flo around to face him. She looked pretty and almost young, her thick layer of powder hidden by the darkness. He leaned over and gave her a resounding kiss on the lips. "I worked hard for my money, Flo, darlin'. And I promise you, if there's one thing I'm sure as Satan *not* gonna spend it on . . . it's a bride."

Chapter One

Seattle, Washington Territory—May, 1866

So you see, Cassie dear, in spite of your worries and that horrible editorial in the *Herald,* Mr. Mercer has been a perfect gentleman. I must admit I feel a few of what Aunt Minnie would call "palpitations" at the thought of our arrival tomorrow at the Port of Seattle, but I just know in my heart that this will be the adventure I have so long awaited. I miss you all. Kiss the babies for me.

Ever your loving sister,
Emily

P.S. I discover that I have left my patent slippers. You could try them with newspaper, but if they just don't fit (tiny thing that you are!), please take them over to the mill and see if one of the girls could use them.

"Look at that woman standing on the dock, Emily. Her hair! Have you ever seen the like?"

Emily hadn't. Not in Lowell. Why, a woman like that would be run clear out of Massachusetts. But they were in the West now, and things were going to be different. Without answering Ida Mae, she took a great deep breath of the salty air and leaned precariously over the ship's rail.

"Emily, don't do that!" her friend implored. "You know it makes my stomach turn over to watch you."

Emily swung from the rail and clicked her heels together in excitement. "We're really here, Ida Mae! We're finally in Washington Territory."

Ida Mae looked doubtfully down at the ramshackle wooden buildings of the waterfront. Like everything else in the bustling frontier port, they had been built with a mind to haste and expediency, rather than aesthetics. The town looked as far removed from the orderly streets and neatly trimmed gardens of Lowell as the moon. "Aye, we're here, Emily, for all it's worth," she said solemnly.

Emily refused to be daunted by her companion's doubts. She planted her feet back squarely on the deck and looked out over the city, her green eyes sparkling. Her gaze rested again on the woman with the distinctive red hair, then shifted to her escort, a broadshouldered, well-dressed man whose features appeared from this distance to be extraordinarily pleasant.

"That's what we've come all this way for, Ida Mae," she said enthusiastically, pointing to the couple. "If all the Washington men are as handsome as that one, we'll have no trouble at all finding the right one. And in the meantime, we'll be having the adventure of our lives."

"Aye, and the adventure starts when these Seattle men that you're so excited to meet discover that there's only forty-six of us, instead of the five hundred they were promised,'' Ida Mae huffed.

She slipped a hanky from her reticule and dabbed at her nose. Something on the ship had caused her to have the snuffles ever since they had left Panama. Or maybe it was something she had picked up on that long trek across the isthmus. Emily hoped that the good pine air of Washington would both clear up the problem and restore her friend's good humor.

"Come on, Ida Mae, let's go see if we can disembark yet." Emily pulled at the dark blue taffeta of Ida Mae's sleeve. Toward the middle of the ship a gangplank had been lowered to the ground. Around the base of it men were beginning to gather in increasing numbers, jostling each other for position and hollering to the ladies still on the ship.

"It's like throwing Christians to the lions," Ida Mae said dourly, but she let herself be led along.

"You were right, Austin," Flo said happily. "You said Mercer couldn't do it, and you were right." With a practiced eye she surveyed the group of eager young ladies lining the rail of the S.S. *Continental*. "Couldn't be more than fifty of them. And not exactly the belles of the ball, if you ask me. Some of them wouldn't be fit for Johnny Faraday's crib houses."

Austin raised an eyebrow at Flo's caustic remark. It was unlike her. Back at the Golden Lady, she was like a mother to the hard-working girls who served up drinks, dances and themselves to the women-starved men of the territory. Of course, the ladies on the ship were supposed to be different, and therein lay the problem. Flo and her girls were the belles of the ball when there were no other women for several thousand square miles. But what was going to happen when these high-class schoolmarm types began lording it about town? Because, Austin decided, taking another long look at the array of females along the rail, besides being uncharitable, Flo's remark was plain wrong. Granted, it had been a long time since he'd seen so many women together in one place, but they looked mighty pretty to him, young and . . . blooming. There was one in particular with hair that turned the color of honey when the sun hit it. She was swinging on the rail like a child, but she was definitely no child.

"Austin!" Flo's soft voice had an unusual harshness. "Will you stop ogling like the rest of these rummies? What are we doing here, anyway? Let's get back to the saloon. I have a feeling business is going to be booming today," she added, and gave her companion's arm a tug.

She might as well have been pulling at one of the massive ship pilings out in the water. Austin's strong body didn't move a hair. "I want to stay and see the fun, Flo," he said with an amused look on his face. He nodded toward the growing group of men at the base of the ship. The jostling had turned into shoving, and the shouts were merging into a loud, angry rumble.

Suddenly a slender, dapper young man emerged from among the women on the deck and held up both hands to quiet the crowd below. Some of the men stopped their pushing to listen to him. One burly fellow in logging clothes toward the front cupped his hands around his mouth and yelled, "Where's our five hundred women, Mercer?"

Asa Mercer looked down at the men without fear. He spoke in loud, clear tones. "I told you I would bring as many as I could, and here they are . . . the finest examples of feminine pulchritude east of the Mississippi.'' He smiled broadly and gestured to the women surrounding him with the flourish of a showman.

"How many?" several of the men below shouted.

The smile faltered just a trifle, but stayed in place. "Forty-six of the loveliest belles you could..."

The rest of his statement was drowned out by a sudden swell of sound from below. Toward the back of the group someone threw a punch, and then another. Almost instantly a full-fledged melee erupted. Austin put an arm around Flo and stepped discreetly back on the bank away from the fray.

Before long, male bodies were flying every which way, many of them dressed, Austin noted, in their Sunday-go-to-meeting clothes. He hadn't seen so many suits since they'd buried Frying Pan Jackson last spring. Frying Pan had been the cook for the largest logging outfit in the territory, but it hadn't been the man they'd been mourning, it had been his flapjacks.

For several moments Austin and Flo watched the action in silence. "I tell you, Austin, we'd better get out of here. Before you know it one of those guys is going to come up here and take a swipe at your pretty face."

"It's not my fight, Flo," he answered calmly.

By now men were surging up the gangplank toward the women, who were clinging to one another in terror. Many of the women were in tears and some were screaming. Austin searched the group for the golden-haired beauty he'd seen before. He found her immediately. She was up against the rail watching the fracas below. Her face, which had been flushed with excitement a few minutes ago, now looked pale and grave.

Someone had thrown two rope boarding ladders against the side of the ship. Men clamored to get up them, and almost instantly the ladies up on deck were engulfed by a sea of males who pushed, pulled and sometimes carried them off the ship.

After several moments, the girl he'd been watching on deck emerged at the edge of the crowd in the clutches of three Irishmen Austin knew from their regular visits to the Golden Lady. One held her in his arms while the other two grasped at whatever part of her they could reach, trying to stake a claim.

"I demand you put me down this instant, you ruffians," Austin heard her say. Her voice was firm and her eyes were dry.

"Excuse me a minute, Flo," Austin said to his partner. He took a powerful leap from the bank that landed him almost directly in front of the struggling girl. She looked at him sharply as though sizing him up to determine if he were another attacker or a source of aid.

"Boys!" Austin shouted to the rusty-haired trio. "Put the lady down!" He would have gotten a greater response had he been yelling at the sea gulls. Austin looked again at the girl. He shot her a grin and a wink, and a flicker of hope entered her extraordinary green eyes. It gave him a surge of energy.

He took a step forward and tapped the nearest Irishman on the shoulder. "I said put her down, lads."

The man spun around, his face florid with exertion. As he tried to focus on the man confronting him, Austin clipped him on the jaw with a short, deadly punch that put him out without another word. When his companion saw what had happened, he grabbed Austin's shoulder and bent low to butt his head into his midsection. Austin immediately brought his knee straight up against the man's chin. There was a sick-ening crack, then the second Irishman slid to the ground.

The man who had been holding the girl dropped her abruptly and threw up his hands. "Take her, man. She's all yars, Matthews," he said in a thick brogue. Without a second glance at his two friends out cold on the pier, he disappeared into the crowd.

Austin looked down at the girl at his feet. Her yel-low muslin dress was soiled and torn at the shoulder. Her hair, which had been neatly piled on her head, now fell down around her shoulders in honeyed waves. Her green eyes blazed. "The nerve of them!" she said in-dignantly, looking over at her two unconscious at-tackers without the least trace of fear.

Austin looked down at her in amusement. "In-deed," he said.

She looked around and seemed to take in her sur-roundings. Behind them the riot still raged, though it appeared that most of the women had found protec-tors, and the remaining mayhem was among the men who had not managed to get near one of them. "Oh, dear," she said somewhat less forcefully.

Austin reached a hand down to help her to her feet. "Welcome to Seattle, miss," he said.

"Kendall, Miss Kendall," she introduced herself automatically, still dazed by the unexpected and vio-lent turn of events.

"We'd best move out of here, Miss Kendall," Aus-tin urged. When she continued to ignore his out-stretched hand, he leaned over and grasped her shoulders, gently pulling her to her feet.

"Yes, of course." Emily looked back at the angry crowd. Mr. Mercer was nowhere in sight. "But where are we to go?"

Austin took a quick survey of the situation. There appeared to be no order at all. "I don't rightly know, miss, but for the time being I would say anywhere but here."

He started to pull her up the bank to where Flo was waiting with narrowed eyes, but she stopped him. "Wait. Ida Mae. I have a friend here. I have to see if she's all right."

Before he could open his mouth to argue with her, she had slipped out of his grasp and headed right back down into the thick of the fighting. Austin watched her incredulously for a few seconds, then he flexed his sore right hand and followed her with an exasperated sigh. The girl might be beautiful, but she was plumb crazy.

Emily spotted Ida Mae immediately. Two well-dressed men had planted themselves on each side of her and were warding off all other comers. Her dress was in ruins, and her plump bosom heaved with sobs.

"Ida Mae," Emily called to her friend.

"Oh, Emily," she managed through her tears, "what are we to do? This horrible place, these horrible men . . ."

Emily reached her friend, and one of the men relinquished his post at Ida Mae's side so that Emily could put her arms around her. "It's all over now, Ida Mae, don't take on so."

"But what are we to *do?* We can't stay here. And what about my piano?"

Ida Mae's prize possession was the enameled traveling piano that her mother had bought in Vienna. It was a veritable work of art, decorated with painted Muses and opening to reveal a mirror and sewing box. Ida Mae had adamantly refused to leave Massachusetts without it.

"Your piano will be fine, Ida Mae. We'll get it later."

The two men who had been guarding Ida Mae looked harmless enough, Emily thought, as they sent guilt-stricken glances at the tears running down Ida Mae's cheeks, and briefer ones at the heaving of her ample breasts. Emily took another look at the situation. There was certainly no one in charge, and Mr. Mercer had disappeared, though she couldn't say she blamed him with the current disposition of the crowd.

"As I was saying, the main thing is to get away from the waterfront," said a calm, deep voice behind her.

Emily turned to face her rescuer. "You are absolutely right, sir. Would you be so kind as to escort my friend and me away from this area?"

"That's what I've been trying to do for several minutes now, miss," Austin answered.

He took her arm again and headed up the bank, followed by Ida Mae and her two defenders. When they reached Flo, he ignored her sour expression and grabbed her arm with his free hand. "Come on, Flo, we're getting out of here."

It was the lady with the shocking hair. Emily had forgotten that she had first seen her handsome rescuer with this woman. She bit her lip. Who were these people? What kind of a situation had she gotten herself into? When she had imagined her Western adventures, somehow she hadn't thought they would begin the second she stepped off the ship.

"Where are we going, Austin?" the red-haired woman asked grumpily.

Austin looked over at her and grinned. "For the time being, I think they'd be safest at our place. What d'ya say, Flo?"

Flo gave the two New Englanders a long, slow look from their starched lace collars to their pointed kid leather shoes. "I say...this is going to be very interesting."

"Lord save us, Emily, it's a saloon!" Ida Mae said in a breath.

Austin was holding open the swinging doors to the Golden Lady and motioning the two new arrivals to enter. His lips twitched with amusement as he watched Emily Kendall's eyes widen, but he kept his expression neutral.

"This is the Golden Lady, and Miss McNeil here and I are the proprietors."

Emily's gaze went across the room to the huge painting that hung behind the gleaming redwood bar. It was of a woman clad in some sort of drapery that covered only the smallest portion of her anatomy. Her fulsome breasts were completely bare.

Austin noted the direction of Emily's glance and gave a careless wave. "The Golden Lady herself," he said nonchalantly.

Ida Mae sounded as if she had choked on her tongue. Emily took a shaky breath. "I'm sorry, Mr. Matthews. We appreciate your help at the pier, but we cannot possibly enter a...an establishment such as this one."

Talk in the bar had stopped, along with the tinkling piano they had heard from outside. Even the clink of glasses had ceased. As her eyes became accustomed to the dim light, Emily could see that the room was about half full of men. The only female in sight was a dark-haired girl who was playing cards with several men at a rear table. She was dressed in a purple silk dress that revealed almost as much of the upper part of her body as the woman in the painting over the bar.

Flo gave an audible sniff and shouldered her way past the two New Englanders to enter the room. Austin patiently continued to hold the door open. "I regret offending your maidenly sensibilities, Miss Kendall, but I think you'd better put aside your principles for the moment before your friend there passes out on the sidewalk."

Emily looked back at Ida Mae. The skin around her tightened lips had turned a frightening bluish-white. She leaned heavily on the arm of one of the men who had helped her on the dock. Emily looked helplessly once more at the flagrant painting, then threw her shoulders back and set her teeth. "Very well, sir, we will avail ourselves of your hospitality until my friend recovers herself."

Under Austin's amused gaze, she walked proudly into the smoky barroom and sat down at the nearest empty table. Still supporting herself on her defender, Ida Mae followed her and sat down heavily with a whoosh of air.

"What can I get you ladies in the way of refreshments?" Austin asked.

"I don't suppose you'd have tea?" Ida Mae asked wanly.

From where she had taken up position behind the big bar, Flo looked over at the group with disgust. But Austin's expression stayed solicitous. "No miss, I'm afraid you're right on that one. Let me see, I could get you—" he looked at a loss for a moment, then his face brightened "—some lemonade."

Ida Mae just sank lower in her chair, but Emily gave their host a polite smile. "Lemonade would be very nice, sir."

"Austin...Austin Matthews, at your service, ladies."

"Thank you, Mr. Matthews. I believe my friend, Miss Sprague, would do well with a glass of lemonade." Emily tried to keep her voice steady and sophisticated, as though she drank lemonade in a saloon every day of her life.

Austin hollered to a stout, gray-haired man who stood at the opposite end of the bar from Flo. "Jasper, could we get some lemonade for these ladies?"

The man's handlebar mustache did a peculiar zigzag jump. "Lemonade, Austin?"

"Yes, please," he answered calmly.

The man shrugged and disappeared behind a door at the back of the bar.

The two men who had accompanied Ida Mae had by now sat down at the table with the two ladies and introduced themselves as Mr. Briggs and Mr. Smedley. Ignoring Ida Mae's obvious lack of interest, they began presenting her with escalating accounts of their prospects in Seattle.

"My house is almost finished, with wood floors and glass windows and the pump not more than ten yards out the back," Mr. Smedley said. He had a round, happy face framed by bushy sideburns that moved from side to side as he talked.

"...The land is already platted, Miss Sprague, and I'm only waiting for the right woman to tell me what she wants in the house of her dreams...." Mr. Briggs' words came tumbling on top of Mr. Smedley's, but neither seemed to mind. Ida Mae ignored them both and dabbed at her nose with a nearly shredded hanky.

Austin remained standing, but leaned over Emily, lifting a booted foot to a rung of her chair. "So, Miss Kendall, you've come to Seattle to find a husband?" he asked with studious politeness.

He towered over her, and Emily wished he'd either sit down or go away. His bent leg nearly touched her. He was wearing fine serge trousers that fit smoothly along the muscles of his upper leg. Emily swallowed. She'd expected the men of Seattle to be clad in denim or something rough, linsey-woolsey, perhaps. She swallowed again. She didn't think she'd ever been quite so close to a man's thigh.

"Miss Kendall?" he asked again.

Emily gave herself a little shake. "We came to Seattle to make new lives for ourselves, Mr. Matthews," she stated. "Many of the ladies you saw on the ship today are war widows."

She was gratified to see that her comment had dimmed the man's falsely charming smile. Though he had been the soul of politeness, she had the feeling that Mr. Austin Matthews was laughing at her, and it was a feeling she didn't like. Any more than she liked the flutters in her stomach when his eyes looked at her as if she were a confectionery treat.

"I'm sorry to hear that," he said gravely. "But you and Miss...uh...Sprague are not...?" He left the question hanging delicately in the air.

"No," Emily answered reluctantly. "Neither Ida Mae nor I has ever been married."

Austin nodded just once. Emily squirmed in her chair. She looked over at Ida Mae, who seemed to have a more natural color now and was actually smiling weakly at Mr. Briggs as he told her in graphic detail about his tannery shop.

"Perhaps we should be going," Emily said. "I don't believe I care for any lemonade, after all, and by now Mr. Mercer should be seeing to the arrangements for our lodging."

Her arm brushed against Austin's side when she started to stand. She had a fleeting impression of a body that was rock hard, a very different feel from the girls she had worked with side by side back at the mill in Lowell.

From the little door behind the bar a woman emerged carrying a tray and two glasses of lemonade. She was even more scandalously dressed than the woman in the purple dress playing cards. One side of the skirt of her taffeta gown was gathered up almost to her waist, revealing a long leg clad in black netting and nothing more.

Emily looked over at Ida Mae and watched her friend's eyes grow wide as the woman approached their table.

The woman gave the visitors a curious glance as she put the glasses down, then turned to complain to Austin. "I'm telling you, Matthews, I'm not doin' Hiram Carter again for any amount of money. He hasn't had a bath in this century, and his rod's so pickled in whiskey, it wouldn't stand up for the President of the United States."

Austin winced, then found himself having to hide a grin at the shocked expression on Emily Kendall's face. Almost immediately, however, her look turned to concern. He followed the direction of her gaze and saw that Ida Mae was slipping slowly under the table, her eyes rolled back in a dead faint.

Smedley and Briggs each grabbed an arm to keep her from sinking out of sight. Emily jumped from her chair and ran to her friend. "Ida Mae!" she cried, reaching to massage her pale cheeks. When there was no response from the inert girl, she looked up helplessly at Austin.

"Your friend needs to lie down, Miss Kendall," he said gently. Without waiting for an argument, he reached over Smedley and lifted Ida Mae easily in his arms. With brisk strides he carried her across the room to a long stairway. The newel post, Emily saw, was carved in the form of yet another scantily clad lady.

Austin shifted Ida Mae in his arms and looked back over his shoulder at Emily as he started up the stairs. "Coming, Miss Kendall?" he asked.

Ida Mae's even breathing had deepened to a gentle snore. Emily stopped pacing the length of the tiny bedroom and sank down in a tufted, perfumed damask chair. This was definitely not how she had imagined her first evening in Seattle, she thought to herself.

Perhaps all the pessimists back home had been right. She had been crazy to get on a ship and travel practically halfway across the world all alone. Her sister, Cassie, and brother-in-law, Joseph, had been horrified when she had told them her plans. But with three new little ones in as many years, even they couldn't deny that their tiny house on the edge of town was getting entirely too crowded.

Of course, when Cassie and Joseph had married, Emily had thought she soon would be establishing a household of her own...with Spencer. Though the

Bennetts had assumed that she and Spencer would live with them in their big brick mansion up on the hill, Spencer had assured Emily that he would see to it that they had a place of their own.

Dear, gentle Spencer. What irony that a man so fine, so dignified, so *peaceful,* should meet his end in a savage barrage of cannon shrapnel during the bloodiest three days in American history. She shuddered. Gettysburg. The war was over now, but she still couldn't even bear to hear the word.

Emily sighed. What *was* she doing here in the middle of what was obviously a bawdy house? The girls back in Lowell would never believe it. Her eyes wandered around the room. A small dressing table held bottles of mysterious-looking oils and unguents. Emily didn't even want to *think* about to what use they might be put in this very room. Over the bed were four small lithographs with the names of the seasons engraved underneath. The seasons were depicted by appropriate outdoor scenes and four beautiful maidens, each again clad only in drapery. Dear Lord, didn't the women of the West ever wear clothes?

Emily's thoughts were interrupted by a soft tapping. In a moment the door opened and the very male presence of Austin Matthews dominated the small, feminine room.

"How's your friend doing?" he asked in a low voice.

"She's fine, I think. She's sound asleep." Emily stood, trying to gain some measure of equality, but her head reached only slightly above the man's chin. "But really, Mr. Matthews, I think I had better awaken her so that we can be on our way. I'm certain Mr. Mercer will be wondering what has happened to us by now."

Austin shook his head. "Mercer's disappeared. He's left word that he will meet with the men of the town tomorrow night after tempers have calmed. In the meantime, the town's full of very confused young ladies. You're as well off here as anywhere."

"But this is someone else's room," Emily protested, looking wanly around the tiny bedroom. The open wardrobe against the wall revealed shockingly colored clothes, and hanging over the door was a nightrobe that was entirely transparent. "Surely there must be a hotel..." Her voice trailed off tiredly.

Sympathy flickered for just a moment in Austin's dark eyes, but his voice was level. "Dixie says she has no problem with you ladies using her room for the night."

"Dixie?"

"The...uh...lady who served you the lemonade."

"Oh." Emily's cheeks burned. "Well, it's very kind of you, Mr. Matthews, and of Miss...er...Dixie, but I hardly think it would be proper...."

Before the words were out of her mouth she knew she'd made a mistake. One of Austin Matthews's thick eyebrows shot straight up and a muscle twitched along the strong line of his jaw.

"That—that is..." Emily stuttered and tried to recover her wits. "I don't mean to sound ungrateful. I don't know what we would have done without your help at the pier, but—"

"But you're too damn good to spend a night in my establishment, right, Miss Kendall?" Austin interrupted brusquely.

Emily bristled. There was no call for the man to use such language. Anger made her tone haughtier than she had intended. "I didn't mean to imply, Mr. Mat-thews—"

"Listen, lady...you can stay or you can go, it doesn't matter to me. But there are three hundred lonely men out there who've been waiting over a year for you women to arrive. After the free-for-all at the dock, most of them went out and got drunk. If you want to sashay on out among them to look for another place to spend the night, go ahead."

Emily willed herself not to flinch at the harshness of his words. She did a quick assessment of her predica-ment and decided that the man was probably right. She and Ida Mae would be better off staying here, at least for the night. She looked up, directly into her host's eyes. "It appears to me that we have little choice, Mr. Matthews. Ida Mae and I are grateful to you for your hospitality."

Austin nodded and turned to leave, then stopped. His powerful frame filled the tiny doorway. "Just re-member, Miss Kendall, 'proper' is a relative term. You're not in Massachusetts anymore."

Then he left the room, closing the little door behind him without a sound.

Chapter Two

"You don't have to bite my head off, Austin," Flo snapped, facing her partner with her hands on her hips. "You've been insufferable all evening. It's as if havin' those two fancy ladies under your roof has put a burr under your saddle."

Austin tipped back in his chair and rocked on its two back legs. "Ah, Flo, I'm sorry," he said with an apologetic grin. "You're right. Prim and proper females make my skin itch."

Flo walked behind him and began to massage his shoulders with both hands. "Whatever did they do to you, Austin Matthews? The girls here in the bar say they've never met a more charming fellow. Half of them are crazy in love with you. But when it comes to the good, upstanding ladies of the town, you turn as prickly as a porcupine."

Austin closed his eyes and groaned while Flo continued her ministrations. "There...just a little lower," he said with a low growl of satisfaction.

"'Course...half of *them* are in love with you, too. It don't seem to make no never mind that you treat them like pariahs."

"'Pariahs'...what a fancy word." Austin smiled lazily. "You've been reading again, Flo."

"I'm serious, Austin," she said with annoyance, digging her fingers a little more roughly into the thick muscles of his upper back. "We've been partners for three years now and I still don't know anything about you."

"Maybe there's not that much to know, darlin'." Flo had marvelous, large hands that were working wonders on the stiffness that had begun in his neck and shoulders as he'd watched the New Englanders on the ship that afternoon. He should have been elated, actually. Mercer had been unable to come through with the kind of numbers he had promised. Forty-six ladies wouldn't even make a good dinner for the women-hungry men of Seattle, much less the feast they had all been anticipating. It would send even more customers over to the Golden Lady looking for nourishment.

But he felt as peevish as a pregnant grizzly bear. Perhaps it was the lace collars. He'd stood looking up at the ship and been faced with row after row of starched lace collars. Like the one his mother had been wearing the last time he saw her, before they closed the casket. Like the ones his grandmother had spent endless hours tatting up until the day she died just two years after Ma... on his tenth birthday. His sister had been wearing one, too, on the day she'd left him and Pa to run away at fourteen with the theatrical troupe, sobbing angrily that she was too young to run a household, too young to be a mother. He figured it was his sister who had broken what was left of his father's heart. After that it had been just the two of them—him and Pa—and they'd done all right. No more lace collars for them.

"Fine!" Flo pushed his chair back down flat on the floor with a crash. "If you don't want to talk, we'll just forget it."

Austin looked up at her with one of his practiced smiles. "It's those magic hands of yours, Flo. You were putting me to sleep."

Flo reluctantly smiled back. As usual, when Austin Matthews turned on the charm, she was helpless to fight the warm feelings inside her. She really ought to know better than to try getting more out of him than he wanted to give, she told herself for the hundredth time.

"So what are you planning to do with those two high-falootin' Easterners?"

Austin shrugged. "They'll be out of here tomorrow. Mercer's planning some kind of meeting to settle the thing. Maybe he'll auction them off to the highest bidder." He shook off the prickle of irritation he felt at the thought of Emily Kendall standing on an auction block in front of the group of angry males they'd seen at the dock today. "How the hell do I know?" he ended with a scowl.

Flo started to say something, then thought better of it. She finished her massage with a couple of strong strokes along his neck. "You want some company tonight?" she asked softly in her deep voice.

Austin stood and put his hand gently along her powdered cheek. "It's been a long day. Thanks anyway, darlin'," he said with a tender smile.

Flo nodded, her eyes glazed bright blue under the scarlet hair. "Good night then, lovey."

"'Night."

, At the top of the stairs Flo turned. Austin had resumed his seat and sat in the silence of the still-smoky barroom, pouring himself another drink.

The barroom looked different in the strong light of morning. Emily descended the stairs cautiously, but there wasn't a drunken logger or a naked woman in sight. She smiled at her hesitation. She'd wanted adventure, after all, and she'd gotten it. Now she'd better be prepared to face the consequences.

Austin looked up just as she reached the shaft of light that slanted in from the three big windows he'd insisted on installing along the side wall when they'd built the Golden Lady. The sun lit up her yellow dress like the warm glow of a whale-oil lamp. Somehow she'd managed to repair the tear in the shoulder from yesterday. She must have relinquished her notions of propriety enough to have asked the loan of a needle and thread from one of the girls. And hairpins, too. Her golden hair was neatly pinned back in a chignon.

"Good morning," he said without much enthusiasm. His thick head was a nagging reminder of the amount of whiskey he'd consumed the night before.

Emily stopped and looked down at him. Again she was impressed at the elegance of his attire. His beige trousers fit snugly along his long legs. He was not wearing a jacket, and his long-sleeved shirt looked to be made of a very fine, pure white lawn. She'd never seen any finer cloth in the mills back home. She told herself that it was the fabric that drew her eye, and not the way it molded itself across the broad expanse of his chest.

"Good morning, Mr. Matthews," she answered stiffly, remembering their words from the night before.

"How's your friend today?" He walked around from behind the bar and extended his hand to help her down the last few steps as if she were a debutante entering a ballroom.

It would be rude to refuse it, Emily decided, but she was not at all happy with the lump that lodged in her throat when his hand touched hers. She swallowed the lump down. It reminded her of the time she'd had oysters at the Bennetts' fancy Christmas party. "Ida Mae's still asleep," she finally managed.

"You're cold," Austin said as she reached the bottom step. He reached for her other hand and rubbed the two briskly between his own. "It can get bitter here, nights. You should have asked for more blankets."

"No, I'm fine...we were fine, really." The sun caught reddish highlights in his chestnut brown hair as he bent over her. His manner was nonchalant. Of course, he probably rubbed the hands of those...girls of his every day, she thought. He had no way of knowing how little experience she'd had with a man's touch.

"Your hands are like ice," Austin said with a frown. "Come sit down and I'll bring you some coffee."

Gratefully she pulled her hands out of his and went to a table. "It's very kind of you, Mr. Matthews. I hate to be any more trouble."

He reached behind the bar and after a moment came up with two steaming cups. "No trouble at all. I was just having some myself." He sat down next to her, entirely too close. Emily wrapped her hands tightly around the coffee cup as though it would jump off the table at any minute. The glint of amusement she had seen yesterday returned to Austin's eyes. "Relax," he said. "I don't bite."

Emily knew he was teasing. She'd been teased before, by Joseph and by Spencer, though Spencer hadn't really been the teasing sort. At least she knew it was not something she should take offense at. She just wished the strange churning inside her would go away. "I'm not sure I believe you, Mr. Matthews," she teased back, giving him at last a genuine smile.

Austin took in a breath. Lord, but she was lovely. She looked different somehow this morning. He studied her face. "It's the freckles," he said aloud. Her high cheekbones and finely chiseled nose were sprinkled with a delightful shower of freckles.

The smooth skin underneath the sprinkles turned pink. "Yes, I . . . normally cover them up."

"Whatever for?"

"Well, they're not dignified, not . . ."

"Proper?" Austin supplied, one eyebrow arching. But this time he did not lose his good humor. He was finding it too delightful to be sharing a cup of strong morning coffee with this fresh, lovely Easterner.

Emily's long lashes swept down. "Not proper, I suppose you would say," she admitted.

Austin laughed. "So how do you hide these most improper blemishes, Miss Kendall?"

The lashes moved and he could again see those bright pools of green. "I make a paste . . . of ground almonds. I didn't have it this morning. It's with my things. Oh dear, Mr. Matthews, do you think they will have recovered our trunks?"

Austin nodded absently. "I'll send Jasper to see about it if you like." The freckles and blushing cheeks made her look more like a tomboy than a highly proper lady. "What did they call you when you were little?" he asked.

"I beg your pardon?"

"With your freckles." He leaned over and brushed his fingers lightly across her cheeks. "They must have called you names to make you want to hide something so pretty."

The blush deepened. "Spotty, sometimes. And Polka Dots. My father used to call me Speckles, but I liked that."

"Well, Speckles Kendall, if you ask me you should take that almond paste of yours and throw it right into the ocean. Your freckles are charming."

"It was the trip aboard ship. It was so stuffy down below that I spent most of my time up on the deck. They come out in the sun, you know." She stopped. What was she doing prattling on about her freckles to this stranger? To the owner of a house of ill repute. Who at this moment had shifted his gaze from her blushing cheeks to the tight pull of her yellow dress over her breasts. Back in Lowell her four-mile walk to the mill each day had kept her figure willow-thin, but the long inactivity on the ship had filled out the natural curves of her body. Her clothes seemed to fit her almost as indecently as the outfits on the women she had seen yesterday in this room. She shifted uncomfortably in her chair. "Anyway, about our trunks," she went on nervously, "it would be very kind of you to have your man check up on it."

Austin pushed himself away from the table. He didn't like the softness he'd felt in his midsection when Miss Kendall was admitting to being teased as a child. He liked even less the hardness he was beginning to feel lower down. This woman had nothing to do with him. She'd come here to be someone else's bride...bought and paid for. "I'll see to it," he said abruptly.

With a curt nod he stood and headed behind the bar. Emily watched him disappear through the small back door. Her cheeks cooled quickly, but her heart continued its erratic thumping for several more minutes.

"So we're all civilized human beings here," the little man at the podium was saying in his slightly nasal voice. "I've kept my part of the bargain. I brought as many women as I could."

Unlike the riot at the pier yesterday, the gathering at the Occidental Hotel had been remarkably calm. Asa Mercer had started the meeting by giving an account of his efforts in the East. It appeared that at one point he had actually had several hundred women signed on with him for the trip to Seattle. A number of factors had intervened, not the least of which was a vicious editorial in the *New York Herald,* which had averred that all of the men of Puget Sound were "rotten and profligate" and that the girls would be "turned into houses of ill-fame." A copy of the article had been passed around the room for those who could read.

"It's as they say," Mercer had concluded. "A lie will travel a thousand miles while the truth is still putting its boots on."

So the men of Seattle had a new, faraway target for their ire, and earnest little Asa Mercer was accepted as one of them again.

Austin had decided to attend the meeting, out of idle curiosity, he told himself. The forty-six brides-to-be sat primly in several rows of chairs at the front of the room, stiffly conscious of the devouring gazes of the onlookers. He could see Emily Kendall and her friend Miss Sprague in the second row.

"This is how it's going to work," Mercer went on. "There were two hundred ninety-seven men who put in the money...that works out to about seven men for each bride."

There was a low rumbling from the crowd, but no one spoke out. Several of the women had begun fanning themselves nervously.

"I've just divided them up alphabetical-like." Mercer squinted at the crowd and singled out a grizzled-looking man who had failed to remove his large felt hat. "Except for Missouri Ike. I don't reckon I ever got your last name, Ike."

"I don't reckon I have one," the man rumbled in a deep bass voice.

Mercer gave a thin smile. "Yes, well...we'll just put you with the *I*'s."

From his vantage point at the rear, Austin could see that Miss Sprague had reached out to take Emily Kendall's hand. He hoped she wasn't going to faint again. Poor Asa was having troubles enough, he thought. He had yet to explain how each one of these ladies was supposed to satisfy seven men.

"It will be a fair contest." Mercer stopped to pull a handkerchief from his pocket and mop his forehead. "Each lady will give fair and equal chance to every man on her list. May the best man win!" He attempted to put an upbeat note in his voice, but it cracked a little just at the end, ruining the effect.

Finally the crowd of men began to make their comments. "What does a fair chance mean, Mercer?" one asked.

"What if they don't like none of us?" another shouted.

Austin grinned. This was shaping up to be the most entertaining event in Seattle since the territorial celebrations when they'd split from Oregon back in '53. He had a wicked impulse to speak up and offer the hospitality of his establishment to comfort the losers, but he held his tongue.

"Now, remember, men, these are *ladies,* chosen for their intelligence, modesty and virtue. They will expect to be treated as such." Mercer stepped down off the tiny stage and headed over to the group of women.

The men meekly began lining up on one side of the room, at Mercer's instruction. Austin marveled at the stylish young man from Ohio. Mercer had only been in the territory three years, but he'd already established a reputation by building and serving as president of the first Territorial University. Now, at just twenty-five years of age, he had turned a crowd of hostile men into a more or less orderly group, each calmly waiting to be assigned "his" bride.

The process would take a while. Mercer was handing a sheet of paper to each of the women. As he reached Emily, Austin began to feel all at once the stuffiness of the room. The rest of the event held no more interest for him. He turned to leave, but his eyes sought out Emily Kendall one last time. She looked up from her paper and her gaze locked with his. He smiled and, as he had back on the pier, winked at her. But this time there was no responding gleam of hope in her green eyes. She nodded politely in return and then bleakly turned her attention to the list in her hand.

* * *

The Empire Room was the only restaurant in Seattle with real linen tablecloths. It had been doing such booming business since the arrival of the brides that the owner, Mr. Vickermann, had moved out the barber shop next door and set up what they were calling The Annex. Even with the additional space, tables were at a premium.

In the past week Emily had practically memorized the Empire's limited selections. She usually ended up ordering the venison stew, which was a safe bet, but she found a thorough study of the menu Mrs. Vickermann had scripted so carefully was the easiest way to start off yet another "get acquainted" dinner.

She'd now met five of the men on her list, counting her current dinner companion, Fred Johnson. None of them had inspired the least spark of interest, much less ardor. The situation did not look promising, for there remained to be met only two men: Dexter Kingsman, who she had learned was the prosperous owner of a steam sawmill, and the man whose name Mr. Mercer had scrawled at the last minute at the bottom of her list, the appointment she most dreaded—the man with no last name, Missouri Ike.

"Now, y'all order up whatever ya like, ma'am. I've been savin' fer this day all year long." Fred Johnson took an oily deerskin bag from the inside of his vest and set it proudly on the clean white tablecloth.

Emily tried to smile her appreciation. Mr. Johnson was a middle-aged man of about her own height. He was attentive, overeager to please. It was, however, hard to ignore the two major gaps in his front teeth. Perhaps, she thought uncharitably, he should have invested in some dental work rather than saving up to show her a good time. "I believe I'll have the stew, Mr. Johnson," she said.

"Back home my mammy makes a coon stew that'll spin your ears right 'round on your head," Mr. Johnson said. They had already established that he was from Tennessee, but that he didn't hold with what he called the "see-cesh" boys, so she didn't have to worry about hitchin' herself to no Johnny Reb.

Emily gave a little sigh. It was going to be another long evening. One week into Mr. Mercer's experiment in alphabetical matchmaking, the atmosphere was gloomy. Already there had been three gunfights over the prospective brides. Ida Mae's two defenders, Mr. Briggs and Mr. Smedley, who had been the best of friends, were now barely on speaking terms, since Mr. Smedley had been on Ida Mae's list of prospects and Mr. Briggs, of course, had not. He had appeared instead on the list of a forty-year-old widow named Rose Bartlett, who had a voice like a foghorn and had left two grown children back East.

The three Irishmen who had first accosted Emily at the pier had the misfortune to be named O'Brien, O'Donnell and O'Leary, and, as such, were to vie for the same bride. The three could be found brawling nightly in the various Skid Road establishments.

"Would ya like a bottle of wine, Miss Kendall?" her companion asked, picking up the dirty leather pouch once more and hefting its weight in his hand. "The sky's the limit tonight."

Before Emily could decline his offer, the frosted glass door to the Empire Annex opened and through it came the man she'd been looking for—but not wanting to see—all week.

He spotted her at once and made his way over to their table. "Good evening, Miss Kendall," he said politely.

Emily's stomach did a little skitter at the deep, pleasant sound of his voice. "Good evening, Mr. Matthews," she answered in what she hoped was a nonchalant tone.

Austin looked from her over to her companion and back again. "You've been enjoying your stay in Seattle, I trust?" The words were correct, but once again Emily had the feeling that the man was laughing at her.

"Very much," she said firmly. "I'd like you to meet my dinner companion, Mr. Johnson."

Johnson halfway stood and the two men shook hands. "How are you, Fred? How's the prospecting?" Austin asked. Most of the territorial residents had abandoned hope of finding in the picturesque mountains stretching out east of Seattle a strike that would rival the California riches of a decade before. But a few stubborn ones still held out for a miracle.

"Not bad, Matthews. No gold yet, but I'm close, I'll tell ya. I kin smell it. It's just around the corner."

Matthews clapped a hand on the man's shoulder and pushed him back down into his chair. "Well, that's good news, Fred. Now, I don't want to interrupt your romantic dinner." He glanced at Emily and gave her one of his outrageous winks. "You two go on ahead."

Emily bristled. How dare he amuse himself at her expense? She reached over and laid her hand gently on top of Fred Johnson's, which sent bright streaks of red shooting up his neck. "Mr. Johnson and I are having a perfectly lovely time," she said defiantly, looking up into Austin Matthews's intense brown eyes.

Austin's eyebrows shot up. "I can see that, Miss Kendall. And I'm very glad to hear it." One corner of his mouth quirked just enough for Emily to see it. "I'll leave you two alone to get better acquainted," he ended solicitously.

With another nod he moved away to a table at the far end of the room. Emily took her hand from Johnson's and the color slowly sank down his neck like the mercury in a thermometer. His eyes were troubled. "How do you know Austin Matthews?" he asked.

Emily tore her eyes away from Austin's impressive figure and turned back to Johnson. "He helped me...rescued me, really. That first day at the pier."

Johnson looked down at the table. "I don't mean to be bold, ma'am, but I think I should tell you that it won't do your reputation no good to be associating with the likes of him."

Emily straightened in her chair. "Why not?"

"Well," Johnson drawled, "the women he works with are not—you know—not decent."

"And just how would you know that, Mr. Johnson?" Emily asked sweetly.

"Er...it's just...well, *everyone* knows it."

She hid a smile at his discomfiture. It was wicked to tease the poor man. But then, there was something about being in the same room with Austin Matthews that seemed to bring out the wicked in her.

Mr. Vickermann himself took their order and before long two steaming bowls of stew were brought to their table. Emily searched desperately for topics of conversation that would not involve the war, Mr. Johnson's mammy or his mining claim.

This supper was even more interminable than those with the other men on her list, and she knew it was due to Austin Matthews's presence. She had hoped Austin would eat his meal and leave, but, though he completely ignored them, he seemed in not the least hurry to move on. He finished his food, then ordered more coffee, picked up a newspaper and started to read. At times he would lean back on the two rear legs of his chair, and Emily feared the flimsy thing would scarcely support his robust form. She knew all this because, much to her annoyance, she found her glance slipping over to Mr. Matthews at regular intervals, sometimes making her lose the course of her conversation entirely.

"I'm sorry, Mr. Johnson . . . you were saying something about a gold mine?"

"Them Colorado people, they think that's where the next big hit's comin', but I tell you it's right here under our noses."

Emily smiled absently and finished the last sip of her coffee. Mrs. Vickermann was bringing Austin Matthews a plate of pie. His smile was twenty-four-carat charm, and the plump little woman bobbed her head in pleasure.

Mr. Vickermann came to collect their bill, and Johnson paid him with another flourish of his heavy money pouch. "Kin I escort you back to your hotel, Miss Kendall?" he asked.

Emily's back grew tense. This was the part of the evening she dreaded. Two of the four men she'd met with so far had tried to kiss her when they'd reached her hotel room. She'd been kissed before, of course, by Spencer. But Spencer's kiss had been a dignified, dry touch of his lips that had been a solemn promise of the lifelong commitment they would make to each other. Kissing her Seattle suitors was more like wrestling with that huge fish the summer she'd gone to the coast with Cassie and Joseph. Slimy and wet and thoroughly unpleasant.

She looked over at Fred Johnson. With a slight shudder, she imagined that gap-toothed mouth against her own. "I'm sorry, Mr. Johnson. I told my friend Ida Mae that I'd wait for her here."

Johnson's face fell, but he recovered gamely. "Then I'll wait here with ya, Miss Kendall."

"Oh, no," she said quickly. "You have that long ride yet up into the mountains. I'll be perfectly fine here."

After several more protestations, she finally got the hapless Mr. Johnson to agree to leave her there. She gave him a firm handshake and a hearty goodbye, then sank down into her chair with relief and put her head into her hands.

Almost immediately, Austin Matthews's deep voice was in her ear. "I surmise that Mr. Johnson is not going to be the lucky man."

Emily picked her head up. "I believe you are entertained by this process, Mr. Matthews," she said sharply.

Austin grinned and motioned to the chair across from her. "May I?" he said, sitting down without waiting for her to answer.

"Actually, I was just about to leave," she said.

"I thought you were waiting here for Miss Sprague."

"Do you make it a habit to eavesdrop on other people's conversations, Mr. Matthews?"

"Absolutely. It's the only way to learn things around here. The newspaper's not worth a damn. For example, it hasn't said a word about all these exuberant marital maneuvers going on about town."

"'Exuberant' is a good word for it," Emily said wearily.

Austin's expression dropped. "None of the men has given you any trouble, have they?" His voice stayed even, but it had taken on a hard edge.

Emily gave a tired smile. "Still trying to rescue me, Mr. Matthews?" she asked. "No, no trouble. Nothing I can't handle, anyway."

A muscle twitched along Austin's jaw. "I hope you'll remember you have a friend if you need one, Miss Kendall," he said soberly.

The easy charm had been replaced by something more dangerous, and Emily felt that uncomfortable shifting inside her once again. "La, Mr. Matthews," she said with an attempt at lightness. "In this town I have nothing but friends . . . ask any man you see."

Austin's smile returned, but it was not as light-hearted as before. "Has any of these 'friends' of yours struck your fancy yet as a bridegroom?" he asked with studied nonchalance.

Emily hesitated a moment. Though she couldn't quite fathom Mr. Matthews's interest in the matter, she decided it would be fun to bait him. "Perhaps . . ." she said innocently. "One or two."

Austin caught on to the game immediately. "Well, congratulations!" he said heartily. "May I expect a wedding invitation shortly?"

"Oh, that would be getting a bit ahead of myself. After all, I still have two gentlemen on my list to meet."

"And who would they be?"

"One is that . . . person with no last name. Missouri Ike, they call him."

Austin sat up in his chair. "They've paired you off with Missouri Ike? Why, that's outrageous," he said angrily. Ike was a bushwhacker, one of the tough breed of men who drove the oxcarts for the lumber camps. They were independent and ornery, and, according to the loggers, their profanity could peel the bark off a tree.

Emily nodded. She'd been of the same opinion herself all week. "So perhaps I may need your defending after all, Mr. Matthews." Her lower lip trembled slightly.

"When are you seeing him?"

"Tuesday next. The men from Piny Ridge Camp will all be back then."

Matthews drummed his strong fingers on the table. "And who's the other man?"

"A Mr. Kingsman, Dexter Kingsman."

The fingers stopped and slowly Austin's hand clenched into a fist. Kingsman was one of the richest men in town and, according to the girls at the Golden Lady, was what they called a "fine figure of a man." He was also a shrewd, respected businessman and a well-liked fellow.

Austin looked over at Emily Kendall. In the light of the single candle at their table her green eyes took on the brilliance of emeralds. The smooth, perfect lines of her cheeks were unblemished. Almond paste, no doubt. He would like to kiss it away to find the freckles underneath, he thought with a sudden, piercing stab.

He pushed back his chair. In the few dealings they'd had, Austin had always liked Dexter Kingsman well enough, but as he stood and looked down at the gentle rise and fall of Emily Kendall's lace collar, he had a feeling that he was about to drastically change his opinion of the man.

Chapter Three

With a sigh, Emily shoved her sister's letter once more into the pocket of her blue dimity day dress. Cassie's dear, familiar handwriting brought intense, almost painful, images of home. Their parents had died of the influenza in the winter of '62, first Papa, then Mama three weeks later. To pay off the hospital bills and other debts, Emily had had to sell the bright yellow clapboard house on the edge of town and move in with Cassie and Joseph, the only family she had left. Now there were the babies, too, of course. How old would they be before she saw them again?

Inside her pocket she rubbed the letter like a talisman. Perhaps it would give her courage for her meeting with her next prospective bridegroom. This meeting, at least, had the potential of actually being pleasant. Several of the other brides had exclaimed with envy to see Dexter Kingsman's name on her list. It seemed that everyone in Seattle knew the man. His foresight in building a steam sawmill just as the lumber industry was beginning to boom had made him wealthy, and his Eastern breeding made him stand out among the town's rough-cut population.

Emily had seen him once, coming out of the livery stable. Ida Mae had pointed him out with great excitement. "There he is, Emily. There's your future husband," she'd sniffed, her excitement aggravating the constant drip from her nose.

Emily had not responded. She had to admit that she didn't have any quarrel with the man's looks. Tall, well-dressed, he had an aristocractically handsome face under perfectly coiffed blond hair. A bit too lean, perhaps, but then Spencer had been on the thin side, too. Quite different from the robust maleness of Austin Matthews. Thank goodness for that, she told herself firmly.

Mr. Kingsman was the only one of her suitors who had approached her with some degree of finesse. The others had simply shown up at her door or accosted her on the street, saying, "I'm the one, ma'am." Dexter Kingsman had sent a messenger, a dozen roses and a beautifully penned note requesting her company at dinner at her hotel, where he had arranged a private room off the main dining room so that they could get to know each other in privacy.

It was the roses that did it. Heaven knows where he found them in this town, she had told Ida Mae that afternoon. With matching sighs, they had both stared at the perfect blossoms, their minds seeing the beautifully groomed gardens of Lowell.

She came down from her room precisely at six, and he was waiting in the lobby. He stood immediately and crossed the room toward her. In his hand was a nose-gay of violets, surrounded by a lovely embroidered hanky. He presented it to her with a little flourish and said, "Miss Kendall, I am so pleased to make your acquaintance. The entire city of Seattle is a brighter place with the presence of you ladies."

Emily reached for the flowers, but found instead her hand clasped in his and brought to his lips. To her surprise, she blushed. She had seen gentlemen kissing ladies' hands at the Bennetts' elegant gatherings, but no man had ever done such a thing to her.

He slipped the flowers into her hand.

"That's very kind of you. They're beautiful," she murmured. Her cheeks were hot and she wondered if her freckles stood out.

"If I may be so bold, Miss Kendall, they're not anywhere near as pretty as you," Kingsman said gallantly.

A newspaper rustled loudly. Someone in one of the red leather chairs of the lobby was holding up a copy of the *Puget Sound Daily* and turning the pages with unnecessary noise. Though the face and upper body were hidden by the paper, Emily recognized the long legs that stretched out below, the muscular thighs straining the fine material of well-made black serge trousers.

She needed no confirmation of the man's identity, but she got it as Austin Matthews peeked around the edge of the newspaper and winked at her. She looked away immediately, the heat in her cheeks intensifying. Didn't he have anything better to do than hang around spying on her? she thought indignantly.

Dexter Kingsman was offering his arm. "Shall we go in for dinner, Miss Kendall?" he asked.

Austin was hidden again behind the paper. Emily summoned her sweetest voice. "Certainly, Mr. Kingsman. I am so looking forward to getting to know a *gentleman* of your quality."

* * *

"I want to talk to you, Austin."

Flo towered over him as he sat at one of the rear tables, her statuesque body blocking out the sun coming in from the big windows. He shrugged. "So talk."

Despite his unenthusiastic response, she pulled out the chair opposite him. "I don't know what's been wrong with you lately." Her voice had an angry edge. "Dixie says you've snapped at her twice, Belle says you ignore her when she asks you a question, and Jasper says if you drink up any more of the profits, we aren't going to break even this month."

Austin raised his shot glass of whiskey to his mouth. The half-empty bottle sat on the table next to his elbow.

"Can't a man be in a bad mood once in a while?"

"Once in a while, but not for days on end. And it's getting worse." Flo put a hand on his arm and adopted a more sympathetic tone. "I'm worried about you, Austin, lovey."

"I'm all right."

Flo gave a huge sigh. "I can't help but think it's that green-eyed Easterner that's got your fur standing on end."

Austin smiled drunkenly. "If you're referring to Miss Emily Kendall, Flo, you're steamin' up the wrong river."

Flo's eyes narrowed. "If I'm so wrong, how come you knew right off who I was talkin' about?"

Austin reached over and tucked an errant red curl behind Flo's ear. "Because, you crazy Scot, you haven't exactly been the soul of St. Mary, either, lately. Jasper says that ever since the brides arrived you've been locking your door to him nights."

Flo sat up straight in her chair, a formidable picture. "He's been complainin' to you?" she asked indignantly. "That little weasel."

Austin put up a hand. "Hold on, Flo. It's a compliment, you know. The poor man's about drained the well out back dry taking cold showers."

Flo gave a little snort. "Maybe he'll start to appreciate what he's missing. All of a sudden it seems that every man in town thinks that unless a woman carries a parasol and talks Boston-like, she ain't no good."

"I haven't noticed any lack of business," Austin said dryly.

"Of course not. Those so-called ladies have got the men so het up that they're waitin' in line to visit my girls, but that's not the point."

Austin grinned. "You're jealous, Flo. And without cause. There's not a one of those Eastern belles that can hold a candle to you."

Flo's frown stayed in place. "Not even that Miss Kendall?" she asked softly.

Austin tipped his head and let the rest of the liquor in the glass slide down his throat. Without answering, he leaned over and kissed Flo on her powdered cheek, then stood and walked out of the room.

Emily could find no fault with Dexter Kingsman's attentiveness. Since their dinner at the Occidental, she had received either a sweet message or a gift—small gifts well within the bounds of even New England propriety—twice a day without fail. Her favorite had been a sweetmeat cunningly formed in the shape of a nest with three baby birds inside.

His courtship was in stark contrast to the rest of her new life. More than anything, Dexter's attentions brought her back to the civilized society she had left behind in Massachusetts. Here even her beloved walks were a trial. She would pick her way along the wooden sidewalks of town, carefully avoiding the wads of spittle and chewed tobacco, and try to ignore the lewd looks and brash comments of the local men. The New England brides were still a novelty in town, and a simple trip across the street to the Empire Room for dinner could cause a major commotion.

Emily closed her eyes, remembering the previous evening's disaster. It seemed that every man in Seattle had chosen that particular Saturday night to get drunk. Emily and Ida Mae had just left fellow brides Parmelia Carruthers and Cynthia Stoddard at their rooming house when they were accosted by the three Irishmen who had grabbed Emily that first day on the pier. While Ida Mae cowered behind her, Emily tried in vain to remember which of the rusty-haired trio was which.

"Mr. O'Brien," she had said finally to the tallest of the group, who happened to be the one swaying the least. "You and your friends should be ashamed of yourselves, addressing two decent women while in this sorry state. You belong in the saloon or, even better, back in your own beds until you sleep off your condition."

Her voice had stayed firm and calm, and the slight tremble in her legs, she believed, was not apparent beneath all her petticoats. To her amazement, the three had hung their heads like scolded schoolboys and meekly disappeared into the darkness.

Emily watched them go with grim satisfaction. "I guess I don't need Mr. Austin Matthews to rescue me anymore," she said in a low voice. She had had a fleeting wish that the exasperating man were there to see how well she had handled herself. Scarcely a day went by when she hadn't been made aware of his arrogant, masculine presence. But last night, when she might have been in real need of a friend, he had been nowhere in sight.

The urge to see him had been strictly due to a desire to show him her independence, she told herself firmly. She did not need Austin Matthews watching out for her. The very idea was ridiculous. Especially since the more she heard about his reputation in town, the more she realized that his presence as a bodyguard was something akin to the proverbial fox guarding the chicken coop.

This morning, again, as she had set out for church with Dexter Kingsman, Ida Mae and Mr. Smedley in Dexter's luxurious black phaeton, she had found herself looking around for some sign of the handsome saloon owner, but had not seen him. Perhaps he had gotten bored with his mission as her self-appointed protector.

Emily sighed and leaned back into the plush leather seats of the carriage. Dexter had explained in great detail that the vehicle had been made in Baltimore and had been shipped around the Horn. It undoubtedly was the only one of its kind in all of Washington Territory.

The church service had been a scant two hours in length, blissfully short compared to the long-winded, fire-and-brimstone tirades of Rev. Gladstone back home. It left the foursome with a long, beautiful day to enjoy the picnic lunch that Dexter had had prepared by the hotel.

"We'll drive up into the mountains as far as the road permits," Dexter told his companions. "The wheels have individual spring action to make for a comfortable ride even over the rocks."

By now Emily had heard enough about the wonders of Dexter's new carriage. "How do people without such a marvel of modern transportation get around with the roads so poor?" she asked.

Dexter looked at her in surprise. "On horseback, of course."

Emily glanced over her shoulder at Ida Mae, who was looking at Mr. Smedley for confirmation of this troubling fact. "Everyone rides horses here?" Ida Mae asked, then gave a kind of distressed sniffle when Smedley nodded.

"Don't you ladies ride?" Dexter asked.

Neither woman answered for a moment. "You mean as in . . . get up on the back of a horse and ride?" Emily's usual determination was missing from her voice.

"How do folks get around where you come from?" Mr. Smedley sounded perplexed.

"In Lowell, we mostly walk where we want to go. My brother-in-law, Joseph, has a wagon we use sometimes."

Ida Mae giggled. "Our horse at home was called Hobgoblin. Once my brother tried to climb up on its back and got thrown clear into the neighbor's garden."

"Well, you're Westerners now," Dexter said firmly. "You'll have to learn to ride."

The two women shared another disturbed look, and Ida Mae pulled out her ever-present hanky. Her sniffles had only grown worse since their arrival, in spite of elaborate efforts to stop them. Today, for example, Mr. Smedley had brought her a concoction made from the pitch of the balsam fir. With a beet-red face he had rubbed a generous layer of the pungent stuff under Ida Mae's chin and along her neck before they set off that morning. Emily couldn't see that the remedy had had much effect, other than to give the impression all day long that the foursome was traveling inside a pine tree.

"Well, we can't very well learn to ride when we don't have horses," Emily concluded, sounding relieved.

Dexter turned to look at Emily, his eyes warming as they skimmed quickly over her splendid figure. "That's not a problem. I'll give you one of mine."

Emily gasped. The man would give her a horse? "Thank you, D-Dexter," she stammered. "But, of course, I could never accept such a gift."

Dexter smiled confidently. "We'll call it a loan, then, until such time as it doesn't make any difference. The little bay, I think. She's gentle enough for a beginner. I even have a handsome little sidesaddle trimmed with silver that I got in Mexico last year. You can ride properly—like the ladies back East."

In Lowell, Emily had never even thought about riding. But now that the opportunity had arisen, there was something appealing about the idea. What freedom! She wondered if the mere *loan* of something so valuable would be considered beyond propriety. In Lowell, undoubtedly it would, but then she wasn't in Lowell anymore.

"Thank you for the offer, Dexter," she said, her green eyes glowing. "I'll give it some serious consideration."

"Nothing to consider," he said indulgently. "I'll have her transferred to the hotel livery tomorrow, and you may ride her at your will."

This time Ida Mae's sniff was deliberate. "Not me. You won't catch me up on one of those beasts."

Mr. Smedley reached over and gave her tiny hand a little squeeze. "I'd be happy to take you anywhere you need to go in my buggy, Miss Ida Mae," he said tenderly.

She beamed at him in return, and Emily turned her attention back to the scenery. Austin Matthews had been right about one thing—Washington Territory was breathtakingly beautiful.

As soon as the name entered her head she clucked her tongue in exasperation. She was on an outing with a handsome, generous man with impeccable manners and excellent taste. There was absolutely no reason for her to be thinking about a notorious saloon keeper whose standard of decency was one step below a pirate's.

"It's a beautiful day, isn't it?" she said to Dexter with a forced smile. She moved a little closer to him on the seat and slipped her hand into the crook of his elbow.

"Miss Emily," Dexter said, giving her hand a pat and letting his eyes wander once again over the gentle curve of her tucked bodice, "I do believe it's the most beautiful day I've ever seen."

Dexter had been true to his word, and a lovely little bay mare named Strawberry had been delivered to the Occidental's stables Monday morning. Emily had not as yet tried to mount her. She had decided to develop a friendship first, and had paid several visits to the gentle animal, admiring her huge brown eyes and sleek coat.

A few days later the horse whinnied gently at her approach. Emily fed it some sugar lumps that she had sneaked from the hotel restaurant and ran a curry brush along its shiny back. But finally the tiny gold watch pinned to her bodice told her it was time to go back to her room and prepare for her evening's appointment. Tomorrow we'll give it a try, my girl, she silently told the bay as she gave her a last gentle stroke, then started walking slowly toward the hotel.

Her meeting that night was the one she had been so dreading—with the bushwhacker Missouri Ike. Though she had never been one to admit to fear, she had slept restlessly the night before in anticipation. It hadn't helped matters that Dexter had chosen that night to show her the imperious side of his nature. When she had confessed to him over supper her nervousness over meeting Missouri Ike, she had hoped for some comfort, perhaps an offer of protection, such as Austin Matthews had made the evening of her dinner with the miner Fred Johnson. Instead, Dexter had become incensed and had demanded—*demanded*—that she refuse to meet the man. She had patiently explained that her obligations to Mr. Mercer required her to honor her commitment to meet with all seven suitors. Dexter had refused to listen and, after throwing a silver dollar on the table to pay the bill, had stalked angrily away.

The next day there had been no tender notes, no nosegays, no gifts. Dexter Kingsman was obviously not a man who tolerated opposition. By afternoon, the warm feelings toward her prosperous suitor that Emily had begun to develop during the picnic in the mountains had cooled considerably. She had been left alone to face the alarming Missouri Ike, and even her usually dauntless nature found the prospect frightening.

She sighed as she walked down the stairs into the lobby. Feeling like a coward, she had gone to Ida Mae's room that afternoon to ask her to accompany her for the evening. But she found her friend in bed in great distress. The previous day Mr. Briggs had brought her some goose oil, which he claimed would cure her sniffles once and for all. Instead, the remedy, combined with the sweet fern tea that had been the contribution of another of Ida Mae's suitors, a Mr. Redmond, had produced intense cramps.

"I'm sorry, Emily," Ida Mae had wailed, her face the color of the bedsheets. "I should be able to go with you. What if that dreadful man tries to..."

Her friend stopped before venturing exactly what it was the mule driver might try to do. Neither woman was particularly sure, though no doubt it could be something calamitous.

"Don't worry about me, Ida Mae," Emily had assured her briskly. "I'm sure Mr.—er—Ike will be no worse than any of the other men we've seen. Are you positive you don't want me to fetch you a doctor before I leave?"

"I'll be fine," Ida Mae had answered in a weak voice.

Emily looked doubtful. "Perhaps you shouldn't be trying any more of these home remedies, Ida dear. I know the men mean well, but—"

"Don't worry about me, Emily. You go on to your appointment, and stop by here when you get back. If you haven't returned by eight o'clock, I'll call the sheriff." Her cheeks took on a bit of color as she said this last sentence with determination.

Emily laughed. "I'm sure that won't be necessary. But I will check in to see how you're doing."

She'd given her friend a kiss on the cheek and then gone downstairs, feeling less confident than she had let on. So far there had been no reports of any dire things befalling any of the New England women. The rough, uncultured Seattle men had proved to be surprisingly well behaved when on their courting appointments. She just hoped she wouldn't be the first to have a problem—to have that dreadful "something" that Ida Mae had hinted at happen to *her*.

Missouri Ike was waiting for her, standing like a statue in the very center of the lobby. At least she *thought* it was Ike. He looked different than he had back at the meeting at the hotel. His cheeks were newly shaven, leaving the bottom half of his face a pasty white color. The large felt hat was held respectfully in his big hands, and he squinted, as if unaccustomed to the light reaching his eyes. His black hair was slicked back severely with some kind of grease that made it glisten like wet tar.

"Evenin', ma'am," he rumbled from somewhere low inside him.

Emily hesitated for a moment at the bottom of the stairs, but recovered herself immediately and moved forward with her hand outstretched. "How do you do, Mr.—er—Ike." she said briskly. As unlikely a candidate as this man may be, she was determined not to treat him differently than she had any of the other prospective bridegrooms. In fact, she found his obvious attempts to make himself presentable rather touching. His clothes were spotless, perhaps new. There was even a fresh crease in his trousers. In his own way, Missouri Ike had gone to almost as much trouble as Dexter Kingsman to impress her.

A tenseness that she had not been aware of left her shoulders. She smiled at Ike, who was a couple of inches shorter than she. "I'm pleased to meet you," she added, surprised to hear the sincerity in her own voice.

Ike was blushing. "It sure is nice to meet you, too, ma'am. Truth is, I was afeared you wouldn't come. The men back at camp took bets on it."

Emily's smile grew broader. "Looks like they lost, then, doesn't it?"

"Yes, ma'am." Ike looked down at his hat, which he wrung nervously in his big hands. "I ain't never talked with a lady like you."

Impulsively, Emily put her hand on Ike's arm. In spite of the warmth of the spring evening, he was wearing a thick wool coat. "Shall we go in to dinner?" she asked in a voice she might have used for the minister come to tea.

Ike looked up at her finally. His eyes were an odd shade of faded blue. "I'd be right honored, ma'am," he said softly.

They had taken no more than two steps into the hotel dining room when Emily stopped. Straight ahead of them, seated at a table in the corner of the room, was Austin Matthews. He nodded to her gravely as his eyes met hers.

This time there was no wink, no mocking smile. He shifted his attention to Ike, and his expression was as deadly as pistols at thirty paces. Emily felt a little chill creep up from under her collar. She wouldn't want to be on the receiving end of such a look.

She had feared the meeting with Ike, longed for a protector, but now felt herself oddly protective of the little backwoodsman who had gone to such pains to make himself presentable. She was about to head toward Austin's table when she saw that he, too, had now taken in the extraordinary change in Ike's appearance. His thick eyebrows rose and the tightness left his features.

Emily looked down at Ike, who was too discomfited by the formal hotel dining room to have noticed Austin's presence. She glanced back over at Austin. His expression had changed back to the familiar sarcastic smile. It was enough to make her believe she had imagined that moment of fierceness. But she knew she had not. While Dexter Kingsman had been off who knows where soothing his hurt pride, Austin had once again made himself available to protect her. What an unusual man, she thought, as she led the hesitant Ike to a nearby table. She hadn't had a serious conversation with the saloon owner since the night at the Empire Room. He didn't accost her as did many of the men in town. He didn't appear to be interested in pursuing any kind of relationship with her. But he seemed to be there, just there in the background, whenever she might need his support.

"I ain't never ate a meal with more than one fork," Ike grumbled as they sat down.

Emily scarcely heard his words. Her eyes were on Austin while he pulled out a newspaper, stretched his long legs out in front of himself and settled back to read.

Horseback riding was not as difficult as she had feared, Emily discovered with relief. She had arranged for the stable boy to give her some lessons on the art. Though the shy, gangly Homer confessed to her that he had never seen the likes of a sidesaddle before, he was a surprisingly good teacher. He led her up and down the length of the stable to give her the feel of the animal, then patiently stood in the back doorway giving advice while she made her first attempts at real riding. She and Strawberry seemed to communicate so well that expertise was not necessary. When at last she and the horse headed off down Washington Street, Emily felt as if they had been riding together for years.

By the time she reached the outskirts of town, Emily felt confident enough to let Strawberry increase the pace from her steady walk. She laughed with delight when the animal jolted into a lively trot, and Strawberry seemed to appreciate her enthusiasm, picking up her feet with dainty pride.

Emily was so fascinated with her new experience that she paid little attention as her ride took her farther and farther away from town. When she realized that it had been quite a while since she had last seen any buildings, she pulled gently on Strawberry's reins. The horse stopped instantly.

"Where have you taken me, girl?" Emily asked, smiling and reaching down to give the animal a pat.

She looked around. The landscape had grown increasingly rocky, with majestic fir trees twisting their way around the boulders and reaching up like straight arrows into the brilliant blue sky. Had the sky ever been this blue back in Massachusetts?

Suddenly Strawberry tossed her head restlessly. Emily immediately sensed the animal's unease. She listened intently. Behind her she could hear the faint hoofbeats of a rapidly approaching horse. She had just come around a long bend in the road and there was no way to see who the rider might be.

All at once Emily felt a hollowness at the base of her stomach. A solitary cloud began dimming a corner of the sun and a sudden breeze felt cool against the back of her neck.

Too late, she realized that venturing out so far alone had been a mistake. She would never have thought of doing such a thing back in Lowell, and here, among all these rough miners and lumbermen, she should have been even more careful. With a gentle swing of her legs, she urged Strawberry forward.

The animal broke immediately into a trot, then, as if sensing Emily's distress, stretched out into a gallop. Emily tightened her hands around the pommel of the saddle, too worried about the rider behind her to be afraid of falling off.

Strawberry's pounding hooves reverberated in Emily's ears. She couldn't tell if the horse behind them was getting closer, but it was definitely racing. This was no rider out for a leisurely stroll.

With a sick feeling, Emily thought back to her dinner with Ike the night before. Though she had been impressed at the beginning by the change in the man's appearance, the atmosphere had become increasingly strained as the evening progressed. Ike had drunk several beers, and by the end of dinner, his pale blue eyes had held an odd glitter when they looked at her.

Could Ike be the man following her? Perhaps she had been right after all to fear the bushwhacker's attentions. She bent low over Strawberry's back and mentally urged her to more speed. Strawberry spurted ahead, but now Emily could definitely hear the hoofbeats behind her growing louder.

She looked around her wildly, searching for a break in the trees where she could leave the road. A few yards ahead the road began to curve to the right, and a faint trail led off in the opposite direction. Just before she reached the spot, she pulled the reins sharply to the left. Strawberry slowed abruptly, hesitated a moment, then turned down the rough trail. The terrain required a much slower pace, but Emily straightened up with relief as the forest seemed to close around her, sheltering her from view of the road. With any luck, the approaching rider would continue down the road right past her. Then she would make her way directly back into town.

She let Strawberry pick her path a few yards deeper into the woods, then pulled her up. It was cool among the sun-dappled trees, and the crisp odor of pine was strong. Emily sat quietly, feeling the quick in-and-out movement of Strawberry's flanks as the animal caught its breath.

Out on the road, the hoofbeats sounded stronger, then faded. Emily let out the breath she'd been holding. It appeared that Ike, or whoever was following her, had continued down the road.

In the stillness left behind she could hear the gentle rushing of water. After hopping off the back of her horse, she followed the sound to the edge of a small stream.

"You deserve a drink before we head back, girl," she quietly told the horse. As Strawberry bent her head to drink, Emily sat down at the edge of the clear water. Parmelia Carruthers had lent her some riding boots this morning, and they pinched her feet. She tugged them off, her socks along with them, and dipped her toes in the water. It was icier than the well back home on a December morning.

Her feet grew pleasantly numb, and she tried to decide if she dared hoist her petticoats and pantalets to wade along the mossy stones of the streambed. Suddenly, a powerful arm clamped around her neck and pulled her back against a rock-solid chest.

Chapter Four

She had scarcely time to gasp before she was lifted completely off her feet and spun around to come face-to-face with Austin Matthews, his expression thunderous. "What in the hell do you think you're doing out here?" he roared.

Emily willed her body to stop shaking and pushed violently against her captor's chest. "Let me go, you...oaf!"

Slowly Austin released his grip and let her feet slide to the ground. "What are you doing out here?" he asked again in a more subdued tone.

"I'm out for a ride," she answered indignantly. "What does it look like I'm doing?"

Her voice was quavery, but she folded her arms in front of her and stuck out her lower lip like a stubborn child. Austin stood back and gave her a thorough perusal, from her disheveled hair to the dampened bottom of her full skirt. His fear-induced anger, which had built into a fury along the trail, drained out of him. He hid a grin and said slowly, "It looked to me as if you were wanting to go swimming in yonder stream."

Emily followed his glance down to her bare feet and flushed. "I wanted to do no such thing. I was trying to

learn how to ride. And you...you scoundrel...
scared me witless following me like that. You should be
ashamed of yourself." She ended her tirade with a
stomp of her bare right foot.

Austin took another step back and pulled her up the
bank to a less precarious footing. "Careful or you'll be
taking that dip, after all."

"Mr. Matthews," Emily continued, "I have appre-
ciated your help on several occasions since my arrival
in Seattle. Really I have. But you're simply going to
have to stop following me everywhere I go. I don't need
a protector, and if I did need one, you'd hardly be the
kind of person I'd call."

Austin tightened his lips. "You'd rather have
Kingsman take care of you, right? Well, I didn't see any
sign of your precious Dexter last night when Missouri
Ike was in his cups. And I don't see him out here today fending off whoever it was following you into the
woods."

"What do you mean? It was *you* following me."

"No," Austin replied with exasperated patience. "I
was following *him*."

"Who?"

Austin shook his head. Her icy feet and the recent
scare had Emily shaking with cold. He pulled off his
leather jacket and put it around her shoulders, then
scooped her up in his arms and carried her over to a
break in the trees where the sunlight made a circle in the
soft grass. "Sit there a minute and get warm," he ordered.

Strawberry had finished drinking and stood watching them with doubtful eyes. Austin walked over to the
animal and gave her a brisk pat, then looped her reins
around a tree branch. Then he picked up Emily's boots

and stockings and walked back over to sit beside her in the clearing.

"Listen to me, Speckles Kendall," he said firmly, grasping her foot in his big hand to pull on a flimsy silk stocking. "They told me at the hotel that like a dad-blamed fool you had ridden out by yourself, so I figured I'd better head out and round you up. When I got as far as the fork at Six Pines, I could hear someone ahead of me, riding hard."

Emily's feet were so cold by now that she couldn't bend them to maneuver her feet into the stockings. He threw the silky garments to the ground in disgust and began rubbing her feet briskly between his hands. "So I took a shortcut over the hill and saw that the rider was a man, and it sure looked like he was after something. I think that something was you."

Emily felt the queasiness back in her stomach, combined with another sensation that was being produced by Austin's warm hands moving over her cold skin. "Who was it?" she asked.

"I couldn't tell. I was above him. By the time I got back down to the road, you had taken off into the woods and he had kept on going up the road. I decided I'd better follow you rather than him." He lifted his eyes to look into hers with a mixture of annoyance and concern. "The only thing I could see was that he was wearing a big old felt hat."

Emily took a deep breath. She didn't bring up her suspicions about Ike to Austin, but she had a feeling she didn't have to. "Why would anyone want to follow me?"

Now Austin's expression was complete exasperation. "If you need to ask that, Miss Kendall, you're in even worse trouble than I suspected."

Emily pulled her feet away from his hands and tucked them under her skirt, trying to sit up straight and regain her dignity. She would have liked to return Austin's jacket to him, but she was still cold, and it would do no good to her pride to face him shaking like an aspen leaf. The problem was, she *didn't* know why someone would follow her, not precisely, anyway. "You mean they might try to rob me?" she ventured.

Austin let out a humorless chuckle. "Among other things."

Her green eyes reflected genuine puzzlement, and Austin suddenly felt like he'd just been kicked in the gut. He'd been too long on the cynical frontier. He couldn't remember the last time he'd met someone so trusting, so lacking in guile. "Do you have any idea how beautiful you are, Emily Kendall?" he asked softly. "What a face and figure like yours can do to a man's insides?"

Emily hunched the jacket closer around her shoulders. Austin's words were making her feel all topsy-turvy inside. "I'll have to ask you to stop talking like that, Mr. Matthews. I'm sure it's highly improper." Her voice dropped to a bare whisper.

Austin's last breath stopped dead in his throat. She looked small, enveloped in his coat. Her lips trembled slightly, full and the color of wild chokecherries. "I'll show you something that's improper," he said huskily, reaching out for her.

She hardly made an armful within the soft, bulky leather of his jacket. Austin settled her across his legs and looked one more time into her confused, swimming green eyes. "Highly improper," he murmured. His face descended to hers. Her mouth looked so ripe that he expected heat, but her lips were cold, like the rest of her. Full and soft as the petals of a flower, but cold. He warmed them gently with his own.

Emily's eyes fluttered closed and she seemed to thaw in his arms, her body melting against his. He deepened the kiss, until he found at last the heat he'd been seeking inside her mouth. He felt her start with surprise when he entered her with his tongue, and he tried to remind himself that Miss Emily Kendall was an innocent, so untutored as not even to know what a man might want with her lushly perfect body. But his senses were not listening. His exploration of her mouth became almost rhythmic as the rest of his body began demanding participation. The blood thundered through his veins, and he pressed her tightly against himself.

Emily made a little whimper in the back of her throat. Experience told Austin that it was in no way a protest, but it was enough to give him pause. He reluctantly pulled his mouth away from hers and looked down again at her flushed face. Her hair fell down around her in complete disarray, covering his arm in a silken blanket. Her eyes remained closed and her lips, now swollen and moist, were an erotic invitation. Once again he tried to ask his racing body to slow itself down to sensibility. He kissed her again, briskly this time, and her eyes opened.

He relaxed his hold on her, but she stayed nestled against him. Finally he said quietly, "I'm sorry."

At that Emily sat up, still on his lap, and leaned back to look into his eyes. The confusion was gone from her expression, replaced by wonderment and, deep down in her green eyes, a hint of mischief. "Sorry for what?" she asked.

Now it was Austin's turn to look confused. He lifted her away from him and set her down a safe distance from him on the grass. "Well, for... kissing you."

"But why would you be sorry?" Now the mischief was definitely there. "It was very nice. I could feel it all the way down to my toes." She stretched her legs straight out in front of her and wriggled her feet. "See, they're not cold anymore."

Austin's throat prickled with unexpected emotion. He had had more women than he would care to claim, but he had never met anyone so refreshingly direct and at the same time so innocent. It was a devastating combination, and one that he decided right then and there that he would do well to stay as far away from as possible.

He had to admit it, he was smitten with Miss Emily Kendall, and there was no way that could bode him anything but ill. She was a proper lady, he a rogue. She had come West to be a bride; he had known before he wore long pants that marriage was not for him. He had sworn that he would never form a family only to watch it slowly and painfully disintegrate as his had. Kissing her had been a mistake, unfair to them both.

He jumped to his feet. "Talking like that isn't proper for a lady, Emily. Didn't your ma tell you that?"

Emily grinned up at him. She felt wonderful. When she had embarked on her new life in the West, she had hoped to find the kind of excitement that was running riot throughout her this very minute. She hadn't known precisely what it would be like or what form it would take, but she had suspected that somewhere there was waiting for her an intensity of feeling such as she had never known before. It was something she would never have experienced in her life with Spencer. Of that she was now positive.

"Of course. This whole thing is improper. I thought we'd already established that. I guess I'm starting to decide that improper is more fun."

Austin suppressed a groan. She looked like a naughty child wrapped up in his coat and hugging her knees against her chest. But her face was still flushed from his kiss and her impossibly long, sable eyelashes swept up and down in unconscious flirtation. In less than a second he could be back down beside her and have her in his arms. In less than a minute he could be feeling her body mold once again to his. In less than five minutes he could have her ready...

He took a deep breath and reached down for his hat. As he brought his baser emotions under control, anger took over once again. Did the woman talk like this to every man she met? Did she know what it could lead to? His voice was unnaturally harsh. "You'll have to put your own boots on. I can't manage the damn things."

Her feet were dry now, and the stockings slipped on easily enough. The boots were more of a challenge. She pulled on them for a few moments, then looked up to Austin, who was glaring down at her as if she were an errant schoolboy. His expression wiped away the last of the good feelings left over from his kiss. "They're too small for me. I borrowed them from one of the other girls," she explained.

With a sigh Austin kneeled behind her and reached around to tug the boots into place. "You'll need some that fit if you like riding," he said gruffly.

Emily's heart sped up as his arms went around her once again. "I do like riding," she said distractedly.

Austin felt the second boot slip into place and stood up quickly, moving away to a safe distance. "But not alone," he ordered. "At least not this far away from town."

Emily bit her lip and tried to concentrate on Austin's words. "But I don't have anyone to ride with me."

"What about one of the other brides?"

"Most of them are horrified at the very idea."

Austin reached out his hand to help her up. "Ride with Dexter Kingsman, then. He's the one who gave you the horse, isn't he?"

The bitterness in Austin's voice made Emily feel better. She could not claim to be an expert at understanding men. Back home Spencer had been her one and only beau. Their dealings had been direct, without subterfuge and without passion. But she did recognize jealousy when she heard it. Austin Matthews was jealous of Dexter Kingsman. She didn't know what that meant, exactly, but it helped make up for the fact that he had been able to end their kiss with such seeming nonchalance.

"Dexter *lent* me the horse," she clarified. "But at the moment, I believe he's angry with me."

"Angry about what?"

"He was upset that I agreed to honor my appointment with Missouri Ike. He didn't want me to see the man."

If Austin had had any say in the matter, his sentiments would have been exactly the same, but now he felt himself resenting the wealthy businessman's possessiveness. "So Kingsman feels that he can tell you what to do?"

Emily smiled at him. "He can tell me what to do till the cows come home. That doesn't mean I'll do it."

Austin's annoyance disappeared. Maybe Kingsman wasn't in such an enviable position, after all. "If you marry him, you'll *have* to do what he says."

Emily laughed outright as she handed his jacket back to him. "La, Mr. Matthews, what a notion. I thought you were supposed to be progressive thinkers out here. Wives don't have to *obey* husbands nowadays, any more than husbands have *ever* obeyed wives."

Austin was beginning to feel uncomfortable. Marriage was not a subject to which he had ever devoted much thought, much less study. He found Emily's viewpoint rather sensible, but he was sure her ideas would be considered revolutionary in Seattle. "I'm not sure Dexter will agree with you."

"He'll have to," Emily replied smugly, and then, apparently to make her remarkable independence perfectly clear, she continued, "Perhaps *you* would ride with me, Mr. Matthews."

Austin breathed deeply of the cool, piny air. He was quite sure that Emily had no idea how close he'd come to losing control with her. Nor did he know what her response would have been if he had. Now she was asking him to ride out with her again, alone, with endless opportunities for a repetition of the occurrence. By God, the woman had better choose her bridegroom quickly, or he wouldn't answer for the consequences.

"I don't think that would be such a good idea, Emily," he said tiredly.

Emily was disappointed. She knew that her first priority was to the men on her prospective groom list. But the contract with Asa Mercer had been very clear that the men had been paying merely for the first *chance* to woo the brides. The brides were not to be forced into any marriage they did not want. After they had given all the men who paid their passage a fair hearing, the women were free to marry whomever they wanted. The only stipulation was that if another man wanted to marry one of the brides within the first year after their arrival, he would have to reimburse Mercer for the three hundred dollars' passage money. And no one, not even Dexter Kingsman with his fine manners and elegant gifts, had attracted her the way Austin did. But, of course, she knew that Austin wasn't the marrying kind. He was a saloon owner, for heaven's sake. He had all those...women working for him. It was an impossibility. A bad idea, as he himself had just stated.

"Then I'll just have to continue going by myself," she said, her lower lip thrust out slightly.

Austin led his horse out of the trees and mounted up, leaving her to climb up on Strawberry unassisted. Fortunately, the wonderful animal stayed rock-still while she made her clumsy attempts, and on the third try she was over the top and perched on the saddle in triumph. She sent Austin a defiant glance, then urged the horse forward.

Austin let her pass without comment, and until they were off the trail and back out on the main road neither said a word. Austin's eyes kept wandering over the up-and-down motion of her shapely back and rear end, though the latter was mostly disguised by the billows of her skirt and petticoats. Not clothes for horseback riding, he noted.

When they reached the road he pulled alongside her. "You need to sit straighter. Don't hunch over like that or you'll end up with an aching back."

Emily straightened her posture and immediately felt the difference in comfort. "You see, Mr. Matthews, if you went riding with me, you could give me lessons."

The words were so close to what he had been thinking in a different context a few minutes ago that Austin flushed. If he did ride out with her again, he knew that the kind of lessons he would be likely to give her went beyond riding. But if he refused her, the woman was fool enough to ride out alone, as she had promised. "I'll take you out a couple times, Emily," he said finally. "At least until your Mr. Kingsman gets over his pique."

A warmth settled in Emily's middle. She knew there was no future in a friendship with Austin Matthews, but at least it appeared that there would be a present. And at the moment that seemed to be enough. With a light heart, she gave Strawberry a nudge and let her stretch out into a run.

When they got back to the hotel, Austin didn't dismount from his horse. He watched her clamber awkwardly down from her horse and hand the reins to Homer, whose blush testified that he, too, was smitten with the hotel's lovely guest. Emily seemed unaware of the boy's adoring gaze, and looked up at Austin. "Thank you for... helping me out there."

With exaggerated courtesy he tipped his hat and said gravely, "It was my pleasure, ma'am." Then his tone took on that deadly seriousness. "If you should happen to see Missouri Ike hanging around you, Emily, send me word."

Emily's smile died, and she nodded solemnly. Then Austin whirled his horse around, sending dust billowing up around Emily's skirts. Before she could say another word, he was gone.

She watched him ride away. On a horse or afoot, Austin Matthews cut a fine figure. But the man was a puzzle, Emily thought as she slowly walked into the hotel. He had now come to her rescue more times than she could count. He obviously cared something for her. He'd even kissed her. But since he'd abruptly cut off their lovemaking back on the trail, he'd been at turns distant, annoyed or sarcastic. Oh well, she told herself, she really ought to put the man out of her mind. She'd already determined that nothing could come of their friendship.

Her happy mood from the ride disintegrated. Perhaps she'd best forget about riding lessons with Austin Matthews. In spite of her experience on the trail today, she wasn't afraid of riding alone. It was true that most of the New England brides she had traveled with would be terrified at the idea. Certainly Ida Mae would. But she herself was made of sterner stuff, she thought proudly. No western rowdy was going to frighten her from doing something so enjoyable.

Her resolve made, she started to cross the lobby to the big mahogany staircase when her attention was drawn to the entrance of the dining room. Ida Mae was there with Parmelia, Cynthia and several of the other brides. They spotted her immediately.

"Emily," Ida Mae called excitedly. "Come join the celebration."

"What are we celebrating?" Emily asked as she entered the room to find most of the New Englanders assembled.

"The first wedding. Parmelia has accepted Mr. Carmichael's proposal." It was petite Cynthia Stoddard who answered. Many of the brides had predicted that Cynthia with her natural blond curls and limpid blue eyes would be the first to wed. But she didn't appear to be the least resentful of her friend Parmelia's success.

Parmelia was accepting the congratulations of her friends with a flushed face and a huge smile that gave a special glow to her rather plain features, making her look almost pretty. Emily made her way through the group to embrace her and add her good wishes. "Mr. Carmichael is a fine man, Parmelia. I hope you two will be very happy," she told her.

Parmelia gave a happy laugh. "Eugene may not be as rich as Dexter Kingsman, Emily, but I don't think I'd trade you now, even if you offered."

Emily gave a polite smile and refrained from commenting on exactly what she would trade Dexter Kingsman for at this moment. "When's the wedding to be?"

"A week from Saturday." The flush on Parmelia's face grew a degree darker. "Eugene says he can't wait any longer."

"A week!" Several of the brides echoed Emily's words. The enthusiastic chatter died down for a moment as the realization came to each of them that this unlikely excursion they had set out on last year in Massachusetts was now coming to its destined conclusion. Any one of them could be next, any day now—wedded and bedded and committed forever to life on the frontier.

As if timed to coincide with their sudden soberness, Asa Mercer appeared in the arched dining room doorway. As usual, he was jauntily dressed and spoke with a brisk optimism. "Ladies! My goodness, but you are all looking well! I can see that the beautiful city of Seattle is proving beneficial to everyone."

The ladies parted automatically to let him make his way to the front of the room where he could address them. "I've come to congratulate Miss Carruthers, here, on the successful completion of her agreement." He stopped to nod at the beaming Parmelia, then ran a slender finger along the inner edge of his collar, as if it were fitting him too tightly.

"I can only hope that many of you ladies are planning to make a similar decision soon." His smile dimmed. "Very soon."

"Well, there's no hurry," Rose Bartlett, the older woman who had been a war widow, pointed out. "Our agreement says that we have a year to decide on a husband. If we don't choose one by that time, you are free from your obligation to provide us with further food and lodging."

Asa Mercer cleared his throat. "It appears we may have to alter those terms just a bit."

"What do you mean?" Several of the women asked the question at once. Emily was silent, but she had the feeling that Mr. Mercer's news did not bode well for any of them.

Mercer continued, "The plain facts are, ladies...the money's just about gone."

At this pronouncement pandemonium broke. Several of the women burst into tears. Others shouted in anger, backing the diminutive Mercer right up against the dining room's potbellied stove. Emily could see the sweat begin to dribble along the man's sideburns.

"What do you mean—gone?" Rose Bartlett's booming voice rose above the din.

Mercer's tone was defensive. "You all know the difficulty we had back East. We had over five hundred women signed up, then the criticism started. It took me

three times as long as I thought to get started back.
And then with only forty-six of you, I've had to re-
fund some of the fees."

"I thought the men knew that they'd have to pay
their money and take their chances," the robust widow
retorted. "What's this about refunds?"

Mercer looked embarrassed. "It's true that the
original understanding was no refunds, but a few of the
men have been, ah, shall we say, more *unhappy* than I
had bargained for."

"So you gave in to them to save that scrawny neck of
yours? Isn't that about it?" Rose Bartlett brought her
angry face within inches of Mercer's. Compared to
Rose's, Mercer's neck looked scrawny indeed.

Emily stayed out of the argument. If the money was
gone, it was gone. Berating the hapless Mercer would
do nothing to change the situation. He himself had no
funds to support them.

"Here's what I have figured," he said, bending
slightly backward to put a little more distance between
himself and the irate widow's heaving chest. "If we can
double you all up, two to a room, we should have suf-
ficient funds to last until each of you has a chance to
make a final decision about a husband."

At this, the women calmed some. This just meant
cramped quarters. They'd been in worse circum-
stances together on the ship.

But the widow Bartlett leaned still closer to Mercer
and demanded, "Exactly how much longer will that
give us?"

Mercer tried to take one more step back and jumped
when his rear end met the overheated brass trim ex-
tending out from the stove. Then, in a move worthy of
the cleverest of foxes eluding a pack of trained hounds,

he scooted around Mrs. Bartlett's impressive form and darted for the door. Turning back to the group of women, he said, "I'd say it will give us all—" his glance fell to the floor and he continued in a low voice "—maybe six weeks." Then he was gone.

This time there was no uproar. One by one the women had come to the same conclusion as Emily. If there was no money left, there was no way to ask Mercer for a miracle. As he had said, they would have to make their choice, and make it soon. It was the only solution. They had no family here, no friends. There was no way any of them could survive in this town without the support of a husband.

Parmelia, whose engagement celebration had been thoroughly dampened, tried to cheer up her friends. "It's really for the best, you know. Why, getting engaged is the most wonderful thing that's ever happened to me."

A few of the women answered her with brave smiles, but most were somber. Six weeks was not much time. There had been no provision in their agreement with Mercer for passage home if the experiment did not work. It had been a one-way trip. Some had families back home who might be able to afford their ticket, but six weeks was not even enough time to get word back home and receive the money.

Subdued, with worried eyes, one by one they gave Parmelia a last embrace and filtered out of the dining room.

Ida Mae was in tears as she came up to Emily. "What are you going to do, Emily?" she asked.

Emily shook her head. "I'm not sure yet. But I do know that I'm not going to commit to marriage for the rest of my life just so I can have a place to sleep."

"But it doesn't appear that we have any other choice," Ida Mae said woefully.

"I'm surprised you're so upset, Ida. I thought you and Mr. Smedley were close to making an announcement like Parmelia's today."

"I think I love him, but we have a problem."

"What's the matter?" Emily took her friend's hand and drew her out to a settee in the lobby.

"It's Mr. Briggs. He says he's in love with me, too. And if Eldo...Mr. Smedley...and I marry, it will ruin their friendship forever."

Emily was relieved. The problem didn't seem to be insurmountable. Briggs would get over his infatuation in time. "Ida, dear, there are going to be all kinds of disappointed suitors once everyone makes their final choices. Mr. Briggs will just have to get used to the idea."

"Eldo is very unhappy about the situation. The two have been friends since they were boys."

"They'll work it out."

Ida Mae looked hopeful. "Do you really think so?"

"Of course. If Mr. Smedley really loves you, he's not going to let a friend's opposition hold him back."

"I hope you're right." Ida Mae wiped her remaining tears away with the hanky that she now carried as though it were part of her hand.

Emily gave her friend a quick buss on the cheek, then jumped up. "Come on, let's go move your things into my room before one of us ends up with bassoon-voice Bartlett as a roommate."

Chapter Five

Asa Mercer's ultimatum had brought a frenzy of activity to the Occidental Hotel. Hearing of the newly imposed time limits, prospective bridegrooms had redoubled their efforts to woo their assigned brides. There was such an array of flowers and sweetmeats and gifts arriving that Emily told Ida Mae it looked like Jenny Lind's dressing room on opening night.

Dexter presented himself at the hotel the very evening of Mercer's visit to apologize for his peremptory behavior and to present a gigantic bouquet of lilacs that left Emily and Ida Mae's room smelling like a perfume factory. Emily forgave him without a fuss and they enjoyed a pleasant supper together. Though she meant to keep her resolve not to be pressured into marriage, Emily knew that Dexter was the most sensible choice for her—the only choice, really.

For the first time that night he kissed her on the lips. A short, respectful kiss, which sent the blood rushing into her cheeks instantly, not, she was horrified to realize, because of Dexter's kiss, but because it brought her back to those moments in the forest with Austin. Dexter took her confusion for innocence, and even apologized for having taken such a liberty. However, he followed his apology with a gentle reminder that time was rather of the essence.

The entire encounter left her depressed and tired. After her ride with Austin, she had fantasized about being able to spend some time with him before she would have to settle down to the business of choosing a husband. Now it appeared obvious that she should stay away from Austin and concentrate on building a relationship with Dexter. And somehow the prospect did not give her the thrill she had imagined when she had pictured her Western adventure while still back in Lowell.

Adding to her depression was the fact that five of her other suitors, all on her list except Missouri Ike, who was out of town, also felt the need to make an appearance at the hotel within days after Mercer's ultimatum. One by one she met with them and told them as gently as she could that she did not feel the attraction necessary for a lifelong commitment.

Fred Johnson, the miner, was the worst. An actual tear escaped from his eye and made its way along the sun-baked crevices of his face. It was enough to make Emily wish she were several different people and could marry them all, then, alternately, that she would never have to see another man in her life. Many of the other brides were experiencing similar dilemmas.

Fortunately, Parmelia's wedding at the end of the week distracted them all from thinking about their own futures. Friday night they gave her a party—ladies only—in the hotel dining room. A determined effort was made to steer away from any discussion of the fast-approaching deadline for choosing husbands. Many of the brides already had a good idea whom they wanted

to marry, and those who didn't appeared to be re-
signed to making the best of the available candidates.

Emily felt herself being pulled along by the momen-
tum. Dexter had become more possessive and sure of
himself with each suitor that she dismissed. He knew
that she had turned down all the others on her list except Ike, who, apart from his absence, was not even
worth considering.

By the time of the wedding Saturday night, Emily
herself, was assuming that an understanding with
Dexter was imminent. Perhaps they would become engaged that evening. But she couldn't get over her feeling that somehow she ought to be happier at the
prospect.

Dexter had offered the use of the cookhouse behind
his sawmill for the wedding party. Emily and several of
the other brides missed the church ceremony in order
to decorate the big cedar room and lay out the food. By
the time guests began filtering over from the church,
the room had been transformed from a cookhouse to
a ballroom, with tables pushed to each end and room
for dancing in the middle.

Three of the burliest lumberjacks Emily had ever
seen had formed an unlikely orchestra. Two of them
played fiddles that looked impossibly small and frag-
ile in their big hands, and the third added a sprightly
accompaniment on a nine-inch harmonica.

The newlywed Mr. and Mrs. Eugene Carmichael led
off with a waltz. Parmelia, her face wreathed in smiles
and her hair in early summer wildflowers, never took
her eyes from her new husband's face. That is what it
should feel like to be married, Emily said to herself,
watching them glide by. She turned to Dexter, who was
standing impatiently beside her, waiting for the signal

that would allow the wedding guests to join in the dance. He was impeccably dressed in a dark blue suit and snowy white shirt and string tie. He *is* handsome, Emily admitted. Perhaps the day would come when she would look at him in the same way Parmelia was looking at Eugene.

The dance ended just as Ida Mae and Eldo Smedley came up beside them. Ida Mae was radiant with her arm tucked securely in Eldo's. A faint odor of vinegar clung to her. She'd been using Rose Bartlett's vinegar plasters faithfully around her neck all week, and they seemed to be doing some good. The sniffling had subsided considerably and her nose had practically resumed its normal color.

"Isn't it romantic, Emily?" Ida Mae asked dreamily. "It's just like we imagined back in Massachusetts. Our dreams are all coming true."

Emily smiled. "It certainly appears that Parmelia's dreams have come true," she agreed, nodding at the bridal couple, who were now, amid much laughter, attempting to drink ale together from the same mug.

"You see, that's why you women get into trouble," Dexter interrupted. He was half smiling, but his underlying tone was serious. "Marriage is not a dream. It's a very serious, practical arrangement and should be entered into by both parties with the utmost thought and analysis."

Emily bit her lip. "Just like one of your business ventures?"

Dexter's blond hair stayed immaculately in place as he nodded vehemently. "Exactly! If only every move we make in life could be planned as carefully as a business, we'd all be much happier."

Emily made a face at Ida Mae behind Dexter's back, then grabbed his arm. "Does your careful planning allow for dancing, Mr. Kingsman?" she asked brightly.

Dexter's serious expression relaxed as he looked down at his partner. His eyes looked almost tender, then he bowed slightly and said, "Dancing with you, my sweet Emily, will always be good business."

They moved out onto the dance floor, where many couples now swayed to the slow strains of a waltz. Dexter danced extremely well, and Emily was moved with the sheer enjoyment of the rhythm. She didn't object when he tightened his hold on her and moved her closer than the prescribed arm's length. She looked up into Dexter's eyes, which were as blue as the Washington sky, and let herself be lulled by the gentle music, the happy emotions of the night and the feel of strong arms around her.

"May I cut in?"

Both dancers started at the interruption and halted in midstep. The rest of the couples glided around them as Dexter asked irritably, "What are you doing here, Matthews?"

Austin smiled benevolently. "Same as you, I expect. I'm a wedding guest. And I'm asking for the favor of a dance with Miss Kendall here."

Dexter's eyes clouded. "This is a party for decent folk. You don't belong here."

Emily watched as Austin's eyes narrowed. His tone was dangerously silky. "I guess Eugene Carruthers figured that if my money was decent enough to bankroll his smithy, that makes me decent enough to dance at his wedding."

Dexter's jaw clenched. In another minute one of them would be taking a punch at the other. Emily didn't want Parmelia's wedding to end in fisticuffs, so she put a soothing hand on Dexter's arm. "I perhaps owe Mr. Matthews a dance after his help the day we arrived here," she told him gently. "Why don't you go get us both some punch, and I'll be with you directly."

Dexter glowered but did not protest as Austin seized the opportunity and whirled her into the middle of the dancers.

"Playing peacemaker?" he asked sardonically.

"I was merely trying to prevent you two from ruining Parmelia's wedding reception with your stupid quarrels."

"I didn't have a quarrel with anyone. The only reason I came tonight was to have a dance with you."

His words made her flush. He held her even more tightly than Dexter, and she could feel a strange heat developing between their bodies. She closed her eyes. Perhaps if she could not see how intently he watched her movements...

The music switched to a slower tempo. Closing her eyes hadn't helped. Austin's thighs brushed against her as he turned her in perfect time. "Open your eyes, Emily," he said softly after several moments.

Her long lashes fluttered open. "I've never seen such eyes as yours. Green as emeralds. A man could lose his soul for those eyes." His voice was low and deep, a husky caress.

The heat that had smoldered between them flamed suddenly and seared her cheeks. She missed a step, then another, but Austin's strong lead kept her steady. "Has it gotten very warm in here?" she asked weakly.

Austin made a quick survey of the room. He spotted Kingsman over by the punch table talking with his mill foreman, Ethan Witherspoon. Before Emily knew what he was doing, Austin had waltzed her out the big open double doors of the cookhouse and several yards off into the black summer night.

"Where are you going?" Emily protested, but without pulling herself out of his arms. The sound of the music and the laughter grew muted, replaced by a nighttime cacophony of insects in the trees and the mating call of frogs in the millpond. There was no breeze, but the sudden change from the heated dance floor made Emily shiver.

"You said you were warm," Austin answered nonchalantly. He had stopped dancing and now put an arm around her and led her gently along the path down to the water.

Emily looked back at the light streaming out from the cookhouse. "We shouldn't be out here," she said.

"Don't worry. Your boyfriend is busy talking business. He won't miss you." He stopped when they reached a fallen tree trunk at the edge of the little pond. Without hesitation he took off his immaculate cream-colored jacket and threw it over the tree, then motioned for her to sit. "Of course, if you were *my* girl, I'd never let you out of my sight. And if any other man tried to touch you, I'd knock him to kingdom come."

He spoke so mildly and looked so handsome and impeccably attired that it was hard to associate him with violence. Emily couldn't help but laugh. "What makes you think Dexter won't do that very thing?"

Austin lifted an eyebrow. "I suppose he could try," he said with unruffled confidence.

"We should go back in," Emily said more seriously. Both Dexter and Austin were strapping, dangerous men. She didn't want either hurt. Her ideas of adventure had never included the least desire to be fought over like a medieval damsel.

"We'll go in shortly," Austin said without concern, seating himself next to her on the tree trunk. He put his arm around her as she shivered again. "Are Easterners naturally cold-blooded or is it just you?"

Emily shrugged, warming immediately at the feel of his body next to hers. "Maybe Washington Territory is just too cold for us."

"It hasn't seemed any too cold for a lot of you lately. I hear tell there's been more engagements celebrated at the Occidental this past week than at a bawdy house at the end of a cattle drive." His voice was rich and teasing.

She smiled. "I don't think I approve of your analogy. We're not talking about the same kind of engagements."

Austin grinned. "We're not?"

Emily shook her head in good-humored reproof. Back in Massachusetts she would probably have been horrified to be discussing such a subject with a gentleman. Or with anyone, for that matter. But her association with Austin had gradually broadened her notions of propriety.

"Anyway, the rumor is that Mercer's making all you ladies choose a husband by the end of July. Any truth to that?" His tone was still light, but had taken on that serious edge she had come to recognize, and his dark eyes looking down at hers were grave. His strong features looked devilishly handsome in the moonlight.

"None of us can be forced to choose against our will. But Mr. Mercer has told us that there will be no more money after that date. We would have to make our own way."

A muscle flinched along Austin's lean jawline. He hesitated for a moment, then said, "If you need help, Emily, I want you to know it's available...money to get you back home again, whatever." Then, as if to prevent any accusation of good-heartedness, he twisted his smile into an exaggerated leer. "No strings attached, my pretty."

Emily shook her head. "Why do you want to help me, Austin? You'll have to pardon my frankness, but you just don't seem the philanthropic type."

Austin gave a self-derisive laugh. "Damned if I know. Maybe I've never had a beautiful woman land in a heap at my feet before. Or maybe it's those freckles you try so hard to hide." He ran a gentle finger along the bridge of her nose. The moonlight reflected off the pond as brightly as a lantern and clearly revealed the sprinkle of brown along her finely etched cheeks.

"I'm serious," Emily said, swallowing hard. Austin's touch on her skin was as light as a wisp of air, but she felt it all the way down to the base of her stomach.

The smile dropped off his face. "So am I, Emily. If you're set on marrying Kingsman, then fine and dandy, but I don't like the idea of you having to sell yourself to the highest bidder just because Mercer can't keep his finances straight."

Emily didn't answer. The protectiveness in his voice was more seductive than his earlier compliments. Tears threatened behind her eyes.

"Are you?" he asked grimly.

"What?"

"Are you set on marrying Kingsman?"

She looked away from the scrutiny of his magnetic eyes. "No," she said sharply. Then more softly,

"Maybe. I don't know. It's still so soon. He's been very kind...and generous. He'd make a good husband...."

"A right proper one, eh?" Austin said with a half snort of disgust. "Has he even kissed you yet?"

Emily pulled herself upright in annoyance. "I don't see how that's any of your business."

Austin's teeth gleamed white. "So he hasn't."

"You're insufferable, Mr. Matthews. As I said, it's none of your business, but as a matter of fact, Dexter has kissed me."

Austin's dark eyes flared. "But not like I did—like *we* did—out on the trail last week."

"I wouldn't care to make comparisons," she said loftily.

Her little nose tilted upward slightly. Austin turned her in his arms. "Perhaps you've forgotten what it was like. Shall I refresh your memory?"

This time there was no gentleness in his kiss. His mouth took hers in a hungry fervor that had him instantly stiffening with passion. He slipped to his knees in front of her, oblivious to the muddy ground against his expensive trousers. Folding her back against his arm he moved his lips from her mouth to the tender hollow of her neck where her pulse beat in counterpoint to his own. His hand was at her waist, then he shifted slowly to run it along the smooth taffeta of her gown up to the base of her breast, where a first soft stroke with his thumb elicited a gasp.

This time Emily had been ready for the heady dizziness of his kiss. Sensation sluiced down through her body as she closed her eyes and let her mouth respond to his. His face blotted out the moonlight, and the slow touch of his hand along the front of her dress blotted out all other senses. He stroked gently, through her dress, but it was enough to make her take an involuntary breath.

She turned slightly, allowing his hand to sample the fullness, his palm encircling her hardened nipple with exquisite skill. Her head fell back onto the tree bark while he lifted himself away from her and began to concentrate on learning the swells and curves of her through his touch. His exploration was almost reverent, completely ridding her of any embarrassment. The unfamiliar buildup of feeling from her breasts down to the area between her legs was exquisite.

Austin's hands burned. Experience told him she was barely corseted underneath the thin material of her dress. Her waist was naturally tiny, a tantalizing contrast to the fullness above. He fought an overwhelming desire to strip the covering from her, to feel her skin. Instead, he sought her mouth once more for a long, drugging kiss.

When he pulled away again, her eyes in the moonlight were full of wonderment, as though she had just seen something unexpectedly beautiful. Austin felt a strange constriction in his chest.

"You take my breath away, Emily Kendall," he told her softly.

Emily continued watching him, her green eyes sparkling with unspoken emotion. She lifted a hand and smoothed his hair back from his forehead. As the world came back into focus, she could feel the rough bark behind her head, smell the musty dampness of the night air.

Gently Austin pulled her upright and brushed a few clinging pieces of wood from the back of her hair.

"You didn't answer my question. Are you going to marry Kingsman?" he asked soberly.

Emily took a deep breath of the damp night air. Once again she had completely lost herself to the attentions of this man. And once again, he had been the one to pull away. It seemed to her somehow unfair, almost cruel. Austin was able to turn his lovemaking off and on like the wick of a lantern. And then he had the audacity to ask about her marriage, as casually as if he were asking if she would be going to church on Sunday. She felt a surge of anger. "Do you think I would let you kiss me like that if I were promised to another man? I'm not one of your...*doxies*, you know."

"More's the pity," Austin said, a rueful edge to his light tone.

They both sat in silence for several moments, listening to the resonant croak of a bullfrog at the edge of the pond.

Gradually Emily's anger drained away, leaving in its place the melancholy she had been unable to shake for the past few days. Finally she said wistfully, "What would you do if I *were* one of your doxies, Austin?"

He gave a humorless chuckle. "Why, Miss Kendall. What an utterly improper question!"

Then he looked down at her, his expression grave. "If you were a...doxy...I wouldn't be sitting alongside you with my hands in my pockets. I wouldn't be wasting time talking when there would be other, more pleasurable uses for my mouth. And when I got through with you there would be absolutely no question about whether you would ever even look at Dexter Kingsman...or any other man but me."

A tear made its way down Emily's cheek. "But I'm not," she whispered.

"No," Austin said harshly. Then he stood and offered her his hand. "Though you might be accused of being one if I don't get you back inside."

She stood and he retrieved his coat, shaking it once to remove the wood dust. He didn't bother to put it on, just flung it carelessly over one shoulder as he put his opposite arm around her and steered her up the bank toward the cookhouse. He didn't feel much like dancing anymore. He'd take Emily back where she belonged and then head back to the saloon, his bottle, perhaps one of those "doxies" Emily had mentioned. Though the prospect didn't much appeal to him at the moment.

He recognized Dexter's blond hair before he could see the features of the man who came out of the darkness toward them. The mill owner stalked toward them, the stiffness of his body reflecting his fury.

"Where have you been?" he demanded angrily.

Emily's hand on Austin's arm tightened, but she spoke directly and with soft dignity. "I'm not sure I like your tone, Dexter."

Austin took a step away from her. If he were Kingsman, he, too, would be mad as hell. As much as he hated to admit it, Dexter Kingsman would be a good husband for Emily. He had money, brains, good looks and comported himself like a man. Austin couldn't deny that he and the beautiful New Englander had a strong mutual attraction. The decent thing to do would be for Austin to step back and let her make for herself the kind of life she deserved.

"Miss Kendall felt a bit faint with the heat while we were dancing," Austin said mildly. "We just walked out a few steps so she could get some air."

Dexter looked pointedly at the soiled jacket slung over Austin's shoulder, then back to Emily, whose green eyes looked at him without flinching. Finally he said, "Well, thank you, then. But now I can look after her myself."

Austin gave a little nod. "Certainly. I was about to take my leave." He turned to Emily with a polite smile. "Thank you for the dance, Miss Kendall." Then he turned and faded into the darkness.

Emily watched him leave with a lump in her throat. What demon fate had made her fall for the one man in Seattle who didn't want a bride? Why did Austin Matthews have to be the one man who made her heart sing and her body ache?

"Are you feeling all right now, Emily?" Dexter asked stiffly.

She blinked her eyes impatiently over the threatening tears. "Yes, thank you, I'm fine. Weren't we going to have some punch?"

"That was quite some time ago, Emily," he said pointedly.

Emily lowered her eyes. Dexter had a right to be angry with her. It had been wrong for her to disappear with Austin, wrong and foolish to kiss him. Her one chance at happiness in Washington was the man standing beside her. She had better make up her mind to accept that fact and start acting accordingly. "I'm sorry, Dexter." Her tone was contrite. "I really did need some fresh air. But I'm fine now. Let's go on back in and dance some more."

Dexter took immediate advantage of her apparent surrender. "I'd rather not have you talking to Austin Matthews anymore, Emily. He's not our sort of people, you know."

Emily felt herself bristling, but fought to keep control. She had no intention of letting her husband tell her whom she could or could not talk to, but Dexter had reason for his anger tonight, and she would let it pass. With a smile she put her arm on his and walked with him into the dance.

Ida Mae and several of the other brides had formed a quilting society with the goal of producing one quilt for each new marriage. Parmelia's was almost finished, and following church the day after the wedding, the group had gathered in Cynthia Stoddard's room to work on it. Ida Mae had urged Emily to join them, but she had refused.

The truth was she was feeling unusually low in spirits and didn't think a quilting party would do much to raise them. It was too much like the tedious mill work back in Lowell that she had come West to get away from. She had hoped that Seattle would have more excitement to offer, but everyday life here seemed even duller than back home.

Dexter had been attentive the night before, and when he brought her back to her room, his kiss had held the first hint of a kind of rough, possessive passion. But the evening had left Emily confused and unhappy. She couldn't have Austin. Not only was he not on *her* list of prospective bridegrooms, he had made it very clear that he would never be on *anyone's* list—ever. So she ought to be happy with Dexter. He was the ideal man. She was the envy of all the other brides. So why had she lain awake that night watching the moonlight stream through the tiny hotel room window until tears blurred the view?

She stood up. Sitting inside her room all day would do nothing to improve her mood. With sudden decision, she decided she would ignore Austin's warnings and take Strawberry out. A brisk ride in the country should chase away the gloom, she told herself.

She began pulling on Cynthia's boots, which she had neglected to return, when there was a knock on the door. She hurriedly tugged the difficult boots into place, then crossed the room and opened the door.

It was Mr. Smedley's friend, Ephraim Briggs. Emily greeted him with surprise. "Hello, Mr. Briggs. Ida Mae's not here just now."

Briggs turned his hat around and around in his hands and ducked his head a couple of times before he spoke. "Actually, Miss Emily, it was you I wanted to see."

Emily hesitated. She had the feeling that Briggs was going to ask her help in his infatuation with Ida Mae, and she didn't know what she would answer. Her friend was very happy with Eldo Smedley, and the couple would probably be engaged by now if it weren't for the man standing in front of her.

"I guess I could go down to the lobby and talk with you a spell," she said finally. Though he seemed harmless enough, she wasn't about to invite Briggs into her hotel room.

"I'd appreciate it, ma'am."

"Let me just get my shawl." She snatched her shawl and room key from the dresser, then joined Briggs in the hall. "What did you want to see me about?"

Mr. Briggs shuffled his feet along the Persian carpet. "It's about Miss Ida Mae." For the first time he looked Emily directly in the eyes. "I love her."

Briggs was not a handsome man. He had a bulbous nose that marred the evenness of his nondescript features. But his eyes were a soft, rich brown, and right now they were full of pain.

Emily sighed and led the way down the carpeted stairway. They seated themselves in a secluded corner of the lobby and Briggs continued, "I don't mean to put it to you so bluntly, but it's the plain truth. I love Ida Mae, and if I can't have her, I think I'd just as soon crawl away like a wounded coyote and die."

"Now, surely you can't mean that, Mr. Briggs." Emily was at a loss to comfort the man, who was obviously every bit as distressed as Ida Mae had led her to believe. "There are quite a few wonderful women who have not yet been spoken for, and they say more women will be coming into the territory every day now. Somewhere out there is the right one for you."

Briggs shook his head. "Ida Mae's the right one for me. I knew the minute I laid eyes on her. It was just this stupid alphabet system of Mercer's that gave Smedley first chance with her. Now he thinks he's got some kind of right to her. And he ain't. She's mine."

His assurance was frightening. Emily spoke gently. "Now, Mr. Briggs, I think in the end that decision is up to Ida Mae. Don't you agree?"

His nose moved oddly in the middle of his face as he shook his head. "I agree just fine, as long as the one she chooses is me."

There was no arguing with the man. Emily tried several more times to make him see that Ida Mae would marry the man who captured her heart, but he didn't even seem to hear what she was saying. Finally, she excused herself, saying she had an appointment to ride, and not bothering to mention that her appointment was with her horse.

*   *   *

By Monday morning, Emily was feeling better. She had been right about the horseback ride. It had lifted her spirits and given her back some of her typical energy. And during the course of the ride, an idea had taken shape in her mind that just might allow her to put off committing to Dexter or any man until she was good and ready.

She had lain awake thinking about it most of the night. At first light she could not wait any longer to tell someone. She shook her sleeping friend.

"Ida, wake up."

Ida Mae's first few words each morning were accompanied by long pauses while she cleared her nose. Emily had come to the conclusion that whatever Ida Mae's problem was, it was *not* a cold, and she had begged Ida to stop troubling herself with more home remedies.

"What is it, Emily?" Ida Mae asked sleepily.

"I need to talk to you. I have an idea about what we can do when Mercer cuts off our funds."

Ida Mae sat up in bed and reached over to the bed table for her hanky. "I thought we were all going to be married by then."

Emily nodded impatiently. "He wants us all to be, but that doesn't mean we *have* to be. You and Eldo aren't ready because of Mr. Briggs, and I'm not ready because... well, I'm just not ready."

Ida Mae yawned and leaned back against the pillows. "So what's your idea?"

Emily's eyes gleamed. "You and I, Ida dear, are going to bring *culture* to the Wild West."

Chapter Six

Ida Mae closed her eyes. "Just what exactly do you mean by culture, Emily?" she asked tiredly.

Emily bounced on her knees next to Ida Mae on the bed and grabbed one of her hands. "Well, you know...concerts, dance, oratory. Think about it, Ida. What has there been to do in this town since we've arrived besides fending off suitors?"

"I told you to come with me to the quilting, Emily—"

"Quilting! If I'd wanted to spend my life staring at a piece of fabric, I'd have stayed in Lowell."

"But, Emily," Ida Mae objected wanly, "how are you going to find performers for that kind of thing out here?"

"The same way Mr. P. T. Barnum does it. I'm going to become an impresario."

Ida Mae giggled. "There's no such thing as a woman impresario."

"Maybe not now, but that doesn't mean there can't be."

Ida Mae rubbed her hands along her forehead just above her eyebrows, where she complained of a constant dull ache. "Emily, be sensible. Even if you could become a female impresario or whatever you call it, you couldn't possibly do anything in five weeks. And we only have five weeks."

Emily sat back on her heels and thought for a moment. It was true that she didn't have much time, but she had spent a good deal of the night working things out in her mind, and she had come to the conclusion that it *was* possible. "I'll need to ask Dexter if we could use the cookhouse again until we build the opera house," she thought aloud.

"Opera house!"

"Well, of course. We need a hall for performances. Seattle is booming. There's no reason why this town can't support an opera house."

Ida Mae had seen the same fire in Emily's eyes that day they were working side by side at the cotton loom when her friend had persuaded her to make the journey west. Emily's enthusiasm had always been infectious, and she had a way of making the most outlandish ideas sound perfectly logical.

"How soon do you think you could schedule a concert?"

Emily wrinkled her nose. Ida Mae was a bit too down-to-earth for Emily's tastes, but her attention to details could be valuable. "We'd have to try to get whatever entertainers are on the circuit to San Francisco. It would be several weeks."

"So how do we live in the meantime?"

"We could hold a musicale. I know that Parmelia brought her flute from back home, and you could play your piano. Why, you were the best pianist in Lowell."

Ida Mae accepted the compliment without demure and added reluctantly, "Jessica Emory brought her zither."

"There, you see!" Emily clapped her hands in excitement. "We can start a Friday night musicale and use the proceeds to live on. Anything left over can go to the fund for the opera house."

"Of course, the women would like it. I know quite a few who were members of the Haydn Society back home," Ida Mae said. "But do you think the men around here would really be interested in the classics?"

"If the women are there, the men will be there. You know as well as I do—where we go, they go. Why, you'd have had a dozen of them at your quilting party if you'd allowed it."

Ida Mae giggled again, now thoroughly carried along by her friend's excitement. "Wouldn't it just be something to tell the rest of the girls that we're ignoring the deadline?" she said happily.

"Of course it would! You could tell Eldo and Mr. Briggs to go off and work things out and let you know when they're ready to act like grown-ups. And I could tell Dexter that I intend to marry only when I'm good and ready... and I could tell Austin Matthews..."

Her smile dimmed and her voice trailed off. Ida Mae gave her friend's hand a squeeze. "You like him, don't you? That saloon owner."

Emily nodded glumly. "I have no idea why. He's exasperating and spends half his time laughing at me. And he says marriage is only for buggy-whipped fools who can't think of anything better to do with their time."

Ida Mae made a strangled sound. "What a horrible man! Land's sake, Emily, how could you possibly like him? Of course, he is ... comely."

Emily laughed. "A bit more than 'comely,' Ida, and when he kisses me—"

Ida sat straight up in bed. "Kisses you! Why, Emily Kendall."

Emily pushed her friend back down against the covers. "Don't look so shocked. I told you before we ever came out here that I aimed to find out what life is all about. And one thing I'm finding out is that there's a lot more to a man and a woman than polite conversation on the parlor settee for four years like I had with Spencer."

"But, Emily—"

"No, don't even bother to chastise me, Ida. I've been kissed by Austin Matthews ... *thoroughly* kissed. And if the chance arises I just might let him kiss me again, even though I know there's no future in it. And if Dexter ever kisses me like that ... I just might up and marry him after all."

Ida Mae shook her head but smiled. "And the world would lose its first female impresario."

"Exactly. Which would be a shame, don't you think?"

The two friends began laughing so hard that Emily rolled over on her side on the bed and Ida Mae dabbed at her eyes with her hanky. Their mirth died immediately at the sound of a knock on the door. Emily got up to answer it. She hoped it wasn't Mr. Briggs again. She hadn't told Ida Mae about his visit. Poor Ida was distressed enough about the rift she had caused between the two good friends.

She opened the door a crack. It was Homer, the boy from the livery.

"M-Morning, ma'am," he stammered, the tips of his ears bright red.

"Good morning, Homer. What can we do for you?"

The boy looked dreamily into her face for a few seconds, then dropped his eyes and thrust out a package he held in his hands. "For you, ma'am. From the gent you was ridin' with the other day."

Emily furrowed her brow. Yesterday she had ridden alone. The only time she'd been with anyone else was when Austin had found her on the trail. "You're sure you don't mean the gentleman who has lent me Strawberry?"

"No, ma'am. Not that 'un. The other gent. Mr. Matthews."

Emily took the bulky package from him. "Wait here a moment and I'll get you something," she told the boy, turning to fetch her reticule without exposing Ida Mae, still in bed, to view.

But the boy held up his hand. "No, thank you kindly, ma'am. That's not necessary. The gent, he took care of it."

"Well, thank you, then, Homer."

With another wave of red across his face, the boy was gone. Emily walked slowly back to the bed and dropped the package onto it. The brown paper came loose and out spilled a beautiful pair of polished black leather riding boots. Emily pulled off the remaining paper to reveal an exquisite riding suit. She held it up against her. There was a short, bolero style jacket and a long skirt, split down the middle like gentleman's trousers. The fabric was a thin wool, so fine it ran through her fingers like silk, and it was the most extraordinary blue-green color, unlike any dye she'd ever seen.

"Oh, Emily!" Ida Mae gasped.

Emily was speechless. She had grown used to the posies and sweetmeats from Dexter, but somehow she'd never expected Austin to give her a gift. How could she possibly accept them? Why, the boots alone must have been worth all of twenty dollars, and the suit...

"Oh, Emily," Ida Mae repeated, her admiration tinged by an expression of doubt.

"They're beautiful, aren't they?" Emily said casually. Inside, her stomach was churning. Besides being the most beautiful items of clothing she had ever owned, she *needed* something to ride in. She'd be darned if she'd let old-fashioned New England ideas of propriety deprive her of them.

"Oh, Emily," Ida Mae wailed for the third time. "Are you entirely sure of Mr. Matthews's... intentions?"

Emily laughed. "Don't be a prude, Ida Mae Sprague. I asked Austin to give me some pointers about riding, and he evidently saw that I didn't have the proper attire."

"But, Emily, a gentleman doesn't give a lady—"

"Austin Matthews is not a gentleman," Emily interrupted. "And I imagine he gives a lady whatever he darn well pleases." Now that she was getting used to the idea, Emily was becoming increasingly delighted with Austin's gift. She sat down to unlace her shoes and then slipped on the soft leather boots. They fit perfectly. She could hardly wait to go riding in them. But first she had plans to set in motion. She tapped the heels of her new boots together in excitement. From complete gloom the morning before, the world was definitely looking a lot brighter.

"Get up, you slug-a-bed," she told Ida Mae. "If we're going to be impresarios, we've got to get busy."

Emily sat across from Dexter at the enormous desk in his cedar-lined mill office. She ran her fingers nervously over the carved lion-head inkwell and resisted the urge to throw it at him.

"Seattle's becoming a city," she explained with thinly veiled impatience. "It's not simply a lumber town anymore. And every single one of the brides is behind the idea."

"Fine!" Dexter threw his pencil down on the desk. "I'm all for the idea, too. I'll even help. At next Tuesday's council meeting I'll bring up the possibility of an opera house."

"That would be wonderful!" Emily interrupted, a smile smoothing the agitation from her face.

"But what I'm saying," Dexter continued, "is that this kind of thing is no job for a lady."

Emily sank back in her chair with a groan. "Dexter, back in New England, *ladies* are becoming doctors, lawyers, newspaper reporters—"

"Heaven forbid," Dexter interjected with a dry arrogance that made his aristocratic features look supercilious.

Emily was silent. She had to get Dexter's cooperation or she would never be able to start making money before Mercer's deadline. There was no way an opera house could be ready in a month, even if she did have the funds to build it. So she had to hold her first concerts someplace else. And there was no other building in town like the sawmill cookhouse.

"If you won't help me, I'll just have to look elsewhere," Emily said with an air of nonchalance.

"What do you mean by elsewhere?"

Emily studied her fingernails. "Well, for example, Austin Matthews has been very helpful to me. He might be willing to allow the Golden Lady to be used for the first couple of performances."

Emily had no intention of asking Austin Matthews for help. In the first place, she knew that there was no way the New England ladies would enter an establishment such as the Golden Lady, even for a respectable musicale. In the second place, she had decided that if she were to forge a successful future for herself in Seattle, the sensible thing to do would be to stay away from Austin. But she figured his name would be the most likely to get Dexter's attention, and she was gratified to see his eyes widen with horror at her suggestion.

"You most certainly will not make such arrangements with that man, Emily. I forbid it!"

Emily merely pursed her lips as though in deep thought. "We'd probably have to ask his girls to move out for the evening, but we could offer them some kind of compensation for their time lost...."

Dexter stood and paced nervously to the other side of the room. "All right, you win, Emily. You may use the cookhouse for your Friday night musicales."

Emily jumped from her chair and crossed the room to him. "Thank you, Dexter. I really appreciate this." She was so thrilled with her victory that she wanted to give a whoop of triumph. Instead, she stood on her toes and gave Dexter a brief kiss on the cheek.

"But I want you to give up this nonsense of bringing in other performers and building an opera house.

The men of Seattle will get around to all that soon enough."

Emily had already decided that the best course for her plan was to take one step at a time, so she didn't press the issue. Dexter did not need to know that she had already sent a letter to the manager of the San Francisco Opera House asking aid in adding Seattle to their performers' tours.

She ignored his comment and asked, "Is this Friday night too soon to start?"

"No," Dexter conceded reluctantly. "You can talk with Ethan Witherspoon about what you'll need."

Emily grinned. "You won't regret this, Dexter."

He walked back to his desk and dropped into his chair. "I wouldn't lay odds on that," he said gloomily.

Emily straightened her back and marched up to the door of the Golden Lady saloon. She hoped that the early-morning hour would mean she would be exposed to as few drunken cowboys and scantily clad ladies as possible. She had started to write Austin a note to thank him for the riding clothes, but had decided that it was the coward's way out. Such a magnificent gift deserved a personal thank you. Even if she had decided that she would not see him anymore. Except just this once. It was only decent to say a proper thank you. *Then* she wouldn't see him again.

She was repeating these justifications to herself as she entered the sun-filtered barroom. The room was empty except for the bartender, Jasper, who was stacking glasses behind the bar. He looked up as Emily entered and his graying sideburns twitched. "Can I do somethin' for ya, ma'am?" he asked.

"I'm looking for Mr. Matthews."

"He ain't here."

"Who is it, Jasper?" Flo's deep voice drifted out from the back room.

"One of them fancy Eastern ladies...lookin' for Austin."

In a moment Flo's red head emerged from the door behind the bar. "How d'ye do? Miss Kendall, isn't it?" Flo's smile was pleasant enough, but Emily sensed the reserve in her tone.

"Yes... Miss McNeil? I didn't mean to trouble you. I'm looking for Aust—for Mr. Matthews."

Flo walked leisurely over to Emily, looking her over thoroughly as she approached. All at once, Emily wished she had worn something more sophisticated than her yellow checked dimity day gown.

"As Jasper said, he's not here. Perhaps I could help you with something?"

"No...I was just...no, thank you."

Flo came to a halt in a shaft of sunlight that illuminated her flaming hair. "If you don't mind my asking, Miss Kendall, just exactly what *do* you want with Austin?"

When Emily didn't answer immediately, the older woman continued, "He ain't your kind, you know. The way I got it figured, you've come here looking for a husband. And that's the one thing in life that Austin Matthews is not going to be."

Even though Emily had been telling herself the same thing all week long, she didn't like hearing the words. Especially not from this person who was very probably on much more intimate terms with Austin than she would ever be. "He sent me a gift," she said stiffly. "I just wanted to tell him thank you."

Flo's eyes narrowed. "I can tell him for you."

"That would be very kind." Emily's chin tilted up slightly.

There was a glimmer of sympathy in Flo's eyes and her voice softened as she said, "It would be for the best, you know."

Emily nodded. She only now admitted to herself how much she had been looking forward to seeing him today. And for that very reason Miss McNeil was right. It would be for the best if she forgot she had ever met Austin Matthews.

"Thank you, Miss McNeil," she said with quiet dignity.

"You're most welcome, Miss Kendall. Best of luck to you."

The two women shared a look of understanding for several seconds, then Emily turned and walked out of the room.

"I told you, Austin. She didn't say more than a few words. She wanted to thank you for a gift. That was it." Flo's voice held an edge that she refused to attribute to jealousy of the beautiful and *young* New Englander. The girl had looked so fresh, all dressed in her sweet yellow dress, like the first buttercup of spring. Ready to be plucked, she thought grimly.

"Why is it so goldanged hard for you to get that little gal out of your mind, Austin?"

Austin shook his head. He had asked himself the same question. Frequently. "She's out of my mind, Flo. I promise. From now on I'm staying down here on Skid Road with people I understand."

They were in Flo's sumptuous bedroom upstairs at the Golden Lady. Austin had not occupied it in any kind of proprietary capacity since the first days of their partnership four years ago. But he had taken to stopping by in the mornings and sitting on the edge of the bed while Flo drank her morning coffee, which was laced with whiskey. She claimed it was an old Scottish tradition.

Austin leaned back against the brass footboard, and Flo sighed as she let her eyes wander along the length of his very fine body. She was far from celibate. Of late she had spent many evenings of mutual entertainment with the bewhiskered bartender, Jasper. But since Austin, she had not found a man for whom she wished to give up the luxury of sleeping out the night alone in her big, soft bed. She preferred to think it was the mellowness and wisdom of middle-age, rather than some sort of futile longing for her handsome partner.

"Well, I'm glad to hear it," she said finally. "It won't do you no good to be knockin' around with the likes of those folks. They've got their world and we've got ours."

"You're absolutely right."

"So I suppose that means you won't be headin' on over to the musicale tomorrow night?"

Austin looked down and picked at an imaginary speck on the garish pink coverlet of Flo's bed. "I don't suppose so. Why? Do you want to go?"

"No, you lug. I don't want to go. What have I just been telling you? Our kind's not welcome at their parties. Neither one of us has any business there."

"You *are* fond of music, though, right?"

"There's not a Scottish man nor woman born who's not fond of music." Flo flounced back against her voluminous pillows with a huff.

"Well, I'm fond of it, too, but we'll just find our music somewhere else." Austin stood to take his leave.

Flo looked up at him with an impish smile. "We could make our own music, Austin, lovey, if you were so inclined."

Austin returned her grin. "It's a tempting offer, Miss McNeil. And you'd give a warmer welcome than I'd get from those starched collars up town."

"So we won't go, then?" Flo asked again with just a touch of anxiousness.

"No, ma'am. Tomorrow night I've a date with a certain vintage bottle of whiskey that's had my name on it all week. None of that fancy parlor music for me."

The lines smoothed out of Flo's face. "That's good. You're doing the right thing."

Austin gave a determined nod and left the room.

"What are *they* doing here?" Dexter snapped, nodding toward the ticket table. The well-dressed couple who had just entered the room were unmistakable. Even without Flo's signature hair, Emily would have recognized the two immediately all the way across the room. There was simply no one in Seattle who filled out a suit of clothes like Austin.

Emily was almost as surprised as Dexter at their arrival, but she said mildly, "I suppose they've come to hear the concert."

"I can't imagine that this would be *their* kind of music." He gestured haughtily toward the makeshift stage at the front of the room where Ida Mae's piano had been set up next to a real harp. To everyone's amazement, Harve Ingebretson, the owner of the general store, had produced it out of his crowded and endlessly fascinating "back room."

Emily's eyes were still on Austin. "It's been a long time since most of the people in this town have heard good music," she said. "There's no reason why Mr. Matthews and Miss McNeil shouldn't be looking forward to it just like everyone else."

Dexter turned back to the makeshift music stand he was assembling. Ethan Witherspoon had arrived with three of them this afternoon when Emily, Ida Mae and Cynthia Stoddard had been setting up for the concert.

"Thought you'd need these," the laconic mill foreman had said without a smile.

Emily had bestowed on him one of her most brilliant smiles, and he had turned to leave with a sheepish look on his face.

The women had worked hard all day, and by evening the rough-paneled cookhouse had been transformed, not into a silk-lined salon such as could be found back east, but at least into a semblance of a concert hall.

"Do you think people will come?" Ida Mae had asked anxiously as the three finished hanging a linen drape behind the piano.

"It's all anyone has talked of all week," Cynthia said. She had been one of the few brides who had not scoffed when Emily and Ida Mae had revealed their plans.

"They'll come," Emily said firmly. "And tonight's just the beginning."

Now as she watched the people streaming in through the big double doors, Emily let out a breath it seemed she had been holding all day long. Her optimism was proving correct. Almost everyone she had met since arriving in Seattle was there. All the brides and most of the prospective bridegrooms. Mr. Briggs and Mr. Smedley came in separately. The Vickermanns arrived decked out in finery the likes of which Emily hadn't seen since the last time she'd been to Boston. Mrs. Vickermann's hat appeared to have an entire stuffed bird on top, complete with a little beak that pointed downward toward the woman's prominent nose.

Emily carefully avoided watching the back row where Austin and Flo McNeil had taken a seat. She ignored Dexter's stiff back and turned instead to give Ida Mae a little hug. "We've done it, my friend. It's really happening."

For once Ida's sniffling had subsided and her eyes glowed. "I'm so nervous, Emily. I don't think I'll be able to play a note."

"Of course you will. You'll play like an angel. Everyone will love it."

The early summer night was unseasonably warm, and the crowded room was soon sweltering. The audience seemed to move in ripples as ladies all along the rows slowly moved their fans back and forth. Dexter finished putting together the pieces of the last music stand and set it in place. "Let's get started," he grumbled.

His cooperation throughout the preparations had been given grudgingly. Though, Emily had to admit, he had provided everything they needed, and had impatiently waved off her offers to pay him part of the proceeds for the use of his building.

She took a seat beside him at the far side of the front row and nodded to the performers to take their places. Once plans were underway for the concert, they had discovered that Cynthia Stoddard had brought a violin from back East and that the Widow Bartlett, with her booming voice, was a classically trained mezzo-soprano.

In the short space of a week the women had put together quite a laudable program, with Rose Bartlett serving as impromptu director. The musicians began, Ida Mae on her beloved piano, Parmelia with the flute, Cynthia on the violin, a stoic Swedish emigrant named Hilda at the harp and shy little Jessica Emory on the zither.

They started with four pieces of chamber music, two each from Mozart and Brahms. By the end of the last piece, some of the gentlemen were becoming restless with the heat of the room. There was noticeable squirming and a few discreet attempts to loosen string ties.

But the room grew quiet again as Rose Bartlett took the stage and looked out at the audience with a formidable expression. She was an unusually tall woman. Tonight she wore an accordion-pleated purple silk underskirt that filled out her black taffeta dress and made her look even more imposing than usual.

"Thank you for coming tonight," she announced loudly, "My first song will be 'The Year of Jubilo' by Henry Clay Work."

Emily sank back in her chair and closed her eyes at the first clear, mellow notes. She had never heard Rose during rehearsal and was unprepared for the sheer beauty of her voice. It took Emily away from the crowded room, which smelled of sawdust and sweaty wool, and carried her off to another place. A place of refinement and grace.

It appeared that her reaction was shared by a good portion of the audience. The song came to an end on a sustained note that Rose skillfully modulated into a kind of mournful farewell, and the audience sat for several moments in a kind of stunned silence before breaking into a hearty applause punctuated with whistles.

Rose smiled serenely and almost immediately began another, a poignant song by George Root from the recent civil conflict. From her vantage point Emily could see tears streaming down the faces of several of the women. Across the room, Austin and Flo both looked moved and utterly attentive to the widow's lovely voice.

Emily smiled. It appeared that the first step in her venture, at least, was a success. Even if it took several weeks to arrange for a visiting performer, there was plenty of talent right here to keep the people of Seattle entertained. A few more sold-out performances like this one and they would have enough money to start building the opera house. She could hardly believe it. In Lowell, she would never have even imagined doing such a thing. Suddenly her eyes met Austin's. He seemed to recognize her look of triumph, and nodded to her with a soft smile of congratulations.

Rose had started her third piece when the squirming started again toward the back of the room, more noticeably than before. Like an ocean wave, the movement increased in intensity as it approached the front of the room. Some of the audience actually stood up in their seats. Rose's clear voice faltered in confusion and Emily craned her neck to see what was wrong.

Chapter Seven

> I wish you had been there, Cassie, and Joseph,
> too, of course. The culture-starved citizens of Se-
> attle gave our music a rousing welcome. I do not
> exaggerate when I say that the crowd was on its
> feet at the end of the performance.

Emily sighed and folded the letter to her sister with
care. It seemed that her accounts back home were becoming further and further from strict truthfulness,
and her conscience nagged her. But it was just that life
on the frontier was so very different from the orderly
existence of Lowell.

How could she explain to Cassie that at the grand
and elegant inaugural musicale, some cruel prankster
had set loose a skunk at the back of her makeshift
concert hall? How could she explain the absolute
ruckus that had developed afterward, overheated
bodies scrambling over one another trying to get out of
the room, and the inevitable quarrels over which man
would escort which lady. Why, even the mild-mannered
Tennessee prospector Fred Johnson had ended up the
evening with a spectacular shiner.

But she hadn't actually *lied* to Cassie. The audience *had* liked the music. After people had been able to get out in the air and away from the overwhelming odor, many had come up to her and encouraged her to continue her efforts. No one had asked for their money back. And out of the corner of her eye, she had seen Austin walk up to Ida Mae and put a $20 gold piece in the can she was holding marked Opera House Fund.

Afterward in their room the two women had counted the evening's profits which, enhanced by Austin's donation, came up to a total of fifty-three dollars.

"Not bad for one evening's work," Emily had said resolutely.

"But do you think anyone will come back after...what happened?" Ida Mae looked doubtful.

"Of course they'll come back. You heard them. Everyone thought the music was wonderful. It was just our bad luck that some lowdown, miserable blackguard decided to spoil the party."

"Perhaps the poor little animal wandered in by itself."

Emily shrugged. "Perhaps, but I wouldn't bet on it. I know there are still a lot of people out there who don't believe two women should be setting up concerts and collecting money like this."

Ida Mae gathered the coins into a neat pile. "Dexter says we have to pay for washing down the cookhouse," she said.

"So we pay. We have plenty here." Emily made a satisfied gesture toward the money. "Anyway, Dexter's just ornery because he kept saying we couldn't make this thing work, and now we have. Two women have opened up this city to culture...single-handedly."

"It was a good concert, if I do say so myself," Ida Mae said smugly. "And actually I think the fuss was exaggerated. It was no more smelly in there than Mr. Briggs's tannery shop."

"Or any downtown establishment when the lumberjacks come into town," Emily added.

At that Ida Mae burst into the giggles that Emily found so infectious. "Or those boots of Harve Ingebretson that he sets out to dry by the stove at the general store."

Emily joined her friend's laughter. "Or Homer after he's mucked the stables."

"Come to think of it, that poor little skunk hardly smelled at all!" Ida Mae sputtered.

It felt good to be able to laugh about it. It was true, after all, that out here in the West there were all kinds of sights and sounds that would have offended delicate eyes and noses back home. Perhaps folks wouldn't mind so much the way the first musicale had ended. They would just remember how good it had been to hear music again.

Emily gave a last chuckle and looked gratefully at Ida Mae. "I wouldn't be able to do this without you, my friend."

Ida Mae looked embarrassed. "Pshaw, Emily. You're the one with all the ideas and all the gumption. I just play the piano."

"And you remind me to laugh," Emily said gently. She reached over and gave her friend's hand a squeeze, then started scooping the money into a pouch. "We make a good team."

The incident with the skunk had bothered Emily more than she had let on to Ida Mae. In the first place, it was going to be difficult enough to establish regular concerts for the town without having someone trying to sabotage her efforts, or, at the very least, play mean tricks on her. Secondly, after last night's debacle, Dexter had absolutely refused to let her hold any more gatherings in the cookhouse.

Though she and Ida Mae had gone to bed late after counting the money, she found herself wide awake shortly before dawn, and decided a ride in the country might clear her head.

When she reached the stables, Homer was not yet around, so she hoisted the heavy saddle to Strawberry's back by herself. "Just bear with me here, girl," she murmured as she tugged on the cinch.

The horse stood as still as a statue and paid no attention to her clumsy attempts to adjust the leather. Finally Emily gave a satisfied nod and jumped onto the animal's back. The blue-green riding suit made the effort easy. By the time she was at the outskirts of the city, smelling the damp, piny smell of the early-morning air, she was feeling quite good again.

There had to be some way to continue her concerts until they raised enough money for the opera house. She would just have to find what that way was.

She and Strawberry had developed a mutually satisfactory pace that soon had her reaching the point where she had been followed that day when Austin had found her. She always felt a bit nervous along that stretch. She never had discovered who it might have been behind her. Sometimes she brushed it off, and even thought that perhaps Austin had made the whole thing up to try to scare her. But in any case she found herself looking back over her shoulder and peering into the deep pine shadows.

She didn't actually expect to see or hear anything, but felt the skin on the back of her neck rise as suddenly, sure enough, the sound of approaching hoofbeats grew louder behind her.

She drew Strawberry up in the middle of the road. There was not a cloud in the sky and it promised to be a simply beautiful early summer day. She was not going to let herself be chased away by some phantom pursuer. This time she would just wait right here and find out who the person was and what he wanted.

Strawberry took a couple of nervous sideways steps while they waited. Emily's stomach turned over once, but she gripped the reins and set a firm expression on her face. There was a huge red cedar that stood exactly at the bend, which made it look like it was growing right up out of the road. The rider came around it in a casual lope.

"Austin!" Emily said aloud. She let out her breath with a furious puff. He was following her again. Perhaps he had been the only one following her the other day, as well.

Austin caught up with her and brought his big horse to an easy stop. Emily sat confidently on her horse, as if she had been riding for years instead of just a few weeks. Austin smiled at the striking picture she made. He had known when he picked that unusual color for the riding outfit that it would suit her well.

"Good morning," he said calmly.

Emily ignored the amenities. "Why are you following me?" she demanded.

Austin reached across and made a quick adjustment to Strawberry's bridle. Immediately the horse stopped its nervous prancing. "It seems we've been through this before." His smile thinned.

"Indeed. The last time you claimed to be rescuing me from some mysterious pursuer. I suppose today you're out guarding me against an imaginary avalanche."

Austin grinned in spite of himself, then said sternly, "There *was* someone following you the other day. I told you, it's darn dangerous for a lone female to be out riding in these hills."

"Well, I think I can take care of myself," Emily said loftily. "And I'll thank you not to go scaring me... creeping up on me like that."

"I wasn't creepin' up on you. I ride out this way most mornings. I figure it clears the smoke out of my head after sitting in the saloon all night."

"Oh."

"It's a free country, you know. People have a right to ride where they please."

"Men do, you mean," Emily retorted. "You just said it's not safe for a woman."

Austin conceded the point with a nod. "Well, anyway, as long as I'm here, we might as well ride together."

"Dexter Kingsman says I'm not to have anything to do with you anymore," Emily said with a mischievous grin that made Austin's insides twist.

"Dexter Kingsman can go to Killarney for all I care. What do *you* say about it?"

"I say that I associate with whom I please."

She thrust her lower lip out slightly. Emily looked so young when she got that stubborn expression on her face, Austin thought ruefully. He really should leave her alone. Dexter Kingsman's advice had been correct. "Let's go then," he said roughly, spurring his horse ahead of hers.

The road was wide, and there was plenty of room to ride abreast. From behind, Emily watched the straight, lean lines of his back—broad shoulders tapering down to where his narrow hips nestled easily in the saddle. Then she urged Strawberry to pull even with him. They rode for several minutes in silence.

"Did you enjoy the concert last night?" she asked.

He looked over at her with a smile and raised one eyebrow.

"I mean . . . before . . . you know."

"Before the unwanted and far too smelly visitor? Yes, I enjoyed it immensely."

Emily was surprised at the intensity of his reply. "I hadn't expected that would be your type of entertainment."

"Why? Because I run a saloon?" His question was biting, but his voice became gentler as he continued, "My mother played the piano. I can remember listening to her for hours. My Pa told me she had studied under Karl Czerny of Vienna."

Emily was impressed. It was a side of Austin she had trouble imagining. In spite of the elegance of his dress and manners, she would have judged him to be more at home bantering with rowdies and bar girls than listening to Liszt in a fancy parlor.

"Did you ever play?"

Austin shook his head. "No. Ma said she was going to teach me someday, but she decided to die on me instead." His tone was light, but there was unforgotten pain behind the words.

"I'm sorry," Emily said softly.

"Doesn't matter. It all happened a long time ago." He spurred his horse again and it shot forward, spraying Emily and Strawberry with fine dust.

"Wait," she said. "I thought you said we were going to ride together."

Austin slowed to let her pull alongside him once again. He looked down at her with an odd expression. "You look very pretty this morning, Miss Kendall."

Emily smoothed a hand over the fine velveteen of her riding habit. "Thanks to you. I hope Miss McNeil relayed my message about your gift. I shouldn't have accepted it, but it was simply too beautiful to turn down."

"Turn down?" Austin asked indignantly. "Why, the outfit was made for you especially. I picked the color myself." He ran his eyes quickly over her entire body, down to her black boots. Then he settled his gaze on her face and said softly, "It makes your green eyes sparkle like sea foam on a sunny day."

Emily felt her cheeks grow warm. He loved good music. He created similes like a poet. And he ran a bawdy house. For her own peace of mind, she really ought to keep her resolution to stay away from this man.

"Let's gallop awhile," she said, feeling Strawberry stretch out beneath her almost before she had given the signal.

They raced along until the road narrowed between two rocky cliffs. Austin slowed his horse to a walk and Strawberry followed suit. "Are you ready to turn back yet?" he asked.

Emily shook her head. "It feels so good out here. Crisp and clean. It makes me feel like I never want to go back into town."

Austin nodded with understanding. Huge Douglas firs lined the trail on either side, forming a kind of cathedral around them. "It's beautiful out here. But you'd get mighty hungry after a while, I suspect."

Emily nodded glumly. "That's the problem. Real life intrudes. Food and money and how to make a living for oneself."

Austin narrowed his eyes. "You won't have any problem there living with Dexter. He's got more money than any other ten men in town combined."

"I haven't said I was going to live with Dexter. Or any man. I want to be able to take care of myself if I need to."

"I see."

Emily looked up at Austin sharply, searching for traces of condescension in his remark. But his deep brown eyes were steady and devoid of cynicism. "And I'll do it, too. If I have to hold my concerts in the middle of Occidental Street."

"What do you mean? I thought you were set up in Kingsman's cookhouse until you can build your opera house."

"Dexter's refused to let me use it again. He was against the idea from the beginning, anyway, and the skunk incident just proved him right, to his way of thinking."

Austin grew thoughtful. "So you have nowhere to go."

"Not at the moment. But by next Friday, by golly, I'll think of something."

"How much have you taken in for the opera house?"

"Fifty-three dollars."

Austin gave a low whistle. "You've a ways to go, then. That'll hardly cover the land, what with real estate prices in town skyrocketing like they are."

"I know," Emily agreed. "I have a few funds back East, but I don't know how long it would take me to get them here."

"And in the meantime, you have that little weasel Mercer threatening to throw you out on your ear, while Dexter Kingsman waits in the wings offering you a life of leisure and luxury."

She gave a rueful chuckle. "I guess that sums it up. Don't get me wrong. I like Dexter, really I do. But it's just that I . . . I'm just not so sure anymore that I want to get married right away."

"Then you shouldn't have to."

"Well, tell that to Asa Mercer."

They had reached the end of the cliffs and the road widened once again, with ample room on either side. To the left a stream leveled out from its source up in the hills. "Should we stop awhile?" Austin asked.

"Yes. Let's get a drink."

They led the horses across soft mountain grass to the edge of the water. Austin knelt and scooped water into his mouth, but Emily remained standing. "I thought you wanted a drink," he said, looking up at her.

She gestured toward her velveteen suit. "I don't want to spoil my skirt."

Austin laughed. "It wasn't designed for tea parties, you know. The grass won't hurt it any."

"I know, but I want to keep it new just a while longer."

Austin grimaced, but cupped his hands in the stream and then, standing up carefully, held them out to her. She hesitated a moment, but finally leaned over and drank from his hands. Her lips touched warm, hard skin, then cool water.

She lifted her eyes and was startled to see how close his face was to hers. The brown of his eyes looked as soft and deep as velvet, and his nostrils flared slightly, just as they had before he had kissed her at the wedding dance. She forgot to drink, and the water dribbled through her fingers.

He was the first to draw away. He cleared his throat and dropped down to his haunches, leaning over to put his face in the water for another drink. When he'd finished he looked up at her, his face serious. "Emily, what would you say if I offered you the money to build your opera house?"

Emily's jaw fell open. "What do you mean? You'd give me the money...just like that?"

Austin stood and grinned at her. "What did you think I meant? Do you suspect that I have some kind of nefarious motive?" His eyebrows rose wickedly. "Or do you *hope* I do?"

"N-No," she stammered. "It's just that I—"

"Because I do," he said firmly.

Emily felt a rush through her midsection. "I'm afraid—" she began, but stopped when Austin held up a hand.

"However, not *that* motive, delightful as the prospect might be. No, this would be a business deal. I want to be your partner."

"My partner?"

"Certainly. It sounds like a good business. With all those fancy Haydn Society ladies come to town, Seattle needs an opera house. I heard tell that San Francisco had twelve different opera companies going last year. I think one would do well here."

"But..." Emily's mind was whirring. "I don't have any money, so I wouldn't be able to put in my part."

Austin shook his head. "That's not the way my partnerships work. *I'll* put in the money, you'll manage the enterprise. I did the same kind of thing for Flo."

At the mention of Austin's flamboyant colleague, Emily felt queasy. He was offering her the same kind of deal he had offered Flo McNeil. It was the way out of her financial problems on a silver platter. But how could she go into business with someone like Austin? How could the owner of the opera house also be the owner of a bawdy house?

Austin sensed her dilemma. "I could be a *silent* partner, if you think it's best. No one has to know about our arrangement. You could tell people that your own funds had come from back East."

Emily wavered. "Why would you do this, Austin?"

"I told you...I like music. I also like working with women. They sometimes make better businessmen than the businessmen themselves."

She tried to run through in her head all possible objections. What would Ida Mae say? "Ida Mae would be a partner, too," she said doubtfully.

"Fine."

"I can't believe you're offering this."

"Believe it."

Emily took hold of Strawberry's reins and began walking slowly back toward the road. "So we could begin construction right away?" she asked, excitement building reluctantly within her.

"There's a piece of land just off Washington Street that would be perfect. My bank owns it. We could sign a bill of sale today."

Emily looked back at him with wide eyes. He was still standing by the water, dressed for once in casual buckskins that made him look more like a rough fron- tiersman than a successful businessman. "You've put some thought into this." She sounded puzzled.

He walked toward her, his expression serious. "I've never been one to pass up a good opportunity."

Her heart did a flip-flop as he came near. He looked bigger than usual in the tight-fitting leather. And more...uncivilized. More like a man who takes what he wants without asking questions. Dangerous. She backed away a step, but looked straight into his dark eyes. "We would have to be absolutely clear that this is strictly a business arrangement," she said firmly.

Austin's smile was devastating. A rush of feeling sluiced along Emily's arms down to her fingertips. "I thought we had already established that," he said evenly.

Emily took a deep breath. "Then, Mr. Matthews, you have yourself a partner."

Austin extended his right hand toward hers. After a moment, Emily reached out and shook it. The tingling in her fingertips intensified and she pulled away abruptly. "Let's get back to town and get busy," she said. She turned toward her horse to hide the telltale flush creeping up her cheeks. "We have a lot to do."

"Yes, ma'am," Austin said. Her businesslike tone of voice was not enough to deceive him. He knew the signs. Emily Kendall was as affected by him as he was by her. And if he had a decent bone in his body, he told himself firmly as he swung into the saddle, there wasn't a damn thing he would do about it.

Once she had Austin's backing, Emily couldn't be- lieve how quickly the opera house went up. Of course, it was made of rough-hewn wood, not brick like the elegant buildings in San Francisco or back East. But it had a real stage with a stunning wine-colored velvet curtain and actual theater seats. It seemed a miracle to Emily, but Austin had located the seats, curtain and various accompanying accessories stuck on a ship in a Mexican port. The disintegration of the brief, glittering empire of the Hapsburg, Maximilian, in that country had left the equipment without a home.

Emily had not taken Austin up on his offer to keep the partnership quiet. If she were going to take his money, she decided, she should at least be willing to give him the credit for his participation, even if it meant some unpleasantness.

She felt better about the arrangement after talking to Ida Mae, who, after her initial skepticism, had become her strongest supporter. "If that's what it takes to keep us going, Emily, then so be it," she had said firmly.

Emily suspected that much of Ida Mae's support was due to the fact that Mr. Smedley still refused to make any marriage plans while Mr. Briggs was so upset with the idea. And Ida Mae was not about to marry anyone else. So she was depending on Emily's plan to support both of them until the situation could be worked out to everyone's satisfaction. She had even offered to give piano lessons to bring a little extra money in while they were waiting for their first real profit-making concerts.

The lessons proved to be a good idea. Five of the brides had signed up immediately along with several of the children from the rapidly growing number of settlers in town. Ida Mae had happily set up her little traveling piano in a small room off the lobby of the hotel. When the opera house was finished, she'd continue with the lessons there. A larger piano had been ordered from Steinway & Sons in New York City, but it would be weeks or months before it arrived.

So telling Ida Mae about the partnership with Austin had been easy, and Emily was also pleasantly surprised to discover that the saloon owner's participation in the project didn't seem to make any difference to the brides. They were so excited about the idea of culture and music in their town that Emily figured the devil himself could have been her backer and they wouldn't have cared.

The only real problem with the arrangement was with Dexter. Her announcement about accepting money from Austin had caused such a battle between them that she hadn't seen nor heard from him since. It had done her no good to point out that it had really been Dexter's withdrawal of permission to use his cookhouse that had forced her into looking elsewhere for help. He had stormed on and on about women in business and her reputation and Austin's motives, a terrible tirade that mixed prejudice and jealousy with almost incoherent rage.

Emily had had a few qualms. Perhaps with this move she had cut herself off from her only true chance for a good marriage in Seattle. But she soon convinced herself that new men were arriving every day. Surely some day another Dexter would come along. In the meantime she would be content to establish her enterprise and keep her partnership with Austin on a purely business level.

The first concert in the new hall would be a presentation of the works of the late Stephen Foster, whose reputation since his death in poverty two years ago had begun to flourish, in spite of the fact that one of his songs, "Dixie," had been adopted as an unofficial anthem by the southern states.

Rose Bartlett had brought with her one of his songbooks, and she and Ida Mae had been practicing all week. Emily could hear the strains of "Open Thy Lattice, Love" floating out from the main hall as she walked in the front door of the building, her arms full of antimacassars the brides had sewn to cover the crushed velvet backs of the theater seats. Although everything was in readiness for that night's opening concert, Emily had had a stomach full of butterflies all day.

She walked into the hall quietly, so as not to disturb Rose and Ida Mae. Rose's strong voice carried beautifully all the way to the back of the room. Without putting down her load of linen, Emily stood transfixed by the lovely sound.

"You must be very proud," a deep voice said softly from behind her.

She turned, startled. Austin was standing very close. "This is a wonderful accomplishment," he continued, sweeping his hand out to encompass the room.

Emily took a step backward down the aisle. "It's not exactly *my* accomplishment," she said. "It's mostly your money, after all, and we wouldn't have much of a theater without the shipload from Mexico. I didn't have much to do with it."

Austin reached out and took half the antimacassars from her and began moving along the back row, draping one square of cloth over the back of each seat. "That's not the way I heard it," he said. "Abe Cassidy told me you were out there every day, telling his men how to put one plank on top of another."

Emily blushed. "I just wanted to see that they were spending your money properly."

"An admirable notion, madam partner."

Belatedly, Emily realized that while Austin had come to the end of a row and started down the next, she had just been standing watching him. He was dressed in a black suit, unusually dark for him and in stark contrast to the snowy whiteness of his shirt. In the flickering light of the whale-oil lamps that lined the concert hall, he looked wickedly handsome. She started walking down the row in front of his, neatly placing the squares of linen. When they met at the middle, he stopped, facing her. Without even being conscious of it, she stopped, too.

"Is there anything else that has to be done?" he asked.

Emily was having trouble concentrating. She watched his strong, tanned hands smooth a dainty antimacassar evenly against a seat back. "Excuse me?"

"Anything else that has to be done before the concert tonight. Is everything ready?"

Emily nodded. "I think so. Miss Stoddard and Miss Carruthers—I mean, Mrs. Carmichael—will be selling the tickets. Ethan Witherspoon has volunteered to help out backstage with the curtain."

"Kingsman's foreman?"

"Yes."

"I thought you said Dexter had refused to help you."

"I did. But Ethan can do what he pleases in his free time, and it seems that he's something of a musician himself. Plays the harmonica. We might ask him to join the group for next Friday's concert."

Austin started moving along the seats again. "So the course of true love is still not flowing smoothly with the very rich Mr. Kingsman?"

"It's not flowing at all," Emily answered dryly. "Not that it's any of your business, but I haven't even spoken to Dexter in a month. It seems he didn't approve of our partnership."

Austin frowned and said seriously, "I'm sorry if it caused you problems, Emily. I told you to keep it a secret."

"I'm not in the habit of keeping secrets. If Dexter doesn't want me as I am, then it's just too bad. I'll wait until the right man comes along."

They were at opposite ends of a row of seats and Austin paused to admire his partner for a moment as she turned down to do the next row. She was wearing the simple yellow dress she had worn that first time he saw her on the pier. Her hair was swept up in a careless knot on top of her head and silky, escaped tendrils hung all along her slender neck.

"I wouldn't worry about it," he said softly as she approached him along the row. Ida Mae and Rose Bartlett had finished their rehearsal and were talking quietly up on stage. "Dexter will get over his pique. Before you know it, he'll be back with his flowers and fancy notes."

Emily scrunched up her forehead. It was obvious that she had not yet prepared for the evening, since her freckles stood out clearly, even in the dim theater light. "Why do you say that?" she asked.

Austin took a deep breath and moved his eyes from her full, naturally dark lips up to her clear, innocent eyes. "Because the man's not a damn fool," he said. Then he started moving again along the seats.

Chapter Eight

Emily dressed in her best gown. It was a shimmering green silk, nearly the color of her eyes. It was the only gown she had ever owned that made her feel truly beautiful. She had last worn it to one of the Bennetts' musical gatherings, which they had called a *soiree musicale*. Little had she dreamed then that one day she would be in charge of a performance with an audience three or four times the size of the one that had met in the Bennetts' ornate great room.

It might not be as elegant as the Bennetts', but it's ours, Emily said to herself proudly as she waited in the small loge area to watch the first patrons enter. And I never heard any music at the Bennetts' to equal Rose Bartlett's voice and Ida Mae's piano performing the sweet, poignant melodies of Mr. Foster.

Emily watched with increasing satisfaction while the theater began to fill up. Every single one of the brides had come, which meant that many of their suitors were also in attendance. Mr. Smedley and Mr. Briggs came in together, having called a temporary truce in their rivalry since Ida Mae had declined an escort tonight. She had insisted that she wanted to concentrate on her performance. Even Fred Johnson had ridden in from the mountains for the occasion, Emily noted. But she was not so pleased to see Missouri Ike shuffle in, hat in hand, and sullenly put down his fifteen cents admission. He was cleaned up, as he had been for their dinner together, but he avoided looking at Emily, and his morose expression made her feel queer inside.

Millicent Vickermann had printed tickets for the evening, real cardboard tickets with Inaugural Concert and the date written on them. And she and her husband had offered to serve lemonade and teacakes in their restaurant after the performance as an opening night celebration.

Ethan Witherspoon and a couple of his crew had spent most of their evenings the past week putting in all the new chairs and doing various other odd jobs needed to get the place ready. They all refused to take any money, saying that being able to hear music once again was all the thanks they needed.

Then there was Austin, who, in addition to providing nearly all of the money, had been invaluable every step of the way. If it weren't for him, they would be sitting on crude wooden benches tonight and using a stage curtain made out of gunnysacks. Instead, the big, roughly constructed room had the look of a true theater. No gilt edging or ceiling paintings, but row after row of plush velvet chairs lit by the soft side lanterns. It was hard to believe it had all come together in just a few weeks.

In fact, everyone had been helpful ... except Dexter. He had stayed completely away from Emily, avoiding both the opera house construction site and the hotel. Until tonight. She was accepting congratulations from the Vickermanns when behind Mrs. Vickermann's rather voluminous form, she saw Dexter come in the front door. He held an enormous arrangement of flowers.

She accepted the restaurant owners' good wishes and added her thanks for the reception that was to follow, then she stepped around them and went over to where Dexter was deftly placing the arrangement in the center of Cynthia and Parmelia's ticket table.

"I've brought you some opening night flowers," he said to Emily as she approached.

"So I see. Thank you." She waited.

"It's amazing what you've been able to do here," he said, looking through the doors into the theater.

"I've had a lot of help," she said. And not from you, she added silently.

"Yes. I've hardly seen my foreman this week."

"Is that a complaint?" She felt herself starting to steam. The man didn't come around, didn't speak to her for nearly a month. Then he waltzes in with flowers and acts as if nothing had happened.

Dexter put up his hands. They were finely shaped, just like the rest of him. He was dressed in a lemon yellow suit complete with embroidered waistcoat that no other man in town would have dared wear. But on Dexter it looked . . . princely. There was no other word for it. "Oh, no," he said hurriedly. "No complaints. I'm happy we could help out."

Emily couldn't understand how the actions of his foreman suddenly had turned into a "we," but she let the comment slide. She was too proud and excited tonight to want a fight.

Dexter leaned close. "I've never seen you looking more beautiful, Emily," he said softly.

"You haven't seen much of me, beautiful or otherwise, lately," she couldn't resist answering.

Dexter's expression was properly apologetic. "I know. It was wrong of me. It's just that when you told me that you were going to keep on doing business with that sidewindin' saloon keeper, I got angry."

"We wouldn't be here tonight if it weren't for Mr. Matthews," Emily said.

Dexter took another long look at the building. "Well, it's a start, anyway."

Emily bit her lip. "Are you buying a ticket, Mr. Kingsman?" she asked curtly.

Dexter smiled down at her. "Of course." He turned to Parmelia at the ticket table. "Two," he said loudly, holding up two fingers. "One for myself and one for our gracious hostess, Miss Kendall."

Parmelia looked up at Emily with a questioning look. Emily, of course, did not need a ticket, but she wasn't about to turn down Dexter's money. She gave Parmelia a little nod.

"I may not be able to sit with you, Dexter. I have a lot to see to."

"That's all right," Dexter said gallantly. "But may I have the honor of escorting you to the reception after the concert?"

Emily sighed. He hadn't apologized for his month-long silence. He hadn't admitted that she'd been right, after all, that the opera house had been a good idea. But he *had* brought her flowers, and he had complimented her, and there still was not a man in all Seattle who could hold a candle to him, except, of course, the one man she could not have.

"Yes, Dexter, I'll go to the reception with you. Wait for me here after the concert."

He nodded, then took her hand and brought it to his lips for a kiss. "I'll be looking forward to it, my dear," he said warmly.

Fortunately, Dexter had disappeared into the theater to find his seat when Austin came in. He brought Flo, who looked as if she had gone out of her way to be even more ostentatious than usual. Her dress was an eye-opening pink that stood out in shocking contrast to her bright hair. On most women the combination would have looked hideous, but Flo had a special kind of presence that was almost regal, and her unusual clothes simply added to it.

Emily noticed that both Cynthia's and Parmelia's eyes widened as Flo came through the door, but neither said anything. Austin took out his money clip and smiled down at Parmelia. "How much for two tickets?"

"We should let you in for free," Emily interrupted, walking over to the ticket table. She nodded to Flo, who acknowledged the gesture with a nod of her own, but did not smile.

Austin looked up. "You won't make us rich that way...turning down paying customers." He handed Parmelia a dollar bill. She took it and counted out his change, her eyes still darting over Flo's dress.

"It looks like a full house tonight," Emily said proudly.

Austin's eyebrow went up. "Maybe we should have built it bigger."

"It's a good beginning." They smiled at each other. She felt an immense satisfaction in sharing this moment with Austin. Together they had really produced something fine, and it made her glow inside to stand here with him and contemplate the results of their efforts.

Austin was having similar feelings. Emily had a special radiance tonight. Her natural beauty was enhanced by the flush of triumph, of a battle fought and won. There was a rose blush to her cheeks and a sparkle to her green eyes. He felt something akin to pain in his chest.

He looked down at the ticket table. "Someone sent flowers?" he asked.

Emily hesitated. "Dexter brought them."

Austin's jaw clenched for a moment, then he said easily, "What did I tell you? Kingsman is too savvy a businessman to let a good thing slip through his fingers."

Emily's smile disappeared. Suddenly the evening didn't seem quite so joyous. "I'm not exactly a business deal," she said.

"Everything's a business deal," Austin replied.

Flo, who had been listening to their exchange, stepped forward and took Austin's arm. "Are we going to hear a concert, Austin, or stand here yammerin' all night?"

With a last glance at Dexter's flowers, Austin nodded to Emily and said wryly, "Congratulations again, Miss Kendall. Your venture is a smashing success."

Emily sank back against the wall. The rough paint felt cool against her overheated back. At Austin's insistence, they had ordered flocked *tapis* paper for the walls from Baltimore, but it would be weeks before it arrived.

"Lordy," Cynthia was saying, "that Austin Matthews has got to be the most superb specimen of manhood west of the Mississippi."

"Cynthia!" Parmelia admonished. "He's a saloon owner, and he goes around with...well, you just saw the kind of woman he goes around with."

"I'm not saying I'd marry the man, Parmelia. But there's nothing wrong with looking."

"Anyway, they say he doesn't even like decent women," Parmelia added in a self-righteous tone.

Cynthia looked over at Emily with a sly smile. "He seems to get on all right with Emily. Isn't that right, Em?"

Emily pushed herself upright. The palms of her hands were sweaty. "We have a business deal. That's all."

"He didn't appear to be thinking much about business when he was looking at you just now," Cynthia retorted.

Emily gave a big sigh. "You heard him yourself. To Mr. Matthews, *everything* is a business deal."

Cynthia giggled. "I wouldn't mind doing some business with him myself. Ouch!" she yelped when Parmelia gave her an elbow in the ribs.

Emily bit her lip. "I'm going around backstage to tell them to start."

Parmelia looked up with a glimmer of sympathy in her eyes. "Don't pay no never mind to Cyn, Emily. She's just teasing."

"No matter," Emily said breezily. "What people say about Austin Matthews is of no consequence to me. Thanks again, ladies, for helping with the tickets."

There was no direct connection from the loge to backstage without going through the theater, so Emily went outside to walk around the building. The cool night air felt good against her cheeks. She was angry with herself for letting Austin's presence and her friends' comments upset her. What she had said to Parmelia *was* true. Nothing regarding Austin Matthews should be of any consequence to her. This was her night to enjoy, and she was not about to let anything spoil it.

Emily leaned back against the velvet seat with a sigh of satisfaction. The concert had been a success. There had been no mishaps and no pranks. No little animals running through the theater. The audience had responded so enthusiastically to the music that even the unflappable Widow Bartlett had tears in her eyes at the last curtain call.

Emily could breathe again. She was on her way. Of course, the real beginning would be when they featured their first touring performer. Then they could charge twenty-five cents a ticket . . . or perhaps as high as fifty. She made a mental note to write to the manager of the San Francisco Opera House to ask about prices.

"Are you ready to go, Emily?" People were filing out of the theater, heading over to the Vickermanns' restaurant for the party, and Dexter had made his way through the crowd to her.

She looked up at him with a smile. "What did you think? Did you like the concert?"

Dexter nodded. "I've always been fond of Foster," he said crisply.

Emily gave a little shake of her head. She surmised that she was not going to get any more enthusiasm out of Dexter for any project that was not his own. "Well, I thought it all went wonderfully. And we took in a lot of money."

"Good." Dexter looked around the nearly empty theater. "Are you ready to go over to the Vickermanns'?" he asked again with a touch of impatience.

Emily grasped the seat back in front of her and pulled herself up. It was easier to talk to Dexter when they were on the same level. "Why don't you go on ahead? I should see that everything is secure here. I'll join you in a few minutes."

"All right. But don't be long." He paused and bestowed on her one of his dazzling smiles. "We need to make up for some lost time," he said. He lifted his hand to give a gentle, loverlike stroke to her cheek, then headed down the aisle toward the door.

Emily watched him leave with mixed feelings. He could be tender when he wanted to be, and courtly. But he hadn't offered to stay with her and help.

Austin had seen Dexter's parting gesture from across the room. He felt the burn inside and welcomed it. He may have complicated his life by going into business with Emily Kendall, but the sooner he got any other notions concerning her out of his head, the better.

"Do you want to go over to the Empire Room?" he asked Flo.

Flo had seen both Kingsman's caress and Austin's reaction to it. "I think we should be heading back to the Golden Lady. No telling what Jasper's up to with both of us gone."

Austin nodded distractedly. "Would you mind going on back by yourself, then? I'll just ask if there's anything that needs to be done closing up here."

Flo grimaced, which Austin didn't see, but she said pleasantly, "Sure. Take your time. I'll see you back at the saloon whenever you get there."

Austin nodded his thanks, then moved out of the row of seats and started over toward Emily, leaving Flo behind, shaking her head.

"Congratulations again, Madam Impresario," Austin said with a broad smile.

"And to you, too, partner," she answered beaming. "It was wonderful."

"Yes, it was." Emily rocked forward onto her toes. "It really was, wasn't it?"

Austin chuckled. Emily's entire body looked as if it wanted to explode with excitement. "Absolutely. The audience loved it."

"Do you think the sound was good?" she asked anxiously. "Was the paneling the right decision?"

It had been Austin who had suggested cedar paneling as a stage backdrop rather than the traditional cloth. It was his theory that the paneling would make the sound resonate better out into the theater. "The sound was splendid. Everything was perfect, Emily," he reassured her. "I think the Seattle Opera House can be declared a resounding success."

Emily shook her head. "The real test will come when our first traveling performer arrives. Then we'll know if the people here are willing to pay good money for culture."

"Have you heard anything more from San Francisco?"

"Yes, the manager there has suggested that we invite the noted platform lecturer Artemus Ward. And he mentioned a new man who has recently become very popular...a journalist who writes under the name Mark Twain. He's just come back from a tour of the Sandwich Islands, and his lectures on the subject are making him famous in California."

"Great. Send for them both."

Emily had wanted to do exactly that, but she'd been waiting to see that everything went smoothly. "Shouldn't we wait awhile? I mean, what if we don't take in enough money to cover their fees?"

Austin smiled. "You're a businesswoman now, Emily. And part of doing business is learning how to take risks."

Emily gave a rueful shrug. "It can be harder than it sounds. Sometimes I wonder if I have what it takes, after all."

"That's just because you're worn out. You've worked awfully hard this week. I'm not worried about you taking risks. When you left New England to come west you took a bigger risk than most people will take their entire lives."

Austin had a special gift for making her feel strong. With Spencer Emily had felt strong because *he* was basically weak. And she had the feeling that Dexter's strength was something that required *her* to be weak. She had never met a stronger man than Austin, yet he was perfectly content for her to be strong, too. In fact, he made her more so. "All right, I'll do it. The letter will be on its way tomorrow," she said with another excited rock up on her toes.

Austin grinned and began to answer her when suddenly there was a deafening bang from the front of the room. They both jumped and Austin said, "What the hell was that?"

He took Emily's arm and together they hurried toward the stage. Everything seemed in order, but when they moved aside the velvet curtain, they could see that one of the center curtain weights, a heavy metal disk about four inches thick, had dropped to the stage floor.

It had landed less than a foot from the bench where Ida Mae had been sitting at her piano.

"How do you suppose that happened?" Emily asked.

Austin reached over and picked up the weight. It was firmly attached to a stout rope by a metal loop on top, but the rope had come apart about a foot's length from the weight. "Looks like the rope frayed."

"Weren't those ropes new?" Emily sounded puzzled.

Austin nodded grimly. "They were supposed to be." He ran his hand thoughtfully over the end of the rope. "I'll have someone check them all out tomorrow."

"Imagine if that had fallen and hit someone," Emily said with a shudder. "What a terrible accident."

Without replying, Austin walked over to the side of the stage to put the weight down.

A horrible thought came to Emily. "You *do* think it was an accident, don't you, Austin?"

He nodded. "Most likely. We'll check things out tomorrow. In the meantime, you ought to trot yourself over to your celebration party. You deserve it, you know."

"Aren't you coming?"

Austin shook his head. "No, this is your night with your friends."

"But you're my partner. You should be there with me."

"It appeared to me that Kingsman will be taking good care of you," he said with just a hint of resentment. "I think I'll head back over to the Golden Lady where I belong."

"You're welcome at any gathering that I have any say about," Emily's words were firm, but her expression was troubled as she looked up at him.

Austin gave in to the impulse and bent down to press his lips softly against hers. He savored the sensation for just a moment, then pulled away. "Don't worry about me, partner. I'll have my own personal celebration over at the saloon."

Emily still looked doubtful, but Austin smiled reassuringly. "Let me know if you need anything more before the next performance."

Emily nodded. She hated to let him go. Dexter was waiting for her over at the Empire Room, but it wasn't Dexter she wanted to celebrate with. With a prickling feeling in her middle, she wondered if Austin's "own personal celebration" would involve Flo McNeil. "I'll let you know. And, Austin..." She put a hand on his arm as he turned to leave. "Thank you again, for everything."

"It's been my pleasure, Miss Kendall," he said. He lifted her hand from his arm and kissed it. Dexter had kissed her hand earlier in the evening, and it had felt no different than a handshake. But the touch of Austin's lips on the soft skin of the back of her hand felt like a jolt from one of those electric shock machines that came around with the carnivals back home.

Their eyes met for several long seconds, then Austin gave a little bow. "Good night," he said. He cleared the huskiness out of his throat, then continued in a stronger tone, "Send word if you need me, and—" he gestured upward toward the broken weight rope "—be careful when you're working around here."

Emily nodded. "I will."

* * *

It had become a habit for Emily to take Strawberry out for a short ride each morning. She enjoyed watching the landscape change as summer filled every available space with lush greenery. The mountain mornings were still cool and quiet, but they held an air of expectation, as if anticipating the warmth of the day ahead.

On the morning after the concert, Emily awoke with reluctance and considered skipping her ride this once. Ida Mae slept alongside her, breathing heavily through her stuffy nose. They had come in late after the reception last night, too tired to even count the ticket money, which was carefully locked away in Emily's jewelry box.

I should take the money over to the bank, Emily thought lazily. The banker, Jebediah Overstar, had been hesitant about opening an account in Emily's name, but Austin had convinced him with a very few well-chosen words.

Emily stretched out under the covers. Through the window of their room she could see that the sun was already high. She really needed to get up. They had a lot to do today. She and Ida Mae had decided to move to two rooms backstage at the opera house. They would live there until one of them decided to get married or until they became rich enough with their new enterprise to afford better quarters.

With a sigh Emily threw back the covers and forced herself to climb out of bed. She would make her ride with Strawberry a short one today, then get the money to the bank, send the letter off to the San Francisco manager and start getting ready for their move. She dressed quickly and, with a last glance at Ida Mae, who still rumbled away in peaceful sleep, she left the room.

She walked to the stables humming one of Stephen Foster's tunes and greeted a sleepy Homer, who had Strawberry saddled and ready for her.

It *was* a beautiful morning, she decided as she headed down the now-familiar mountain road out of town. Her spirits had been dampened last night by Austin's refusal to come to the celebration, but in the broad light of day, she saw that it had probably been for the best. Dexter had behaved impeccably all evening and had congratulated her twice on her achievement in building the opera house. Perhaps he would become adjusted to the idea. And, as for Austin, she could still work with him, still be his friend, even if there would never be anything more than that between them.

Her life seemed to be sorting itself out nicely, and the only niggling worry was the accident with the curtain weight, which could have proven deadly. Was it merely a coincidence that both the concerts they had presented so far had ended with near-calamities?

Missouri Ike had been there last night, and he was someone she didn't fully trust. There had also been someone following her that day of her first ride, if she was to believe Austin. And he didn't have any reason to lie to her.

She had lost track of time as she went through it all in her mind. Suddenly she was at the familiar red cedar curve, and, as if in the middle of a bad recurring dream, she heard fast hoofbeats coming up behind her. Perhaps it was Austin again, but a sick feeling in her stomach told her that it was not.

She knew that a little way up the road was a gentle cliff. If she could get to the top, she would be high enough to see back down the other side of the road before the other rider could see her.

She urged Strawberry ahead until she found the spot she wanted, then turned her off the road and coaxed her up the steep grade to the top of the cliff. Below her, the other horse and rider were already in view. She couldn't recognize the man, couldn't even tell if the big hat he wore was the one belonging to Missouri Ike. In a panic, she looked back into the woods behind her. There was no trail, but there was room to maneuver between the trees. She gave Strawberry a pat and wheeled her around. "C'mon, girl. He's not likely to look for us up here," she said to the horse quietly.

Trying to stay calm, she let the horse take her farther and farther back into the woods. They came to another hill, and Strawberry gallantly pulled her way up it without complaint.

They continued into the back country for another quarter of an hour as Emily's heart gradually slowed to normal. Finally she stopped, convinced that once again she had eluded her pursuer. But as fear subsided, anger took its place. Who was this person? she thought indignantly. Was this the man responsible for spoiling her first concert with the skunk? And what about the broken rope at the opera house? If that had been deliberate, it was a sight more serious than a prank. Someone could have been badly hurt, even killed.

Slowly she turned Strawberry back in the direction they had come. The horse was breathing heavily. "We'll stop and rest when we get back to the road," Emily promised.

She looked up. They were surrounded by trees. Had Strawberry turned completely around? All at once she was unsure of her way. She looked up at the sun. It was almost directly overhead. A little nip of disquiet pulled at her. "Take me out of here, girl," she whispered to Strawberry.

The horse turned its head back and twitched the black tips of its ears.

"Back to the road," Emily said more insistently. "It's got to be down there somewhere."

After another moment's hesitation, Strawberry started forward. These animals always know the way home, Emily said to herself with relief.

Chapter Nine

Ida Mae walked across the small hotel room to look out the window for what was probably the hundredth time. There was still no sign of Emily, and by now it was apparent that something had to be wrong. Emily had specifically said that now the first concert was behind them, they would spend the day getting their new rooms ready. Mr. Mercer would stop paying their hotel bill at the end of the week. But Emily had been gone when Ida Mae awoke, and it was now midafternoon without any word from her.

Ida Mae reached for her bonnet, her mind racing. She could go to the sheriff, but it might be too soon for him to do anything about Emily's absence. After all, she had ridden out of town on her own. This morning Ida Mae had gone to the stables, where Homer had told her that Emily had gone off on Strawberry for her accustomed morning ride.

She thought of going to Eldo, but as fond as she was of the mild-mannered silversmith, she didn't see him as much help in the present situation. Then there was Dexter Kingsman. He would be the logical person to go to. So why, Ida Mae asked herself, were her feet taking her directly down the street toward Skid Road?

It was more instinct than anything else. Austin Matthews had seemed to be Emily's guardian angel since the moment they got off the ship. If Emily was in trouble, Mr. Matthews was the one person Ida Mae would trust to help her. Even if it meant going in...*that place* again, with the golden, naked women.

She hoped she was doing the right thing. Emily, she prayed silently, please be all right.

His horse stumbled for the second time and Austin let out a blistering stream of curses. The feeling of dread that had locked into his throat when Ida Mae had timidly walked through the doors of the Golden Lady that afternoon had grown stronger as the slow summer twilight faded into darkness.

Austin had ridden several miles without seeing any sign of Emily. He remembered the first day she had gone out. She had left the road to ride up into the mountains in order to avoid being followed. If someone had been following her that morning, she might have done the same thing. Which meant that she could be anywhere. Perhaps this time the man had caught up to her.

He pulled up and angrily turned his horse around. He would go back along the way he had come and look more carefully for signs of a horse leaving the road. Though how he would see tracks in the dark, he didn't know. There wasn't even a damn moon yet to provide a bit of light.

Carefully he picked his way back along the road, straining his eyes in the darkness. Why hadn't he gone to the sheriff? By now they could have had a whole troop of people out here with torches looking for her. Damn. If I find you, Emily Kendall, I'm going to hogtie you to your danged opera house before I'll let you ride out alone again.

It was simply too dark to see. Austin had just about decided to give up and ride back into town for help when he rounded a curve, and there, standing like a ghostly apparition in the middle of the road, was Emily's horse.

He dismounted and approached it cautiously. Its reins hung dangling in front of it. Austin reached out carefully and took them in a firm grip. "Where's your mistress, girl?" he asked the animal in a soothing voice. "You want to take me to find her, eh?"

At first Strawberry didn't seem inclined to move, so Austin gave her a gentle slap on the rear. "Let's go find Emily," he said again, jumping on his own horse to follow while Strawberry slowly started to move up into the nearly black woods.

The animal picked her way in and out of the trees in a slow walk with no clear direction, and Austin felt his muscles grow stiff with frustration. They reached the foot of a small hill, and Strawberry stopped.

"C'mon, girl," Austin urged. "Take me to Emily." He leaned over to give the horse another gentle nudge, but this time she refused to move. Then above the night sounds he heard a moan.

In an instant he was off his horse and running toward the sound. In the darkness all he could see was a shapeless mass, but as he drew near, the moan sounded again, stronger.

"Emily!" he called. He reached her side and knelt beside her. She was at the base of a jutting rock about six feet in height. He lifted her against him. "Emily, it's Austin," he said, his voice loud and urgent.

Her eyes were closed, but she appeared to be breathing normally and he couldn't see any obvious injuries. He touched her cheek. It was frighteningly cold.

"Emily, wake up."

There was a flutter of her long lashes, then her eyes opened. "Austin?"

Austin took a ragged breath. "I'm here, Emily." He held her close to his chest. "Are you hurt? Can you tell me what happened?"

Emily closed her eyes again. It took her several moments to remember, but then things began to come into focus. "We slipped…Strawberry slipped coming down the hill, and I fell…" She clutched Austin's sleeve. "Is Strawberry all right?"

Austin lifted her to a sitting position. "Strawberry's fine, but my concern is for you. Where are you hurt?"

Emily stretched out her legs and gave an experimental twist to her back. "I think I'm fine," she said slowly, sounding confused. "I don't know what happened. How did it get so late?"

"You must have hit your head. You've been unconscious."

"We need to get back. Ida Mae must be frantic." She struggled to get up, but Austin's firm hold on her kept her where she was.

"Just wait a minute. It was Ida Mae who sent me. I told her that I would find you, and that if I couldn't, I would send for more help."

"Ida Mae went to you?" Emily asked, amazed.

Austin smiled. "She marched right into the Golden Lady, brave as you please. You mean a lot to her."

Emily nodded. "She's a good friend, and I should get back—"

"We're not starting back until we see that you aren't hurt. There's an abandoned cabin just up the road—the leavings of one of the placer miners who thought he'd find his fortunes in these mountain streams. Do you think you can ride?"

"I think so." Leaning on Austin's arm, she stood, but when she tried to take a step toward her horse, she swayed and almost fell.

"Maybe not," Austin said. He lifted her easily in his arms and boosted her up on his horse's back, then swung up behind her. He steadied her against his chest. Her body felt cold. He reached for Strawberry's reins and started toward the cabin. If they were lucky, there would be wood for a fire to help warm her, and he'd be able to see for himself that she was unhurt.

By the time they reached the simple wooden structure, Emily began to notice that her head ached. Austin lifted her off the horse, then dug in the saddlebags for his matchbox. Emily tried to walk toward the cabin door, but was again overtaken by dizziness and stopped to wait for Austin's help.

Once inside the cabin, he let go of her. "Steady yourself against the wall for a minute while I try to get a fire going," he told her. Groping his way in the dark, he was relieved to find a large pile of wood next to the cabin's huge fireplace. The place had only recently been abandoned, or perhaps trappers used it, he thought to himself. The wood was dry and kindled instantly with one match.

The small pieces of tinder flared, brightly illuminating the tiny room. There was no furniture, but in one corner a sleeping area had been made with trading blankets and furs. Austin looked over at Emily, who stood back by the door with her hand against the wall. "Are you doing all right?"

At her nod, he went over to the pile of blankets and began to shake them out. One by one he laid them neatly in front of the fire, making a thick, padded bed. Then he walked over to Emily, picked her up and carried her over to set her down in the middle of it.

He took a fur robe and doubled it over to form a kind of big pillow for her to rest against. "There," he said as he pushed her back against the soft fur. "Just relax for a few minutes, and tell me if anything hurts."

Emily felt as if she were floating. The warmth of the fire reached out to her, and the silky fur cushioned her head. She closed her eyes. "My head was hurting as we rode, but it feels better now."

"You must have taken quite a hit to be unconscious so long." Austin threaded his hands into her thick hair and gently explored her scalp.

His hands felt good, soothing. Her back and shoulders went limp against the fur backrest.

"Here. I can feel a knot right over your ear."

Emily could feel it, too, when he ran his hand over it. She opened her eyes and winced, and immediately he took his hands away.

"Are you still feeling dizzy?" His voice was full of concern.

She smiled lazily. "I'm fine. Warm and relaxed. I suppose we should be getting back to town, but I feel as if I never want to move from this spot."

Austin leaned back on his heels and looked down at her, relief apparent in his strained face. "And nothing else is hurt . . . your arms and legs are fine?"

Emily made an attempt to lift her arms, but they flopped back down. "They don't seem to want to do much of anything at the moment, but I don't think they're injured."

Austin bent over her and ran his hands along her arms. "No bruises, nothing sore?" he asked.

She shook her head.

After a moment's hesitation, he did the same with her legs, gingerly. "Nothing here, either?"

At the unfamiliar feel of a man's strong hands on her legs, some of the lethargy went out of her. A curious wave radiated from her upper legs to her stomach.

"No, I'm fine . . . really."

"Are you hungry?"

Emily tried to sit up. "No, I don't think I could eat. But I would like something to drink."

Austin gently pushed her back down on the furs. "Don't move. I'll be right back."

He stood and moved away from the circle of firelight. In a moment she heard him go out the door. She closed her eyes once again and let the warmth of the fire seep into her body.

She had almost fallen asleep by the time Austin came back. "I've unsaddled the horses and tied them down for the night," he said.

He dropped a wool poncho and his saddlebags alongside the makeshift bed, then sat down at the edge of the blankets.

Austin had had a swift and angry debate with himself when he went out to deal with the horses. In spite of his worry over her condition, seeing Emily spread out lazily beneath him had his insides tightening in a familiar and pleasurable tension. Her hair had looked like a golden cloud, spilled out against the dark fur backdrop, and it had felt like spun silk against his rough fingers.

They were alone in the mountains. It would be at least morning before anyone would be out looking for them. The anxiety that had built up as he had searched for her had now turned into raw desire, as if by possessing her he would be finally sure that she was safe. But he was not a fool. He knew that taking her tonight would be the last thing he should do to ensure Emily's well-being. And he was not a bastard. He knew that making love to her tonight could bring nothing but heartache to either one of them.

"You unsaddled the horses?" Emily asked in confusion. "But shouldn't we be getting back?"

Austin shook his head. "We'll let you rest here a spell. Sleep if you can. They won't start wondering about us before morning."

Emily nodded. If Austin thought it was all right to stay, it was all right with her. She was perfectly comfortable where she was, and she was content just to lie back and enjoy watching the firelight flicker over Austin's strong, handsome face. The anxiety was gone from his expression now, replaced by the familiar look of strength, of control. He turned and reached out a long arm to his saddlebags, and she admired the movement of his back and broad shoulders.

"You said you were thirsty." He pulled out a leather flask. "It's whiskey, but if you take it easy, it should go down all right."

She took the flask from him and lifted it to her lips. The drink burned, but her throat was so dry that she took a big swallow, and followed it with another.

"I said to take it easy," Austin said, reaching for the flask with a smile. "You'll be as drunk as a sailor."

Emily giggled. "It might be kind of fun. I've never drunk spirits before."

"Not even ale? Wine?"

Emily shook her head. "No. My parents were against it. The Bennetts used to serve champagne at their parties, but I never tried any."

"Who are the Bennetts?"

Emily hesitated a moment. "The family of my fiancé."

"Fiancé?" Austin sat up straight. He couldn't explain why her revelation had come as such a surprise. She was bright and smart and an extraordinary beauty. It would have been absurd to think she had reached her age without numerous offers of matrimony. But in spite of her natural sensuality, she had that underlying air of innocence, a spirit of childhood, that made it hard to picture her as experienced in an intimate relationship with a man.

"Spencer Bennett. We were to be married, but he was killed at Gettysburg."

There was nostalgia underlying the words, but no real pain, Austin decided. Perhaps the intimacy had never had time to develop. "How long were you engaged?"

Emily gave a bittersweet laugh. "Four years. At first Spencer said he wanted to wait until he had enough money to buy us a house. Then he had to go into the army, and he didn't think it was proper for a soldier to leave behind a new bride."

Four years. Then again, perhaps Spencer Bennett had simply been a damn fool, Austin concluded. "So you joined with the other war widows to find a husband out in the Wild West."

Emily's laugh was softer this time. "Not to find a husband as much as...I don't know. I wanted to build my own life for myself. Back in Lowell I was Ralph

Kendall's daughter. The Bennetts' future daughter-in-law. Then Joseph Jackson's sister-in-law. Poor Aunt Emily. I guess I just wanted to be me...Emily Kendall."

Austin took a long pull at the liquor flask, then held it out to her. "Well then, go ahead and drink up, Emily Kendall. You're out West now. If you want to get drunk, nothing's stopping you."

Emily took the flask from him, but shook her head. "I didn't really mean it." She took another drink. "Anyway, it tastes awful." With this swallow she could feel the liquor stretching itself out along her limbs. "It does make my head feel better, though."

Austin had been watching her with an odd half smile, but at her words he frowned and moved over beside her. "Does it hurt a lot? Maybe we should get you in town to a doctor."

Moving slowly as if he were about to touch a butterfly, he rubbed the sore spot on the side of her head. "It's not swelling up or anything, is it?" he asked anxiously.

His face was over hers, his velvet brown eyes apprehensive. "I'm fine, Austin," she said softly. "It doesn't even hurt anymore."

The fire caught the mahogany highlights of his thick hair. He was close enough for her to see the stubble of beard along his chin. Their eyes held for a long moment.

His hand moved from her head down the satiny skin of her neck. Emily drew in a quick breath. Her mouth opened slightly of its own accord.

"Dammit, Emily," he said with a groan. His hand dropped to her chest, then molded itself carefully around her breast. He bent his face to hers and took her lips in an exquisitely gentle kiss.

He kissed her eyes, then, slowly, the rest of her face, tasting the faint trace of almond on her freckled cheeks, as he had once fantasized. Her arms had come around his neck, and her breasts pressed against his chest, firm and tantalizing.

He tried to remember the things he had said to himself just a few minutes before out with the horses. He told himself that she was hurt, that he had no business touching her. But his mind blotted out all other thoughts as their mouths met once again in a whiskey-flavored mating. He pressed her down against the fur and moved his body over hers. Her curves met his leanness with erotic perfection. So much for good resolutions, he said to himself.

Emily had never known such intensity of feeling. The tips of her breasts tingled, and below her waist a delicious kind of pain radiated downward. Austin moved against the area with the lower part of his body, which had grown rock hard and seemed to generate heat. It felt mysterious and wonderful. In a move of incredible daring, she reached down to his firm rear and pressed him more closely against her.

Austin gave a rough, thrusting movement and made a strangled sound in the back of his throat. Pulling himself back into control, he lifted his head to look at her.

"Emily, wait." His voice was raspy. "You don't know what you're doing to me...where this will lead...."

Emily ran her hand through the thick hair that fell down over his forehead. "Show me," she said gently.

Austin shook his head and pulled away, trying to regain his senses. "You don't know what you're saying. It's the liquor talking...or the bump on your head. I have no right...."

"Shhh." Emily stopped his words by running her fingers down to his lips. Then she lifted her head and replaced her fingers with her mouth. "Kiss me again, please."

He did, so expertly and so thoroughly that both were short of breath when they finally pulled apart. Austin's face was grave as he looked down at her in the glow of the fire. "You don't know what you're doing, sweetheart," he warned again.

Emily let her head fall back on the furs and smiled up at him. "You're right. I have no idea. But it feels wonderful."

Austin dropped his head to her chest and spoke in muffled anguish. "Emily, I have to be honest with you. You've come here for a husband. If we make love tonight, it could ruin everything for you."

Emily answered slowly, "I'm not so sure any more that a husband is what I want. I told you, I came to make a life for myself. And maybe one of the things that means is learning about this mysterious thing that can happen between a man and a woman."

She put her hands on either side of his head and lifted it so that they were looking in each other's eyes. "Maybe I want to understand why it is my insides turn to mush when you kiss me."

Austin felt a quick, desperate stab at his own insides. He pulled himself up to her mouth again, this time with an urgency that made the kiss rougher than he had intended. When he finished, her lips were red and swollen, but her eyes held nothing but acceptance. "Teach me," she said softly.

Austin gave up. If this was really what she wanted, he was tired of fighting the increasingly demanding messages of his own body. But he would make it good, he vowed. He had grown used to the quick and casual pleasures of lighthearted sex with saloon girls or experienced, married women. But being with Emily took him back to a more innocent time, back in St. Louis. When the warm summer breezes found new lovers along the banks of the Mississippi. And satisfaction was sought with inexperienced fumbling and furtive haste to the accompaniment of the river's gentle rush.

Emily's green eyes were wide with expectation. He kissed them shut, then her mouth, her chin, her neck, all the while loosening the velvet buttons of her riding jacket and moving his hand to the silky blouse underneath.

"What should I do?" she whispered.

Austin smiled gently. "Just relax. You'll know." He lifted her slightly to remove her jacket, then did the same with his own. "You're not too cold?"

She shook her head. Her mouth was dry again and the truth was, she was nervous. But it was an exhilarating kind of nervousness, a hollow waiting at the pit of her stomach. She ran her hands down Austin's chest over the fine linen of his shirt. "You have beautiful clothes," she said.

Austin's laugh was deep and rich. He was at ease now, savoring. Now that he knew she was his, he could wait. He could listen to her voice, feel her slender hands on him. Without hurry.

He leaned over and nuzzled her neck. "Do you prefer me with my beautiful clothes or without?" he whispered wickedly just before he sucked gently at her earlobe.

Emily felt a rush in her head. "Without would be nice." She had difficulty forming the words.

He backed away out of the circle of light. When he appeared again, standing in front of her, he was naked, his lean, muscled body a reddish-bronze in the glow of the fire.

He appeared quite at ease and stood for several moments, letting her run her eyes up from his powerful thighs to his lean hips...and the male organ which sprung proudly from a nest of black hair.

"You're beautiful without clothes, too," she managed finally and held out her arms as he joined her once again on the furs.

"Your turn now, sweetheart." He kissed the bridge of her nose. "Now I get to see just how far those freckles travel down this lovely body." With more impatience now, he struggled to open the tiny buttons of her high-necked blouse. "You can help if you like."

Between the two of them, her blouse was disposed of, and the rest of her clothes soon after. She fought back the impulse to reach for a cover, and instead stretched out naked, allowing herself to feel the sensation of her bare skin against the silky furs.

"And you are *definitely* beautiful without clothes," Austin said hoarsely. Then he ran his hand slowly down from her breasts to her stomach. As he reached the area between her legs, he bent to take her mouth in a series of drugging kisses that made her head spin and left no room for any embarrassment at the touch of his hand at her most private place.

As the kiss ended, he moved his hand back up to caress her breasts, leaving her with a hollow feeling at the pit of her stomach. She made a little murmur of protest and involuntarily moved her hips against him. He laughed and kissed her briefly, before moving his mouth down to join his hands in lavishing attention on her breasts. "We're just taking it slow. I'm the teacher, remember?"

Emily would have been hard put to remember her own name, as his insistent sucking on her nipples made her tremble with unknown desire. "I want..." she began, then stopped with a confused moan. Flushes of heat raced up her cheeks.

Austin looked up at her suddenly, feeling the tension, knowing the signs. Quickly he positioned himself above her and gave her a deep kiss while at the same time entering her with as much restraint as he could stand. She called his name and clutched at his back. Almost immediately he felt her spasms. In a great rush of relief, he relaxed his control. He moved within her, barely, then climaxed with a force that left him awed and shaken.

For several moments, neither moved. Emily's world came back into focus. Once again she could feel the slight throb at the side of her head. Her body felt limp, sated. There were tears on her cheeks that she didn't remember shedding.

Austin rolled to one side and gathered her in his arms. "Are you all right?" he asked anxiously.

Emily smiled and nodded groggily. "More than all right, I would say." Her own voice sounded strange to her.

"You're not... I didn't hurt you?"

At the height of their passion, she had felt nothing but intense sensation, but now she noticed a slight tenderness where their bodies had joined. "You didn't hurt me," she assured him. "Did I hurt you?"

Austin bit back a laugh. "It doesn't usually work that way," he said tenderly. "The only thing that would hurt me would be if I didn't...you know...finish."

"Oh, well that's good. Because you did, didn't you? Finish?" she asked with a naïveté that made Austin's throat fill.

He planted a brief kiss on her full lips. "Most decisively," he said with a smile.

"Hmm. So I did everything all right?"

Austin's only reply was to gather her more closely in his arms. He didn't trust himself to speak. An uncharacteristic and unexpected wave of emotion had overtaken him. A few minutes ago Emily had been moving beneath him like the most wanton and sensual of women. Now, as she questioned him with her complete lack of guile, he was reminded that he was her first and only lover. He felt protective and tender and something that felt dangerously like love.

"Austin?" she asked.

"You did just fine," he said finally, not able to say anything further. He reached over for his wool poncho and pulled it over the top of them. Emily nestled against him and gave a sigh of satisfaction. For several minutes the only sound was the crackle of the fire.

Emily's breathing was deep and even, and Austin thought she had fallen asleep until she suddenly spoke. "Austin, can people do it twice in one day?"

"I beg your pardon?"

"Lovemaking. How often can it be done?" She leaned under the blankets to plant a kiss on his hard chest.

Austin shook his head. He had never met a woman quite like Emily Kendall. "Are you sure you're feeling all right? Your head doesn't hurt anymore?"

Emily moved against him, learning the feel of his hard body against her soft skin. "I'm fine. I was thinking I'd like to try it again, but of course, if you don't feel like it... I've heard that some men only like to do it once."

She had heard no such thing, and Emily was amazed at her own boldness. But she had felt a... *weightiness* come over Austin, and she wanted to turn him back to the lighthearted lover of a few minutes ago.

Austin let out an exclamation at her words and immediately snapped to life. He grabbed her wrists and turned her over on her back, looming up over her like a great pagan fire god. "You've heard that, have you?"

Emily smiled saucily and bobbed her head. Her hair was in hopeless tangles and her eyes shimmered. "And you think you want to try it again?"

A flush started up the side of her body. "Yes, please," she whispered.

Chapter Ten

Emily awoke with a throbbing head and some unusual, but not entirely unpleasant, aches in various other parts of her body. It took her a minute to realize where she was and to discern that she was not alone. Austin slept on beside her, and she took a moment to enjoy the sight of his bare chest. She had never slept beside a naked man before. In fact, she had never herself slept naked. She stretched out on the furs, feeling wickedly wanton.

Her movements awoke her partner, who opened and shut his eyes three times before they came to focus on her with a sleepy, sexy look. "Hey, look who's here," he said with a teasing smile. "I do believe it's that famous New England beauty, Speckles Kendall . . . right here in my bed."

Emily giggled. "I wish you'd forget about that name."

Austin reached for her shoulders and pulled himself over on top of her. "I certainly couldn't forget it now," he said with mock gravity. "Not when I now know just exactly how far down those freckles reach. . . ." He started to make a trail with his lips. "From this pert little nose, to these perfect cheeks . . . and finally a bare smattering all across the tops of these delectable breas—''

Emily put her hand across his mouth before he could finish the word. "It's not proper to talk about those things," she protested, but her body gave a reflexive surge up toward his mouth, which had ceased to track the freckles and had fastened on a more prominent target.

Emily closed her eyes and let the delicious tugs radiate sensation deep inside her. An ache began to build, low and insistent. Suddenly, Austin pulled back. "Is this all right?" he asked with concern. "You're not . . . uncomfortable after last night?"

Emily lifted her head and nipped the edge of his chin. His whiskers felt rough against her soft lips. "I thought you told me last night that I was supposed to be a little uncomfortable. You know . . . when you kept kissing me and I wanted to go ahead and—"

Austin stopped her words with a long, hungry kiss. He was utterly aroused, but combined with the familiar sensation was an unusual uncertainty. His pupil was getting ahead of him. He couldn't remember ever having such conversations with any woman about lovemaking. He was confident of his physical skill in the area, but the thought of talking about it intimidated him.

After several moments in which they both nearly forgot the original question, Austin backed off and smiled at her. "We're talking about two different sorts of discomfort here. Last night I was talking about a kind of *edge,* the exquisite pleasure of waiting until you want it so much it *almost* hurts. But I don't want you to really hurt. And we did get . . . thorough last night, at least for your first time."

Emily gave a long sigh of pleasure, remembering. "I never knew anything could be like that, Austin."

Her declaration was made with absolute simplicity. Austin looked down into her clear green eyes and felt his heart constrict within his chest. He had, perhaps, had physical sensations to match the ones he had experienced with Emily, but never had they been combined with such intense feelings.

He rolled to one side and pulled her into his arms. For the moment, he didn't even want to make love. He just wanted to hold her against him. He buried his face in her sweet-smelling golden hair and fought back the very first tears he had shed since the death of his mother twenty years ago.

Emily was taken aback by Austin's fervor. Last night, he had seemed in such complete command. While she had been completely at sea, lost in the incredible new sensations, he had gently instructed, guided, teased and, as he had said, held back with merciless control until she had reached a fever of intensity. This morning there was something different. She felt a special tenderness and something she couldn't quite define. An instinctive compassion. As if she could fill a place in his soul that was empty. But even as she held him, she sensed that the closeness would not last. He had lived so many years guarding that empty space, she didn't think he would ever allow her to enter it.

As if in answer to her thoughts, he abruptly let her go. "We can't be doing this," he said, his voice steady again. "They're going to be out combing these woods for you before long. All you'd need is to have Dexter Kingsman ride up and find you here with me."

Austin deliberately let the mill owner's name intrude into their idyll. He was entirely too close to feeling something for Emily that he swore he never would allow himself to feel for anyone. He had given up the idea of loving anything feminine when he was a boy.

He had made love to Emily Kendall. Nothing could change that. But one night of passion didn't have to mean that either of their lives had to be affected permanently. Perhaps now that he had satisfied his desire, it would be easier to let her go about making a life for herself. Though he had a suspicion that Emily was one woman who would not be forgotten easily.

She looked at him now with hurt in her eyes. That was for the best, he told himself firmly. The hurt would turn to anger and the anger to indifference. Even if he couldn't forget her easily, he could make sure that she would be able to get on with her life without the hindrance of a hopeless relationship.

"You wouldn't want your future husband to find you here, would you?" he asked, more harshly.

Emily pulled the wool cover up around her neck. She was confused and wounded. Just minutes ago, Austin had been holding her in a tender embrace. A few hours ago they had been making passionate love. And now he had abruptly withdrawn and was talking about another man as "her future husband."

"I told you last night that I'm not sure I want to marry anyone," she said, her lower lip thrust out defensively.

Austin felt the constriction in his chest again, but he didn't relent. "You'd be a fool not to accept him, Emily. He could give you anything you ever wanted."

He couldn't give me what you gave me last night, she wanted to say. But his coldness made it impossible to utter the words. "Thank you for your advice, Mr. Matthews," she said stiffly instead.

Austin bit his lip. This was not how he had intended their evening together to end. After Emily had fallen asleep last night, he had lain awake considering the possibilities. He had decided that he would gently, but firmly, explain that, although he would remember this night for the rest of his life, it would be better for them both if they weren't together like this again. She would agree, sensibly, and they would part amicably as friends. He hadn't been prepared for the intensity of feeling that had swept over him when she had awakened him unexpectedly this morning. He hadn't been prepared for the burning in his throat, nor for the way it made him feel to speak Dexter Kingsman's name.

"Emily..." he began. But she rolled away from him and, wrapping herself in his soft wool poncho, stood up. It left him lying on the furs uncovered, but she looked down at his naked body with no apparent emotion and asked, "Would you mind leaving the room while I get dressed?"

Austin stood in one easy movement. Emily wasn't as indifferent as she was pretending, and the view of his long, graceful body in motion as he pulled on his trousers made her insides roll. But she kept her expression even and didn't look away.

He made one last attempt to put things right between them. Placing a gentle hand against her cheek, he smiled sadly. "If there were one woman in the world who could convince me to settle down, it would be you, Emily Kendall. But I'm a lost cause. Too many years, too many women, too tough, too ornery."

Emily remembered the way he had clutched her this morning, as if she had been a lifeline. "Maybe you're not as tough as you think you are," she said soberly.

He shook his head. "Don't get ideas about me. I'm just not worth it. You came out west to find yourself a new life, including a husband. You've made a good start. Why, before long they'll be talking up and down the coast about the female impresario up in Seattle." His voice was warm with pride. "And the husband part will be coming along before you know it. Maybe it won't be Kingsman, after all ... but some lucky man is bound to snatch you up."

Emily dropped her eyes so that he wouldn't see the pain she was feeling. She hadn't thought making love with Austin would change things between them, but she still couldn't believe that it had meant so little to him that he could blithely talk about pairing her off with another man. "We should get back to town," she said quietly.

Austin reached out and grasped her chin, forcing her to look at him. "I've never in my life felt anything like I did last night."

Emily gave him a brittle smile. "Is that what you say to all your women?"

Austin shook his head in frustration. He hated to see the hurt in her eyes, but, as he had told himself before, perhaps it was the easiest way. "You're right, we should be getting back. As it is, we'll have some explaining to do about where we've been all night. We have to think about your reputation."

Emily couldn't care less about her reputation. In her present mood, she wouldn't have cared if Austin rode into the center of town and announced to all concerned that they had spent the night together. What difference did it make anymore? What had been the most thrilling and tender experience of her life had turned into a mockery.

"Say whatever you like," she said drearily.

He had finished putting on his clothes, but he hesitated another moment, looking as if he wanted to say something more. Finally, he said simply, "I'll get the horses ready while you get dressed." Then he headed out the door.

At Emily's insistence, the opera house had been built with strict economy. She knew that there was no way she could duplicate the gilded stages and plush balconies of the houses back East. The building was a simple frame structure which had been finished at a modest cost of $750. Thanks to Austin they had real theater seats and a real curtain, but backstage the rooms were unadorned. Immediately in back of the stage were two small dressing rooms, a wardrobe room and a prop room. In the rear of the building were three somewhat larger rooms. Two would be used temporarily by Emily and Ida Mae as living quarters. The third Emily had made into a small office.

She sat at her new desk, which Dexter, in a magnanimous gesture, had sent over from his warehouse. In spite of Austin's fears, Dexter had not appeared concerned about her day-long disappearance. In fact, Emily didn't think he had really noticed that she was missing. And when she had explained to him the next day that she had been thrown from her horse and Austin had spent the night looking for her, he had merely nodded and warned her once again to stay away from the saloon owner.

Dexter had been in the middle of negotiations for the purchase of an interest in one of the line of steamers that plied the ever-expanding coastal towns. Emily was interested. If she wanted to attract important performers to this area, easy transportation was vital. But Dexter had not felt the subject a proper one to discuss with her, so she had gone back to her hotel to help Ida Mae with the packing.

They had few belongings between them, and the move was made easily with the help of some of the other brides. Little by little, the hotel was emptying. In a veritable matrimonial frenzy, eighteen of the girls had gotten married in the past week. There wasn't even time to hold proper celebrations, and the group was way behind on quilts.

Those who were still unsure were moving out to rooming houses. Some had funds of their own, and some had made arrangements with Mr. Mercer for more time. The whole process had begun to make Emily angry. While it was true that all of the women had come west of their own free will, it wasn't fair that they were being pressured into marrying men they weren't sure they wanted.

She was just glad that she and Ida Mae had found a solution to the problem. Ida Mae's situation with Eldo Smedley had not changed. He wanted to go ahead with the wedding in spite of his friend's feelings, but Ida Mae was holding out for a better resolution. In the meantime, she was happy with her little room in the opera house and was beginning to give lessons on her piano.

Emily was happy, too, she told herself again as she sat at her desk. As she riffled through the sheaf of papers on her desk, she felt that now she truly was an impresario. She had just finished a most persuasive letter inviting Artemus Ward and the new humorist Mark Twain to Seattle. She guaranteed their expenses and, after taking a deep breath, a speaking fee of fifty dollars each. If the performances didn't sell well, she would just have to find the money somewhere. Austin's words about taking risks came back to her.

She had taken a risk with him, and it hadn't turned out very well for her. The more she thought about their night together, the worse she felt. Undoubtedly, for him she had just been another in a long series of women. He probably made love every night over at his saloon. He had meant nothing by it—she'd just been available... and an easy mark.

The thought made her furious. She drummed her fingers on the desk. Perhaps she should go over to Dexter's office and insist that they get married immediately. That would show Austin that she wasn't sitting around longing for his company. Or perhaps she should march right into the Golden Lady and tell Austin and anyone else who wanted to hear what a low-down snake he was.

She was imagining the scene with a nasty smile when Ida Mae poked her head in the door. "What are you thinking about, Emily?" she asked. "You look like you just stole the money out of the poor box."

Emily looked embarrassed. "I was daydreaming, I guess. How did your lesson go?"

Ida Mae smiled broadly. "They're little dolls, both the Winchesters. And their pa said he'd pay me a month in advance." She held out her hand to show off a number of silver coins.

"It's fun making money ourselves, isn't it?"

Ida Mae nodded. "I'm going to keep on teaching even after Eldo and I get married."

"Are you any closer to getting things resolved?"

Ida Mae pulled out a chair across the desk from Emily and sat, her smile disappearing. "Eldo said Mr. Briggs went to his house last night in a rage, and he'd been drinking. I'm afraid my coming has broken up their friendship forever."

Emily nodded sympathetically. "After you've been married awhile, Mr. Briggs will come around. He won't be able to stay angry forever when he sees how happy you two are."

"I hope you're right." Ida Mae squinted her eyes and looked at Emily. "And what about you? Just exactly who was it you were daydreaming about with that nasty smile on your face?"

Emily laughed. "I'm not daydreaming about anyone these days. I'm going to concentrate on making the opera house a success." She picked up the letter she had just written. "I've invited two of the top humorists on the West Coast to come as guest performers."

"Oh, Emily! I can't believe all this is really happening. Did you ever think when we sat at those looms back in Lowell that we'd be doing something as exciting as this?"

Ida Mae's enthusiasm helped restore Emily's good humor. Her friend was right. Her new life was exciting even without the presence of Austin Matthews. She folded her letter to San Francisco and slipped it into an envelope. "As a matter of fact, I did, Ida Mae. I always knew that something bigger and better was ahead of me if I just had the nerve to go out and look for it."

Ida Mae reached across the desk and squeezed her friend's hand. "You always were so brave, Emily. I would never have come here if it hadn't been for you. Just think, I'd never have met Eldo. I guess I'll be grateful the rest of my life.''

Emily smiled. "Well, I just hope things work out for you two before too long. Now, aren't we supposed to be over at the hotel for Cecilia's ceremony?''

Ida Mae looked at the tiny silver watch that was pinned to her bodice. "Goodness me! We're going to be late.''

They hurried out the office door, but just outside, Ida Mae stumbled, then looked down and gave a little shriek. On the new wood floor was the bloody carcass of a rabbit.

"What in the world!" Emily exclaimed.

"How horrible!" Ida Mae shuddered. "How in heaven's name could that have gotten here?''

Emily looked up and down the hall. The doors were all closed and there was no sign of an intruder.

"Do you think a dog could have dragged it in?" Ida Mae asked.

Emily walked down and one by one pulled open the doors to the rooms behind the stage, then the ones to her bedroom and Ida Mae's. All the rooms were empty. She walked back over to Ida Mae, who was still standing by the office door, looking at the dead animal with distaste. "I've never seen a dog that could open doors," Emily said grimly.

"But what's it doing here?''

"Someone must have put it there." Emily had not told Ida Mae about the broken curtain weight after the first performance. She had not wanted to alarm her friend, and she had hoped that she was wrong about someone trying to sabotage her performances. But with this new incident she couldn't avoid the obvious conclusion any longer. For an unknown reason, someone was out to harm her or, at the very least, scare her. Without mincing words, she told Ida Mae about the frayed rope.

"Oh, Emily, perhaps we have...you know...one of those opera *ghosts*." Ida Mae's gray eyes had grown wide.

Emily gave a bleak smile. She wished she could believe the troublemaker *was* a ghost. She wasn't afraid of spirits. But she had a terrible feeling that the perpetrator of these hateful tricks was a flesh-and-blood human. One with a sick mind. And she had to find out who it was before his mischief ended in tragedy.

It had been Ethan Witherspoon who had suggested a special shantyboys' concert. Before he became Dexter's foreman, he had worked logging camps himself and spent many hours entertaining the loggers, or shantyboys as they were called after the ramshackle buildings that usually made up most of the camps.

Ethan played the harmonica, and Pete Spicer, one of his crew members, played the fiddle. One or the other of them knew just about every logging song ever written, and they put together an evening of some of the most popular, with the mill crew boys singing along. The ballads were rough-hewn and earthy. It wasn't exactly the kind of culture that the New Englanders were used to back east, but the hearty grins on the faces of the men in the audience were satisfying to see.

There was special laughter when they launched into a cleaned-up version of "Once More a-Lumb'ring Go." The last verse was significant for many who had given up their logging jobs and were now, in fact, vying to win one of the New Englanders as a "little wife."

Emily tapped her foot and smiled as Ethan sang in a surprisingly strong tenor voice:

> When our youthful days are ended
> And our jokes are getting long,
> We'll take us each a little wife
> And settle on a farm.
> We'll have enough to eat and drink,
> Contented we will go;
> And we'll tell our wives of our hard times
> And no more a-lumb'ring go.

There were tender looks exchanged between many members of the audience. Sitting in front of Emily, Eldo Smedley reached for Ida Mae's hand. Emily glanced at Dexter in the seat next to her. He appeared unmoved. Of course, Dexter had most definitely never been a shantyboy.

Emily would have enjoyed the concert more if she were not so worried about another appearance by Ida Mae's so-called opera ghost. She had asked several of the new husbands of some of the brides to be a kind of special security force. Since an hour before the concert, they had stationed themselves, one on the inside and one on the outside, of both the back and front doors. When she had checked with them just before the beginning of the performance, they had reported nothing suspicious. She herself had stood just behind the ticket table and checked every person coming in. Missouri Ike had not shown up, which made her feel somewhat better. Perhaps there would be no trouble.

On stage, Ethan changed the mood by launching into a poignantly beautiful version of "Bonnie Doon." Emily sat back and closed her eyes. In addition to the worry about the prankster, she was concerned because she had not heard anything from her San Francisco contact. She wondered if the opera house would continue to be so popular if she kept having to offer nothing but local talent. Although, tonight was another full house. She really should not worry so much, she told herself. But sometimes it seemed that being an impresario wasn't quite as much fun as she had hoped.

It would help to have someone to talk things over with. Dexter loftily changed the subject whenever she mentioned the opera house. Ida Mae was no help. Any mention of concern made her sniffles worse. And since their night together, Austin had been nowhere to be seen.

The music ended with a sprightly tune called "The Jam on Gerry's Rocks" that had Pete's fingers moving so fast on his fiddle that they looked like a blur. The men whistled and stomped their feet and called for more, but the proud musicians had already jumped down into the audience to be congratulated by their friends.

Dexter stood and stretched. "A pleasant little performance," he said, taking Emily's arm to lead her out of the row of seats. "Would you care to go get something to eat?"

Emily hesitated. Lately she had turned down more of Dexter's invitations than she had accepted, and one of these days he was going to get impatient. But she wanted to talk with the men who had been watching the doors and check the theater to be sure nothing was amiss.

"How about if we plan a more leisurely dinner some other night," she said, trying to make her refusal sound contrite.

"Tomorrow?" Dexter's jaw had tightened. He looked annoyed.

"Yes, tomorrow. That would be fine." With her sweetest smile, she ushered him out of the theater and said good-night. Then she turned to walk back up the aisle. The four men who had been helping her had agreed to meet on stage after the concert.

Parmelia's husband, Eugene Carmichael, had taken charge of the group. "None of us saw anything unusual, Miss Kendall," he said as she approached. "Couple of kids tried to sneak in the back door without paying, but that was it."

"Did any of you see Missouri Ike coming around?"

"Ike's workin' out at Piny Ridge Camp, and none of them boys are in town right now," one of the other men said.

Emily nodded. "Well, I certainly do appreciate your help." She looked at Eugene. "I could pay you all something...."

Eugene rubbed his whiskers and looked embarrassed. "Aw, Miss Kendall, 'tweren't nothin'. We're happy to help out if it means keeping the opera house open ... and keeping our missuses happy." He looked around at the other three men and they all nodded vigorously.

She felt a warm glow. It was touching to see to what lengths many of the rough-and-tumble frontiersmen would go to please their delicate eastern brides. She'd seen men bigger around than a redwood tree pass an entire afternoon sipping tea from a wafer-thin china cup and making polite conversation, just to be near the women.

"I certainly appreciate your help," she said again.

"Maybe those things you were worried about were just coincidence," Eugene said with just a touch of male condescension.

Emily smiled politely. "Let's hope so." And with a few more reassurances, the men left her alone. She was relieved that there had been no incidents, but she wasn't comforted by Eugene's words. There was nothing coincidental about a dead rabbit.

She walked along the side aisle, turning off the wall lamps one by one. Slowly the theater dimmed, until there was just one lamp left lit, near the stage. Back East, some theaters had fancy lighting systems that could be dimmed during the performance, so the audience was in darkness while the stage was illuminated. She looked out over the now-dark rows of seats. It was more dramatic, she thought. A darkened room could add to the magic of a theater experience.

Lost in her study of the room, she let out a shriek when a hand grasped her elbow. Blood pounded in her ears and her heart raced.

"Emily, it's me."

Emily sagged and let out a breath. Austin. In the muted light, he looked powerful, almost menacing, as he stood over her. "You scared me," she said in an irritated tone.

"I'm sorry. You looked like you were lost in thought. Is anything wrong?"

Recovered from her scare, she looked up into his face. "No, nothing's wrong. I was just thinking about lighting."

"Lighting?"

"Yes, lighting the theater. How we could change the lighting during the performance."

Austin looked as if this wasn't the answer he expected. "Oh. But you're sure nothing's wrong?"

Emily turned the wick on the last lamp, plunging them into blackness, then she pushed by him to go through the curtained doorway that led backstage. Her body brushed against his in the dark, and she stiffened. "I told you, nothing's wrong," she said to him over her shoulder as he followed her through the curtain.

"You're lying."

The words were so cold, they made the hair stand up on Emily's neck. "What are you talking about?" She turned around to face him, hands on her hips.

"You had men posted at the doors before the concert. Front and back. I saw them. There must be a reason."

Emily hesitated. During the performance she had been sorry that she had no one to talk to about her worries, but now that Austin was here, standing too close to her in the narrow backstage hall, she found herself reluctant to confide in him. The last time they had been together they had made love. Then she had not heard from him all week. Finally she said, "I was just playing things safe. There was an incident the other day."

"What kind of incident?" Austin's mellow voice was unusually insistent.

"Nothing important. Some prankster left a dead rabbit backstage. I probably would have ignored the whole thing if it hadn't been for the weight falling the other day."

"And the skunk, and someone following you through the woods," Austin added. He sounded angry. "Why didn't you tell me about the rabbit?"

Emily's anger matched his. "You haven't exactly been around to tell lately, now have you?"

"The Golden Lady's a five-minute walk."

"Maybe I didn't want to go into a place like that."

"You could have sent word."

"You could have come around to check on your investment."

They glared at each other for several moments. Finally Austin broke the silence. "I didn't think I had to check. I thought I could trust your judgment." His voice was quieter, but still angry.

"Oh, and now are you trying to say that you can't trust it?" Emily's tone was shrill. In a sense Austin was right. He was her partner, and he should be informed about things concerning the operation of the opera house. But both knew that their anger went beyond the current discussion.

Austin ran a hand back through his hair. "I do trust you. But I also worry about you...*and* about my investment," he added before she could protest further. "We have to find out who's doing these things before people become afraid of coming to concerts here."

The hair he had smoothed back fell right back down over his forehead. The strong features of his face were taut with concern. Emily felt her temper die. She gave a half smile. "Ida Mae says she thinks we have an opera house ghost."

Austin's expression relaxed a little and he gave a sardonic chuckle. "A ghost I wouldn't mind...it's humans that worry me."

He had echoed her sentiments exactly. Emily felt the stiffness go out of her back. It felt good, after all, to have someone else share her troubles. "I agree. That's why I had the men posted tonight. But they didn't see anything unusual. And it doesn't appear that there were any problems."

Austin looked up and down the hall. "I don't like the fact that you're living here alone, Emily."

"I'm all right. Ida Mae's right next door."

He shook his head. "Why don't you let me pay for you two to move back to the hotel until we get this thing cleared up? It would be part of my investment," he added quickly when he saw Emily begin to bristle.

"Thank you for the offer, but we're fine here, really. Maybe there won't be any more incidents." She smiled at him. "Maybe the ghost has moved on to go haunt Portland or someplace."

Austin's smile was reserved. "Will you promise that you will let me know if anything else strange happens?"

Emily nodded. It felt good to know that he was still concerned about her, despite the way they had left each other after their night together.

"The minute anything happens," Austin insisted.

"I promise."

Now his smile was genuine, and Emily felt the effects. She bit the inside of her lip.

Austin felt his insides twist. She looked utterly desirable, an irresistible combination of vulnerability and sensuality. He wanted to take her in his arms and tell her that nothing bad would ever happen to her again. He wanted to carry her back to the cabin in the woods and make love to her all night in front of the fire. Instead, he tapped the tip of her nose with his finger and said lightly, "That's a good girl." Then he turned on his heel and was gone.

Chapter Eleven

Leave it to Dexter to have taken care of every detail, Emily thought to herself. When he had invited her for a Sunday afternoon drive, she hadn't realized that he would provide a sumptuous meal. She watched, impressed, as he chose the perfect spot, a smooth, grassy place in the sun just up the bank from a lovely mountain stream. He spread out the blankets he had also tucked away in the back of his big phaeton, then took out a straw basket with china plates, glasses and real linen napkins.

"Did you put this all together yourself?" Emily asked.

"I asked my cook to help me out." Dexter looked up at her and smiled. "I told him I had a very special day planned and everything had to be perfect."

"Do you want me to help?"

Dexter shook his head. "You just sit down there on the blankets and enjoy the view. I'll have everything set up in a minute."

She sat and folded her hands in her lap, amazed anew as Dexter brought out a spray of flowers and put them in a vase in the middle of the picnic lunch. "Even flowers?" she asked in disbelief.

"You've told me you like them, right?"

"I love flowers, but I don't think I've ever had them on a picnic before."

Dexter grinned and pulled the cork from an earthenware jug of cider. He poured two glasses of the golden liquid and held one out to her. "There's a first time for everything," he said, an odd note in his voice.

Emily's throat felt dry, and she hoped it was just from the dusty drive. Dexter was acting a bit strange today. She took a swallow of cider and felt better.

Dexter was unwrapping several packets of oiled paper and putting the food out on plates. There was a whole chicken, some cold boiled potatoes and sweet corn cakes. Finally he pulled out a little box that said Hofmeier & Sons, New York on the top in fancy script. He opened it and inside were marzipan candies. Sometime during the long transport west, they had lost most of their intricate shapes, but they looked very tasty.

"This is wonderful, Dexter," Emily said sincerely. In fact, she was surprised at how good it felt. After her parents died, she had had to take care of herself. Since arriving in Seattle she had worked hard, making decisions for herself and others. It was nice to be pampered and waited on for a change.

Dexter held out the box of sweetmeats. "Can I tempt you?" he said with a slightly naughty emphasis to the words. As usual, he was immaculately dressed. Even for a picnic in the mountains, he wore a light brown suit, complete with waistcoat, that would have passed in the finest law offices in Boston.

She turned down his offer with a smile. "No candy until after we eat. That's what my mother always said."

"Your parents are . . . ?"

"Gone. Both of them." Dexter had never asked her much about her family. Or about herself, for that matter. He nodded now gravely, but didn't pursue the subject.

"Well, we'll leave the candy for afterward, then. How about some chicken?"

"That would be lovely."

They ate mostly in silence, enjoying the beautiful summer day. Lazy clouds drifted over their heads, giving vague premonitions of late-afternoon showers to come. The fresh air boosted her appetite, and Emily's plate was soon clean.

"I like to see a woman who can eat," Dexter commented. "I'm glad you're not one of those finicky, skinny types."

"Thank you, I guess," Emily said with dry amusement. "And as long as it's making you happy, I'll have one of those candies now."

Dexter held out the box and she picked out a nice piece, in the shape of a barely recognizable soldier. She looked at it a moment. "They're little works of art. Almost too pretty to eat."

"Perhaps you'd prefer another design." He held out the box. "Didn't you tell me your fiancé was a soldier?"

Emily laughed. "Well, yes, but I don't think it would do Spencer much good to have me refuse to eat this little guy."

"Spencer was his name?"

"Yes, Spencer Bennett."

Dexter set aside his plate and moved closer to her on the blanket. He swallowed and Emily could see the up and down movement of his neck. "Did you love him very much?" he asked. Dexter's tone was different than any he had ever used with her. He sounded nervous, almost shy.

Her smile faded. If she were truthful with herself, she didn't know the answer to Dexter's question. Of course, she had always thought that she loved Spencer, but since coming west, she questioned if what they had had together hadn't been due more to proximity and convenience than real emotion. She certainly couldn't imagine spending a night with Spencer such as the one she had had with Austin. At the sudden memory her cheeks flamed, and Dexter mistook the cause.

"I'm sorry," he said quickly. "That was too personal a question."

"No, don't be sorry. It's just that...my relationship with Spencer now seems like a very long time ago."

Dexter reached for her hand. "That's good, because it means you can move on to someone else with a clear heart."

Emily pressed her lips together. She had the feeling that, thanks to Austin Matthews, it would be a long time before she would have a clear heart.

She watched the progress of another swallow along Dexter's long throat.

"And I think you know, my dear," he continued, "that I am hoping the someone else will be me."

His hand holding hers had grown sweaty. Emily took a deep breath. She didn't exactly know how to respond. Dexter could be very nice when he wanted to be. He was elegant and courtly and, when he wasn't being a high-handed male, he could be very sweet.

He cleared his throat. "I'm doing this badly. It's not as easy as closing a business deal," he said with a rueful chuckle. He let go of her hand and pulled a tiny leather bag out of his pocket. Opening it, he pulled out a beautiful gold ring set with three small emeralds. "Emily, I'm asking you to do me the honor of becoming my wife."

Emily gasped. Even though she had come on a ship almost halfway around the world to become a bride, she was caught off guard. The stones from the ring sparkled in the sunlight. "It's beautiful," she said numbly.

She thought of the gold watch Spencer had given her when they became engaged. She had left it with her sister. "This is going to be a new life, Cassie," she'd told her. "What's past is past."

"I got emeralds to match your eyes," Dexter said a little sheepishly.

The sentiment surprised her. "That was very sweet, Dexter."

He was still holding out the ring. She had made no move to take it. "Ethan suggested it. He goes in for those kinds of romantic notions... it's all those songs he sings, I guess."

Emily smiled. Dexter wasn't perfect, but he had many admirable qualities. Truthfulness was one of them. But she wasn't ready to accept his offer of marriage.

"Dexter, I am very honored," she said gently. "But you know I'm just starting to get the opera house going." She held up a hand as he started to interrupt. "And I know you don't entirely approve. I think it would be better all around if we waited a while longer."

His hand holding the ring slowly lowered. "I wouldn't mind waiting for the wedding, Emily, but I want people to know that you belong to me."

Emily sighed. Sometimes she thought she didn't understand her own mind. She was just beginning to feel the power of being able to provide for herself. The idea of "belonging" to some man—any man—made her cringe. On the other hand, hadn't she been thinking just before lunch how nice it was to be taken care of? And now Dexter was offering to take care of her for the rest of her life. "I need more time, Dexter," she said finally.

He looked discomfited. He was not a man who was used to being turned down, Emily surmised, and she would have to be careful that her refusal didn't turn him completely against her. "I do enjoy being with you, and appreciate everything you've done for me...." She gestured at the spread around them. "Today has been wonderful. But I guess I'm just a person who takes a long time making a decision."

Dexter looked down at the blanket, struggling to control his annoyance. "People who take too long making decisions sometimes miss out on a lot in life, Emily."

She reached out and gently touched his hand that held the ring. "I'll try not to take too long, Dexter." She sounded contrite, and she was. In many ways it would be the easiest thing to just say yes.

Dexter looked up suddenly, his blue eyes narrowed. "It's not Matthews, is it? You're not turning me down because of that saloon keeper?"

Emily looked him straight in the eyes. "Austin Matthews is my business partner...that's it. He's not interested in anything more, and neither am I."

Dexter nodded. He pulled his hand out from hers and carefully put the ring back into its pouch. "I'll just hang on to this for a little while, then."

Emily smiled at him gratefully. "Thank you."

Dexter nodded brusquely, then started putting things away in the picnic basket. The half frown on his face made Emily refrain from continuing on with the subject. The silence grew awkward as they finished picking up and packing everything away in the carriage, but once they started out on the road again, Dexter began a tale about the latest town council meeting. His voice regained its normal tone, and by the time they got back to town, they were back on a friendly basis.

There was just one last uncomfortable moment when Dexter took his leave. He held her a moment as he helped her down from the carriage, then leaned down and kissed her, a half-angry kiss that was more possessive than loverlike. Then he set her down and patted the side pocket that held the ring and said again, "Remember, don't take too long, Emily."

She had ducked her head in confusion and thanked him again for the nice day, then escaped through the back door of the opera house with a sigh of relief.

She knew she had done the right thing, but it made her head hurt to think about, and she rubbed her temples as she walked down the hall to her office. By refusing Dexter, she may be giving up an excellent chance for happiness. Perhaps doing some work on her books would remind her of the life she was building for herself.

The door to her office was slightly ajar and she felt a queasy sensation in her stomach. Had they had another visit from the mysterious intruder? Cautiously she pushed open the door. There, seated with his feet up on her desk, was Austin. He had a sarcastic grin on his face. They both spoke at once.

"Have a nice ride?"

"What are you doing here?"

They were glaring, much as they had the other night, and almost at the same instant, it struck them both as funny.

"It seems we have a tough time carrying on a civil conversation these days," Emily said, letting a reluctant smile break out on her face.

Austin smiled in response. "Flo says I'm the most even-tempered person she's ever met, but you'd never know it when I get around you." He lifted his feet off her desk and sat up straight.

Emily sat in the chair across from him and asked, "Well, what *are* you doing here?"

His smile grew broader. He picked up a sheet of paper from her desk. "You got a letter."

"And you read it?" She started to bristle again.

"It was addressed to the Seattle Opera House. You hadn't been by the post office in a couple of days so Hector gave it to me." Hector Finnegan was the postmaster and knew more about most people in town than they knew themselves.

Emily half stood to snatch the paper from his hands. "It's from San Francisco," she said eagerly.

She plunked down hard in her chair and read rapidly, running the words together, "...will be very pleased to perform...earliest convenience..."

Austin had already read the letter, which was from Mr. Twain himself, whose real name was Samuel Clemens. He had written that he was about to embark on a tour of Europe, but would be happy to make a detour up to Seattle to appear at their opera house.

"He's coming!" Emily's eyes snapped wide with excitement.

Austin nodded and they grinned at each other. "We have to be sure it's a sellout, Austin. Do you think we should put an advertisement in the paper? I could get the brides to help with handbills. And what about the lighting? Do you think we could work it somehow to dim them during his lecture?"

Austin gave a warm, rich laugh. When Emily's brain started into action, her whole body came alive. She looked as if she were about to come right out of her chair. Her smile of enthusiasm was pure delight. "Hold on there, partner. Mr. Clemens said he would be here next month. I think we have time to work things out."

Emily sank back in her chair and let out a happy sigh. "It's really happening, Austin. Just like I imagined. I can hardly believe it."

Austin nodded. "Yup, I can see it now... you'll be famous. 'Speckles Kendall, the greatest impresario in the West.'" His smile turned bittersweet at the sudden, vivid memory of the last time he had called her by that name. She'd been beneath him, and he'd been kissing her.... When she'd arrived earlier he'd seen her kiss Dexter, and he'd been unprepared for the cruel wrench it had given him.

His grin died suddenly. Emily sensed his shift in mood, and wondered at the cause. "Well, not *the* greatest, maybe," she teased, trying to coax the smile back into place.

"Anyway, you've got your first guest performer," Austin said briskly, standing up. "If you need anything to get ready—money for an advertisement or anything like that—let me know."

Emily stood, too. She was tired of trying to follow the moods of this man. One minute he was looking at her tenderly and saying nice things, and the next he turned cold and businesslike. Well, two could play at that game. She extended her hand and spoke unemotionally. "Thank you, Austin, but I'm sure I can handle everything from now on."

He reached across the desk and shook her outstretched hand. His eyes traveled briefly down her pink gingham dress. "You never answered me about your ride. It looked like you and Kingsman had a very good time."

He nodded toward the window behind the desk, from which he would have had a perfect view of Dexter's farewell kiss. Good, Emily thought with perverse pleasure, let him think what he likes. "We had a lovely time," she answered breezily.

Austin nodded. "Well, I just wanted to be sure you got the letter. I'll be heading on back to the Golden Lady."

"I thought you weren't supposed to be open on Sundays anymore," she said, referring to a recently passed ordinance.

Austin's customary grin returned. "It's going to take more than a town council to shut down Skid Road. I'd like to see some of those council members try to close us down when a camp's arriving at the end of a log drive."

"Face it, Austin, civilization is coming to Seattle, whether or not the Skid Road owners want it to."

Austin picked his hat up off the desk and gave a mocking bow. "It's been a pleasure, Miss Kendall. Perhaps you'll invite me to tea one of these days."

He clapped his hat on his head and went out of the room, leaving Emily watching him with a frown on her face. The man did infuriate her, she thought as she moved around to sit at her desk. Some of her enthusiasm had disappeared, and she didn't feel much like working. It had been, all in all, quite an afternoon. A marriage proposal, the letter from San Francisco, and another frustrating encounter with Austin Matthews.

She leaned back in her chair. She would put the first and the last occurrence out of her mind and concentrate on the upcoming performance. There would be time enough to deal with the men in her life later.

Ida Mae had become increasingly skittish. She asked Emily to see her to her bedroom each night and wait on the outside of the door until she heard the key turn in the lock. Even Emily's excitement over her first touring performer could not raise her friend's spirits. Ida Mae appeared to have lost interest in making the opera house a success. She just wanted to go on giving her piano lessons and planning her marriage to Eldo.

The two were walking back from a quilting session at the house of Cynthia Stoddard, who was now Cynthia Smith. Last week she had married a brawny livery stable owner with the unimpressive name of John Smith.

"I don't care what anyone says, I think it's wonderful that Parmelia is in the family way," Ida Mae was saying.

"It's only the Widow Bartlett who says it's indecently soon," Emily answered absently. She had many things on her mind, and the women's gossip had not held its usual interest for her today. It had occurred to her, however, to be grateful that it was not *she* who was in the family way. The appearance of her monthly courses had confirmed that fact. She supposed that now that most of the weddings were over, one by one the brides would be making announcements such as

Parmelia's today. They'd have to leave off their quilting to make baby blankets.

She was happy for Parmelia, but she gave a little shudder as she imagined what the reaction would be to such an announcement from her, unwed. Not even engaged. It would be the scandal of the town. She had been a fool to let herself get carried away like that with Austin, and she was determined that it would never happen again.

"Emily, I'm talking to you. Where's your head today?"

"I'm sorry, Ida. What were you saying?"

"I was asking if you thought Dexter would stand up with you for our wedding if Mr. Briggs still refuses to be a part of it."

"I don't know." The thought of *any* wedding made Emily's head ache. "I'll ask him."

They walked in silence for several minutes, taking the shortcut behind the livery stable to reach the back door of the opera house. "Emily..." Ida Mae said slowly as they approached the building. "Are you getting tired of living here?"

"What do you mean?"

"Well, we don't have anywhere to cook our meals and the rooms aren't exactly beautiful...."

"I like it here just fine," Emily answered, pulling open the back door. "It's convenient for me to be near the office so I can work any time I want. It's convenient for you, too—you're available any time for your piano lessons."

Ida Mae nodded and meekly followed Emily into the building.

"Besides, it's free, which is important to both of us at the moment."

The back door opened on to a small hallway that went between the bedrooms and the office. Emily stopped to turn the wick up on a lamp that had been left low, then she stepped into the main back hall and glanced toward her office. Behind her, Ida Mae gasped.

At eye level sticking into the door of her office was a hunting knife. It held a sheet of paper in place. Emily felt herself grow cold. She looked up and down the hall, then walked over to the door. The knife had an intricately carved handle made of bone. Its blade was caked with dried blood. The notice said in bold block letters: Jezebels—Go Back East Where You Belong.

Ida Mae began to cry softly. Emily pulled open the door to her office and looked inside. The room was empty. One by one she checked the other rooms, the theater and the loge. There was no one in the building. At least no one that anyone could see.

She walked slowly back to the door, where Ida Mae stood trembling. "There's no sign of anyone," Emily told her.

"I don't think I can take any more of this, Emily," Ida Mae said shakily. "Whether or not it's a ghost— someone is doing these things."

Emily walked over and pulled the knife out of the door. The sheet of paper drifted to the floor. "At least this time we may have a clue to follow up on," she said, looking carefully at the weapon.

"How can you be so calm?" Ida Mae demanded angrily. "What if that knife had been stuck in one of us instead of in your door?"

Emily shook her head. "We have to find out who's doing this. That's for sure."

"I think we should pack up our things right now and move over to the hotel."

"Running away isn't going to solve anything. So far the person has never come around when we're here."

"So far. What about when he followed you out on the trail?"

"That's nothing definite." She hefted the knife. "But this is. I'm going over to the sheriff's and see if there's any way to find out who this belongs to."

"What about moving our things?"

Emily sighed. "Ida, I'm not letting any ghost or any red-blooded man chase me out of my opera house. If you want to move, go ahead."

"And leave you here alone?"

Emily shrugged. "If you insist on leaving."

Ida Mae dabbed at her eyes with one of her tattered hankies. "I couldn't do that."

"Good. Then we'll stay here and we'll find out who's been doing this and stop him once and for all." She headed toward the door. "I wonder if the men from Piny Ridge logging camp have arrived in town yet."

"Why?"

"Missouri Ike's with that outfit."

"And you think he may be the one doing these things? I know he's odd, but why would he do something like this, Emily?"

"Why would anyone? I'm not saying it's Ike, but we have to consider all the possibilities." She headed out the door.

"You're not leaving me here alone," Ida Mae said hastily, following her down the steps. "I'm going with you to the sheriff."

"C'mon then. We've got a varmint to catch."

After finally pacifying Ida Mae and saying goodnight, Emily found she wasn't the least bit sleepy. The manager of the San Francisco Opera House had sent her a packet of Mark Twain's articles, and she stayed awake well into the night reading the clever essays. They took her mind off the latest disturbing incident.

Sheriff Cutler had really been of very little help. He had not recognized the unusual knife, and he said that although some of the Piny Ridge men had been in town, he hadn't seen Ike. Nor did he put much stock in that theory. "Ike's a bit odd, but he's all right," he'd said dismissively.

All in all, it seemed that the sheriff resented the fact that the arrival of the New England brides had placed more emphasis on the importance of law and order to the community, which meant that he would have to do some work for a change. He didn't appear eager to help Emily and Ida Mae discover the perpetrator of what he called "practical jokes."

Ida Mae had tried once more to persuade Emily to move to the hotel, at least for the night, but Emily had held firm, and Ida Mae had meekly followed her friend's lead, as she had during the entire course of their friendship.

Emily finished up one of Twain's essays on "Curing a Cold." Perhaps she should pass it on to Ida Mae in the morning, she thought with amusement, though Mr. Twain's advice of drinking a half-gallon of whiskey every twenty-four hours—since two different people had recommended his drinking a quart, and two quarts make a half-gallon—had obviously been more tongue-in-cheek than practical.

She laid the paper on the nightstand next to the bone-handled knife, which the sheriff had seen no reason to keep. "It's not as if it were used to commit a crime," he'd said.

Back in Lowell, sticking a knife into someone's door would most definitely have been considered a crime, Emily mused. But, she said to herself for the hundredth time, she wasn't in Lowell anymore.

She turned off the whale-oil lamp and flopped back down on her pillows. Maybe now she could sleep. And dream of a concert hall with lights dimmed, ringing with laughter as Mr. Twain regaled them with his outlandish tales. And not dream of bone-handled knives. She dozed.

It wasn't exactly a sound that awakened her, but more like an overwhelming *feeling,* a presence. It brought her instantly to consciousness from a deep sleep. The back of her neck prickled. Her mouth was utterly dry.

She didn't move, just lay still in the darkness, straining to hear a sound. It was several minutes, but then, yes, she did hear something. There was someone in the hall outside her room, soft footsteps. If there were footsteps, she reasoned, it had to be a person— not a ghost.

Slowly, trying not to make any noise, she swung her legs out of bed and reached for the knife on the table beside her. Her hands closed around the slippery, cold handle. She stood and crept with tiny steps toward the door. A pulse beat urgently in her throat, and her brain was sending signals that she ought to be crawling under her bed, not going out to meet the intruder. But she was sick of being afraid. If the man who had been doing these things to them was outside in that hall right now, she was going to find out his identity once and for all.

As slowly as she could she turned the knob on her bedroom door. When she heard the click of the latch, she pulled the door open all at once. Outside a massive black shape swooped toward her. She stumbled backward and let out a shriek.

Chapter Twelve

"Hellfire and damnation!" The oath was low and heartfelt.

"Austin!" Through the moonlight filtering into her room, the shapeless mass gradually came into focus. Emily could now see the ghostly whiteness of Austin's dress shirt, and vaguely make out his strong features, which were twisted into a grimace.

"What did you hit me with?" he asked indignantly.

Emily looked down at her hand, which held the hunting knife with a death grip that made her hand shake. She couldn't remember having used it to strike at Austin, but he held the lower portion of his left arm as if in pain. She backed into her room where there was more moonlight. "Come in here," she said, still sounding dazed.

Austin followed her into the room and closed the door behind him. He had let go of his arm, but held it dangling strangely. After a few seconds, he walked over to the lamp, struck a match and lit it. The room filled with light. Emily blinked, then focused her eyes on Austin's arm. On the gray wool of his sleeve was a slowly expanding stain of red.

"I d-didn't realize..." she stammered. The knife clattered from her hand. "I didn't even know I had brought it anywhere near you."

"I'm lucky your aim's not any better," he said with a dry chuckle, sitting on her bed and pulling off his jacket.

"How can you laugh? I could have hurt you badly. What if I had—."

"Killed me?" He examined his arm. The knife had torn through his shirt and gouged the skin enough to cause an annoying amount of blood, but the wound did not appear to be at all deep. "That would have been a good scandal—'Well-known saloon owner murdered at opera house in a crime of passion.'"

"I don't know how you can joke." Now that her fear was subsiding, Emily felt her temper rise. "What in the world were you doing here at this time of night?"

Austin didn't answer. Blood was dripping from his arm on to his trousers. He began to unbutton his shirt with his good hand. "I'm going to have to bandage this up or I'll bleed all over your floor."

Emily's temper died when she suddenly realized that Austin was really hurt, and that she had been the cause. "Let me see that."

She moved over to sit beside him on the bed. The cut was about four inches long, straight down his left forearm. "Do you mind helping me off with this thing?" he asked impatiently.

She reached across him to take over unfastening his buttons. Her fingers brushed against his warm chest, but she forced herself to ignore the sensation. In a minute, she had freed him as far as the top of his pants. There she stopped. Suddenly she was very aware that she was undressing him, and that she sat next to him on her bed dressed in no more than a thin cotton night shift. She looked up into his face and found the expected grin. "You can do the rest yourself," she said sharply.

With one hand he pulled the shirt out of his pants and over his head. After all the time they had spent together, she had gotten used to the way his muscular body filled out the fine clothes he wore, but she was not yet immune to his nakedness. She had forgotten the breadth of his shoulders, the solid hardness of his stomach.

Austin was watching her with amusement. "If you're done lookin'," he said mildly, "I could use a kerchief or something in the way of a bandage."

Emily colored to the roots of her hair. She jumped up from the bed and walked over to the open steamer trunk that served as her wardrobe. After rummaging in one of the drawers, she pulled out a clean cotton neckerchief. "Are you sure you don't need to see a doctor or something?"

"That'll do fine," he said, nodding toward the kerchief. "Just wind it around here tight." He extended his arm toward her.

"Well, don't we have to wash it first ... or douse it with whiskey?"

Austin grinned. "You got any whiskey around here? I wouldn't mind some—for myself, not my arm."

She shook her head. "But what about blood poisoning?"

"I'm too tough for blood poisoning." He dropped the grin and gestured vaguely. "C'mon, Emily, just put on the danged bandage."

She moved next to him on the bed again and began to wind the kerchief around his bloody arm. "You still haven't told me what you're doing here."

Austin winced as she pulled the end of the cloth tight and began to tie it. "Sheriff Cutler came into the saloon tonight and started talking about what happened over here this afternoon."

"He didn't seem to think it was very important."

"Yeah, well...I think he's changed his mind." Austin's face was no more than a foot from hers. His eyes looked almost black as they bore into her. He set his jaw in the way he did when he was controlling his anger. "I thought I told you to let me know if anything else happened."

"I was going to tell you about it," Emily said. Then, as he raised his eyebrow and waited, she added defensively, "Listen, I had enough trouble with Ida Mae tonight. I didn't think I needed a mother hen clucking about. I'd planned to send word over tomorrow."

"Which wouldn't have been much help if something more had happened tonight."

Emily gestured dismissively. "I figured our ghost had done his dirty deed for the day."

"So why was your back door open just now?"

Emily's mouth dropped open. "The back door was open?"

Austin nodded. "That's why I came in. I had closed up over at the Golden Lady and decided I would check things out here before I turned in. When I got here the back door was wide open."

A chill went up Emily's spine. "Oh," she said meekly.

Austin's face was grim. "In fact, I think I'd better take a look through the building and be sure our uninvited visitor isn't still around somewhere."

He stood, and Emily slowly did the same. "What about your arm?" she asked.

Austin gave his bandaged arm a dismissive glance. "You stay right here," he told her, pushing her gently back down on the bed. "I'll look around and be back in a minute."

Emily sat stock-still on the bed. It was terrifying to think that the malefactor had been inside the building while she and Ida Mae were sleeping. And the realization that she had actually stabbed someone with a knife made her stomach feel queasy. Much as she hated to admit it, Ida Mae had been right. They should have moved back into the hotel until this mystery was solved. She thought about waking her friend up. Even with all the commotion, she didn't expect her to be awake. Ida Mae slept as soundly as a bear in the winter, and, with her poor stuffy nose, sounded much like one, too.

The door opened quietly and Emily jerked her head toward the sound. It was Austin. "All's quiet out there, except for your friend's snoring. How did you sleep in the same room with her, anyway?"

Emily managed a weak smile. "I'm a heavy sleeper. Thank you for coming tonight," she said. Her voice had a quaver that went right to Austin's chest. She looked vulnerable and small, sitting on the edge of her big bed in her simple, unadorned night shift. He wanted to hold her, and there was nothing lustful about the impulse.

He walked slowly over to the bed and sat down beside her. She smelled of powder and sun-dried cotton.

He reached out and brushed a long sweep of hair from her shoulder. "Are you all right?" he asked. His voice was velvety soft.

Emily gave a rueful laugh. "You're the one who got stabbed," she said remorsefully.

"But you're the one who had a knife stuck in your door, a harassing note, a dead animal left in your hallway..."

Emily shuddered. "I guess I was foolish to think this thing would go away. I've decided that Ida Mae and I will move back to the hotel tomorrow."

Austin nodded. "Tonight would be better."

Emily took a deep breath. "I hate to wake up Ida, and anyway, we're probably fine for the rest of the night. What time do you suppose it is?"

Austin shrugged. "Must be close to three o'clock."

"Not too much longer until dawn. We'll be all right."

"Maybe I'll just hang around and make sure of that," Austin said firmly.

"Stay here?" Emily looked around the tiny room.

Austin grinned. "That would be my choice."

She swallowed hard. "You can't stay here."

"Why not?"

"Well..." Emily paused. Just today, walking home with Ida Mae, she had realized how foolish she had been to become involved with a man who had made it very clear that marriage was not a possibility. Now the man was sitting next to her, his thigh touching hers on the soft bed, his bare arm brushing against the thin fabric of her night dress.

She tried again. "As I said before, Austin, I do appreciate your coming here tonight. I'd hate to think... Well, anyway, I appreciate it. But, as you very clearly have informed me, we are nothing more to each other than business partners. And business partners do not spend the night together."

Austin's eyebrow shot up. "They don't?"

Emily colored at the thought of Austin's other partner, Flo McNeil. "Er, they shouldn't," she amended.

Austin laughed. Emily felt the sound all the way to her stomach. "I think you make an exception when one of the partners is in danger," he said. "Just think of me as your bodyguard."

She was close enough to see the slight flare of his nostrils as he looked down at her. His eyes narrowed, and all at once he looked as if his plans for her body went beyond mere guarding.

"Where will you sleep?" Her voice came out a half whisper.

"Where do you want me to sleep?" he asked huskily.

He hadn't moved a muscle, but there was a difference in the tension of his body that was creating a tightness in hers. His bare chest rose and fell with a little too much pressure. Emily was suddenly aware of the tips of her breasts rubbing against the smooth cotton. Deep inside, a coil of heat began to unwind.

When she didn't answer, Austin closed his eyes, trying to block out the vision of her perfectly defined face, trying to keep from being mesmerized by the flutter of thick lashes around big green eyes. He drew in a long breath. He hadn't come here tonight to make love to Emily. He hadn't even planned on seeing her. And he had resolved after the disastrous end to their night together that he would keep his hands off her in the future.

Even though they had found mutual passion and much pleasure that night, he had to keep reminding himself that Emily wasn't one of the saloon girls. She couldn't love lightly and easily, just for the fun of it. Entanglement with her meant compromise, commitment, family—all concepts he had worked very hard to avoid for too many years.

He felt the soft touch of her hand on his unbandaged forearm. Her fingers were cool, but they almost seemed to burn him. "There's only one bed in this room." She said it so softly, he was not positive that it hadn't been merely the voice of desire inside his head. But then he opened his eyes, and she was looking at him with an unmistakable expression. Her breasts rose and fell under the cotton with her telltale, shallow breaths.

"Emily," he said with half a groan, then lifted her across his knees to sit on his lap. Her lips met his halfway, and they were as pliant and welcoming and captivating as he had remembered. He was instantly, desperately aroused.

She moved against him, her body all lush curves swathed in cotton. He ran his hands along the length of her, learning her again. He felt intensely possessive—of her long limbs, her tiny waist, of the wildness of her golden hair and the generosity of her full mouth. He wanted all of her, her spirit, her soul. He was overwhelmed with an urgent need to make his possession a tangible thing.

He lifted her into the center of the bed. He watched her for a long moment with hooded eyes, then he pulled off her shift. She was naked underneath . . . and his.

Emily had ceased to think. This time she didn't have the excuse of a bump on the head. She simply found herself too awash in the new feelings and sensations inside her to deal with practicality or even right and wrong.

From the moment she had helped Austin off with his shirt, she had wanted this. In spite of his wound, in spite of the fear and anger over the intruder, in spite of all good sense . . . she wanted him.

He was unfastening his trousers, and soon was as naked as she. He glanced over at the lamp, then at the darkened window, where the seersucker curtains provided only partial privacy. He rose from the bed and doused the lamp, then slid the bolt on the door. "There won't be any ghosts in this room tonight," he said softly.

Emily pulled herself up against the pillows and waited for his approach, her body tingling with anticipation. He didn't lie down immediately. Instead, he knelt at the side of the bed and ran his hands slowly up and down her legs. His mouth found a sensitive spot on the sole of her foot, then just above her ankle on the inside of her leg, then, bending, at the back of her knee. Mysteriously, she felt the kisses in a hardening of her breasts. His mouth slid along the tender inside of her right thigh until she arched with tension. Then he joined her on the bed and held her against the full length of him.

"You have me bewitched," he whispered into her ear.

For several minutes they were both lost in the magic of feeling—silky skin against rough, soft curves against lean muscle, skilled lips against untutored, experienced passion against innate sensuality.

At some point their bodies joined. Neither could have said exactly when—it was as natural as breathing. But once merged, the intensity began to build in sharp spikes of urgency. Her nails bit into his back, and his teeth found a tender spot below her jaw. They stiffened, and one or the other cried out.

Emily's world went black for several seconds, then came slowly back into focus. She felt saturated with pleasure, deliciously lethargic. Austin's head lay heavily on her breasts. Their bodies were cemented together with a light sheen of moisture.

"I will never again say that New Englanders are prim," Austin teased tiredly.

Emily tried to chuckle, but it came out as more of a sigh of contentment. "We're only prim on the surface. Underneath lie fiery caldrons."

"I believe it," Austin said, his voice growing firmer.

Emily stretched. Without letting her go, he moved his weight off her. "Is lovemaking always so... intense?" she asked.

Austin reflected a moment. Once again he realized he'd had more experience at practicing the art than at discussing it. "The...uh...completion is usually intense, but the overall effect can be very different. I can't remember anything even remotely approaching what we two seem to have together."

Emily was silent. She knew that Austin had been with many women, but his words had a ring of sincerity, and her own heart echoed their truthfulness. It was not hard to believe that the passion they shared was a rarity. On the other hand, if their two nights together had been as extraordinary for him as they had been for her, how could he get up and walk away from her with no talk of the future?

"I didn't mean for this to happen again," he said soberly.

Emily grew taut. There it was again—he was pulling away. The glow from their encounter had hardly dissipated and already he was establishing his distance. "Well, I didn't exactly invite you here, either," she said defensively.

Austin felt her body tense. A minute ago she had been warm and pliant and willing in his arms, and he had wanted nothing more than to enter her again and continue to lose himself within her the rest of the night. But he knew it was wrong for him to be here. He would only have to hurt her again, as he had in the cabin in the woods. He had been determined not to let it happen, and yet here he was, naked and hot in her bed.

He gently pulled his arms from around her and sat up. He took a deep breath, then looked back down at her. The faint moonlight revealed her cloud of golden hair spread out like a royal blanket beneath her. Her lips were swollen and even redder than usual. Her eyes held a touch of the sleepy sensuality that follows loving, but were rapidly filling with hurt.

"I should probably take another look around the building," he said awkwardly.

Emily made no move to cover herself from his inspection. Her body still felt flushed and warm from passion, but her heart was growing increasingly chilled. "Is this where you say 'thank you kindly, ma'am' and get on your horse?" she asked bitterly.

Austin reached for his pants. "Emily, I..." His tongue seemed to have swelled up in the back of his throat. He had never before dealt with so many feelings all crawling in on top of one another. A combination of possessiveness and frustration, protectiveness and incredible desire, all at the same time.

He stood and dressed quickly. "I'll be right back," he said, and faded into the darkness on the other side of the room.

Emily listened in disbelief as she heard him unbolt the door and open it. This time it was even worse than the night in the cabin. At least then he had held her while she slept and had made an attempt to be tender. Indignation swept through her and banished the last of her languor. She jumped out of bed and went over to the wardrobe. She was getting dressed. She wasn't about to receive Austin in a night shift or even a robe. Dispensing with her corset, she pulled on a serviceable gray dress that had been her mother's, the most un- flattering one she possessed. It was too large for her and made her look like an old maid. Which was what at this moment she had every intention of becoming.

Then she stalked out the door to go find Austin. She would not let him back in her bedroom—not ever again. She found him in the theater. He had lit one of the side lamps and was looking up and down the rows of chairs. Though he had dressed in a minute, he looked perfectly put together with all his natural ele- gance. She, on the other hand, felt like a frump with her hair billowing out in a dreadful tangle and the gray dress hanging on her like a potato sack.

"No sign of anything amiss," he called to her.

"Fine. I think I can handle things from here. You may leave." Her voice was chillier than a newly filled icehouse.

Austin's head jerked up. He knew she was angry, and he knew she had a right to be. But he hadn't known it would make him feel so wretched. "I'll stay out the night," he said, attempting to make his voice even.

Emily walked down the aisle toward him. "Thank you, anyway," she replied haughtily.

He sighed. "I'll stay right here in the theater. I won't bother you."

She shook her head firmly. "No. I'm not planning to go back to sleep tonight, so I'll be here to deal with any problems."

"If that crazy person comes back around here, I don't want you dealing with him at all."

"I'll be fine," she said stubbornly.

"Emily—" he began in a tone of exasperation, but she wouldn't let him finish.

"Mr. Matthews, I know you are a financial partner in this enterprise, but *I* am the manager. If there is a problem, I will handle it. And for now I will thank you to leave the premises. We're not open to the public at the moment."

Austin felt his frustration drain away. She looked dazzling as she stood there proudly, giving orders like an empress, her hair down in regal splendor. The dreadful dress she wore, which was an obvious attempt to cover up the sensuality of the superb body underneath, didn't accomplish its purpose. He now knew that body too well. He could close his eyes and remember perfectly every curve. The knowledge was a precious gift she had given him, and he could give her nothing in return. "I'll go, then. But if you hear anything or see anything strange, you wake up Ida Mae and get the hell out of here."

Emily nodded. Though she held her head up as if she were in complete control of the situation, the truth was she was too miserable to trust her voice to answer. She watched him go up the aisle to the back of the room. He looked at her over his shoulder just before he disappeared through the double doors. "Goodbye, Emily," he said softly.

Austin took the long way home around the mill pond. He had rejected the idea of trying to get some sleep. The sun was making a hazy summer appearance in the eastern sky. The little water community was rapidly awakening—insects, frogs, fish and, off in the corner, a busy muskrat zigzagging back and forth on its own important mission. It should have helped to put life back into perspective, but today all the activity just made his head ache.

When he entered the swinging doors to the saloon, he was surprised to see Flo fully dressed and seated on a stool behind the bar. Mornings had always been her nemesis. In fact, she had always said that one of the reasons for her chosen profession had been that she would never have to face a living soul until afternoon.

"What's the matter?" Austin asked immediately.

"Where've you been?" Flo asked almost at the same moment.

He crossed the room, sat on a stool across from her and reached in his pocket for a cheroot. "Is there something wrong?" he asked again. He sounded tired.

Flo scowled. "It's that bastard Jasper."

"What's he done?" Austin asked with surprise. He would not have suspected Jasper of behaving badly, especially with Flo, whom Jasper had virtually worshipped since he'd started working at the bar almost a year ago.

"He's asked me to marry him."

Austin choked a half laugh. "Marry you?"

"You see?" Flo said indignantly. "You think it's crazy. So would any normal person. It's only a silly fool like Jasper who would even consider such a ridiculous idea."

Austin sobered. "It's not a ridiculous idea, Flo," he said gently. "I think it's very sweet that he asked you."

"Sweet, my as—afetida."

Austin smiled. He was used to Flo's salty language. "I think he's really in love with you, Flo."

"Well, that's just fine. I guess I think he's kind of all right, too. Hell, that's why I let him sleep with me."

"So what's the problem?"

"You know as well as I do what the problem is. People like you and me don't get married."

Austin was silent. Hadn't he just hurt one of the most extraordinary women he'd ever met for the very same reason?

"We don't, do we?" Flo asked, her voice breaking a little.

Austin puffed his cigar, then replied slowly, "I don't think I can give you a square answer on the question anymore, love. I'm a little too befuddled myself."

Flo squinted her gray eyes. "That New Englander again?"

Austin nodded. "That's where I've been. There was another break-in at the opera house yesterday, so I went after work last night to check things out."

"And you did a little more than check things out," Flo said shrewdly. She shook her head. "I told you from the beginning not to get messed up with that kind, Austin."

He shrugged. "You were right, I guess."

"You're damn tootin' I was right."

"But that's a different story from you and Jasper. I don't see anything wrong with the two of you tying the knot."

Flo's face grew sad. She pushed on the bar to slide herself off the stool. "Nah, there's been too many birds in and out of this nest. It wouldn't work to let one think he could take up residence permanent-like."

Austin reached across the bar and gave a pat to her powdered cheek. "Give it some thought, Flo. Jasper's a good man."

For the first time in Austin's memory, Flo's blue eyes welled up with tears. "It just wasn't meant to be, Austin," she said sorrowfully. "Not for people like us."

Then she turned her head quickly and walked away.

Through the open backstage door, Emily could see the light of the new day filtering into the back hall. She supposed she should turn off the one lamp that Austin had lit and go wake up Ida Mae. If they were going to move back to the hotel, they had a lot to get done. But she sat as if glued to the velvet theater seat. She was tired, of course. She had not slept much last night. But it was more than tiredness. She felt drained. Unhappiness had sapped her energy.

All her resolutions concerning Austin had been for nothing. She had let him seduce her again with tender words and expert lovemaking, which she knew very well came from his vast experience in the area. Then she had stood bewildered and devastated while he once again made it clear that his devotion had carefully defined boundaries.

She pounded the heels of her hands on the armrests of the seat, wishing she were pounding on Austin's skull. She remembered when she and Cassie back home had kept themselves enthralled for days reading Jane Austen's novel *Pride and Prejudice*. They had loved the story, but had both agreed that such foolishness over men was not a universally shared feminine trait. Certainly neither of them ever intended to act like such fools over a male. Now she felt like more than a fool. She felt like a miserable idiot.

After the night in the cabin, she had been sure that she could keep her feelings for Austin under control. Obviously, she had been wrong. But this time she was determined to prevent any reccurrence. There was one surefire thing she could do to guarantee that Austin Matthews would never bother her again . . . and she intended to do it immediately.

Chapter Thirteen

Dexter was not yet in his mill office. Though assured by Ethan Witherspoon that he was expected any minute, Emily set out to look for him at the Empire Room, where he usually took breakfast. Nagging in the back of her brain was the disturbing thought that if she didn't follow through with her resolve this very morning, she might lose her courage.

She had just reached the edge of the millpond when she saw Dexter striding briskly toward her, his bright blond hair glinting in the sun. He wore a light-colored summer suit and, as usual, made a striking figure. They would make a handsome couple, Emily thought smugly. Then, somewhat more humbly, she reflected that this might be one of those weddings where the groom outshines the bride.

"Emily," he called. "What are you doing here so early?"

She walked to meet him halfway around the pond. "I wanted to talk with you."

"At this hour of the morning?"

Emily gave her sweetest smile. "I just didn't want to wait any longer to give you some good news. At least, I hope you think it's good news."

Dexter frowned. "Something about your dashed opera house?"

Emily refused to let her purpose be deflected by his continuing resistance to her project. These were things that the two of them would work out together once they were man and wife. He had given in to her in the past, and she expected that eventually she could make him see things her way.

"No, nothing about the opera house. I came to talk about us."

The frown relaxed, but Dexter's expression remained cautious. "About us," he repeated.

"Yes. I wanted to tell you that I am accepting your offer of marriage. That is, if you'll still have me," she added. Dexter always seemed to be happiest when she was just a little self-effacing.

The approach worked again. His smile was instant and genuine. "Emily...darling!" He reached for her hands. "You have just made me the luckiest man in Seattle."

Emily kept her smile in place, but inside she felt all at once an ominous sensation, as if she were about to witness a terrible accident. "And I am the luckiest woman," she said automatically.

"What finally brought you to your senses?" Dexter asked.

Emily might have preferred the question to be asked a little differently. But in view of the fact that she could never be honest with Dexter about what had actually "brought her to her senses," she tried to answer pleasantly. "I just thought about it a lot last night, and decided it was the best thing for me. I think we both could have—will have—a wonderful future together."

"Of course we will." Dexter slipped an arm around her waist, a liberty he had never taken before in the daytime, and they began to walk back toward his office.

"And also..." Emily said slowly, trying to be as forthright as she could be without revealing the truth. "I've decided that Washington Territory is no place for a lone woman."

Dexter stopped and looked down at her. "You haven't had any trouble, have you? Has someone bothered you?"

Emily shook her head. "Just...you know, the incidents at the opera house."

Dexter nodded vigorously. "Quite right. I was horrified to think of you and Miss Sprague alone there. It's like I told you...that's no business for a woman."

Emily switched to a teasing tone. "Well, anyway, I just decided it was time to join the other brides and choose myself a husband. And I think I got myself the best of the lot."

Emily was surprised to see the usually unflappable Dexter coloring underneath his stiff, round collar. "I'll try to make you happy, my dear," he said, not meeting her eyes.

His discomfiture made him seem remarkably human, and she began to lose some of her misgivings. Everything about their match made sense. He was handsome, attentive, well-to-do. She was doing the right thing, she told herself. They had reached the door to Dexter's office and could see Ethan seated at his desk doing paperwork. "I don't have the ring with me to make it official," Dexter said. "I guess I wasn't expecting such an early-bird bride."

He sounded almost boyishly happy, and Emily's heart warmed. "You can give me the ring later. I don't need anything to make it official."

"Can I tell Ethan?"

Emily's heart skipped a beat. This was really happening. "Certainly. There's no reason to keep it a secret. And even if we wanted to, I don't think there's been a secret kept in this town since we all stepped off the boat."

"A shipload of brides did rather dramatically increase the supply of local gossip," Dexter said with a laugh. His good humor seemed more genuine than before.

Emily hesitated at the door. Now that it was done, she felt curiously deflated, not knowing the next step. "So..." she said uncertainly.

"Do you want to come in?" he asked courteously.

"I think I'd better get back to the opera house. I left Ida Mae still asleep."

"We need to set a date, plan the wedding...we've lots to talk about."

"I know, but there's plenty of time now that it's decided."

Dexter's smile grew broad again. "I'll pick you up for dinner tonight."

"Fine. I'll be at the hotel."

"The hotel?"

"Yes, Ida Mae and I have decided to move back there."

"Why? What happened?" He sounded suspicious again.

"Nothing, I told you...it's just these incidents."

His expression lightened. "Yes, well, I'm glad you're getting out of there. And soon you won't have to be in a hotel . . . you'll be mistress of the Kingsman household."

Emily gave a wavering smile. "Right. So I'll see you tonight."

He leaned over and kissed her lightly. "It's going to be pretty hard for me to get any work done today."

Again she was taken by his uncharacteristic joyfulness. She patted his arm. "See you tonight."

She walked slowly back toward the opera house, lost in thought. You have set your course, she told herself firmly. She could now put Austin Matthews out of her mind forever and concentrate on her work and on building a good marriage with Dexter. It was absolutely the right thing to do.

"Miss Kendall!" Suddenly she realized that someone had been calling her name. She looked behind her, and coming up with his slight limp was Sheriff Cutler. She slowed her pace and let him catch up to her.

"I need to talk with you, Miss Kendall," he said, somewhat out of breath.

"What's the problem?"

"It's that knife."

All at once a horrible thought came into her head. Surely Austin hadn't filed a complaint about her stabbing him? He wouldn't be such a cad as to spend the night making love to her and then report her to the sheriff in the morning? "What about the knife?" she asked slowly.

"I guess I need it."

"You need it?"

Sheriff Cutler shifted to his good leg. "I figgered maybe I'd ride out and take a look around out at Piny Ridge Camp. Wouldn't hurt nothin'."

Relief flooded her. The sheriff was after the mysterious intruder, not her. "You think someone out there might be the person who has been doing these things?"

Of course everyone in town knew that Missouri Ike worked at Piny Ridge. The sheriff shrugged. "I don't know. But I guess I'll just take that knife out there and ask a few questions."

The day before he had not felt the situation even worth crossing the street from his office to the opera house. Now he was all set to ride most of the day out to the lumber camp and back on the slim chance of someone recognizing the knife. Austin had evidently been a better persuader than she had been. But she didn't really care, just as long as the mystery was solved. "I'd be much obliged, Sheriff," she said sincerely.

He tipped his hat. "No problem, ma'am. I'll just walk with you over to the opry house and pick that knife up right now, if you don't mind."

"That would be fine." This was her day for getting things resolved. She had gotten Austin out of her life; she had decided on a husband; perhaps now the troublesome intruder would be discovered, as well. She started back to the opera house with a lighter step.

Emily was bone tired. She unpacked the last of her things into the hotel armoire, then straightened and stretched her back. It was amazing how many things one could accumulate in such a short time. All the belongings she had brought from Lowell had fit in two steamer trunks. Now it seemed that she and Ida Mae had spent all afternoon carrying boxes, and she had still left many of her possessions back at the opera house. It was a good thing that the next move she made would be to Dexter's house. And that would be her last move for a long time. At least until they needed a bigger house for a growing family. Strangely, the thought did not inspire her. When she had been engaged to Spencer, she had spent a lot of time thinking about the children they would have, especially after Cassie and Joseph started having their adorable little boys.

She sighed. Her lack of enthusiasm was probably due to her exhausted state. She needed to get to bed. Her dinner with Dexter had been pleasant, except for a few disagreeable moments when she had been adamant about setting the wedding date *after* Mr. Twain's visit. "I want everything to be perfect for this first program, Dexter," she had said in a conciliatory tone. "And perfect for the wedding, too. It only makes sense to take care of first one thing, then the other."

Finally he had agreed, and the rest of the meal had passed without disharmony. But when Ida Mae and Eldo had invited them to go for an evening walk, she had begged off, explaining that she still had things to unpack.

If she was lucky, she could get to sleep before Ida Mae came back. She was not looking forward to being subjected once again to poor Ida's snores in these close quarters. She sat on the bed and had started to unlace her shoe when there was a knock on the door. It startled her. It was late for callers. Perhaps it was Homer, asking whether she would want Strawberry in the morning.

She walked over to the door and opened it a crack, then fell back a step as it was pushed forcefully toward her.

"What in hell do you think you're doing?" a voice shouted.

It was Austin, and his brown eyes were spitting fire. Emily's soon matched them. "Now, wait a just a minute," she huffed. "What am *I* doing? I think it would be more appropriate to ask what you think you're doing...and what you're doing *here*...barging your way into my room."

Austin ran his hand through his hair. There were whisker shadows on his tightened jaw and circles under his eyes. He looked even more tired than she felt. "I'm sorry," he said, but he didn't sound it. "I didn't hurt you, did I? With the door?"

Emily shook her head. "What were you trying to do, pay me back for last night?" She gestured toward his arm, where a white bandage showed beneath the sleeve of his jacket.

He relaxed enough to give a half smile. "No, I just wanted to talk to you."

Emily looked around the room helplessly. She had sworn never to be alone in the same building with him again, much less in a bedroom. "Well, I suppose since you're already here..."

Austin waved his arm toward the settee at one end of the room. "Do you want to sit down?" he asked.

The only alternative was the bed. Emily nodded and led the way. "Just talk fast. I'm very tired and was just about to go to sleep."

"Well I'm tired, too," Austin snapped. "I spent most of last night trying to protect a couple of fool women who have gotten themselves mixed up with a crazy person."

"We didn't ask you to protect us," Emily snapped back, sitting down hard on the rose taffeta cushion.

Austin glared at her, then sat next to her. "No, and you didn't ask me to goad that lazy son of a bitch Cutler into finally doing something about it, either. But I notice you didn't turn him down."

Emily looked down at her hands. "You're right. I thank you for that . . . and for looking in on us last night." She raised her eyes to his. "But that's *all* I thank you for about last night."

Austin scowled. "And we forget the rest of it?"

"That seems to be what you've wanted," Emily said, not bothering to keep the bitterness out of her tone.

Now Austin's eyes went down and his tone softened. "Emily, maybe we need to talk about this."

"It seems to me that you're better at acting than talking, Mr. Matthews."

He bit his lip. "I've never exactly found myself in a situation like this before."

"I find that hard to believe. The experienced, worldly-wise owner of the Golden Lady?"

"I don't mean the . . . lovemaking. It's the rest of it. Somehow it's just more complicated than it's ever been before."

There was real confusion in the depths of his brown eyes, and for a moment she found herself almost feeling sorry for him. Then she remembered how hurt and betrayed—almost *used*—she had felt when he had left her so coldly that morning, and she hardened her heart. "I'm dreadfully sorry to be such a 'complication,' Mr. Matthews, but you won't need to fret your handsome head about it anymore. I'm now an engaged lady."

Austin bristled. "That's what I'm here about. How in hell could you have gone from the night we had together to accept a marriage proposal from Dexter Kingsman?"

Emily sank back against the cushions. She had thought she was looking forward to this moment. To throwing her engagement in Austin's face and telling him goodbye for good. But she didn't feel like gloating tonight. She didn't feel triumphant. She felt weary and a little sick.

"It seemed to be the best thing for me to do," she said in a low voice. "Dexter is a fine man. He'll make a wonderful husband, and you have made it abundantly clear that that is a role you yourself will never fill."

Austin gave a tired sigh. "You can't throw yourself into a marriage with someone you don't love just because I've acted like a cad."

"How do you know I don't love Dexter?"

"Because you're not the kind of woman who could make love to one man while she's in love with another."

Emily didn't answer.

"In fact," he went on, "I don't think you're the kind of woman who could make love to a man at all unless you were in love with him."

She looked up at him with a brittle smile, her eyes filled with tears. "You don't know *what* kind of woman I am, Austin. Maybe I'm just exactly like you. My marriage to Dexter is good business. You're the one who said that was the greatest criterion for a marriage."

Austin's anger dissolved at the sight of her tears. "If it's money, Emily," he said gently, "Whatever you need..."

Emily blinked furiously, determined not to cry. "No, thank you," she said, emphasizing each word. "I don't need money—or *anything else*—from you. Now, if you will please leave... I don't think it's considered proper for an engaged woman to be entertaining a man in her room.''

She stood and folded her arms, waiting for him to move. Austin got up slowly. "Don't do this, Emily," he said. "You'll find a good man to love someday. You don't need to throw yourself away, just because you're angry with me."

Emily felt a welcome surge of outrage. "You flatter yourself, Austin. I'm not throwing myself away. On the contrary, I'm marrying the most eligible man in all of Seattle. And it has nothing to do with you."

"Isn't there anything I can say?" He sounded defeated.

"You can say good night," she said haughtily.

He looked into her brightened eyes a long moment, then finally said. "My offer stands. If you need anything at all, just send word."

"Don't hold your breath."

He gave her a whimsical smile, then left the room. Emily undressed, turned off the lamps and tucked herself into the soft bed. But, tired as she was, all desire to sleep had fled.

"He's there again, Emily," Ida Mae said smugly. "I told you he wouldn't give up."

Emily sighed and continued walking along the wooden sidewalk toward the opera house at an even pace. It had been the same every morning since she and Ida Mae had moved back into the hotel. When they approached the opera house in the morning, there was Austin, seated nonchalantly on the iron bench out front.

The first morning she had been indignant. After the confrontation they had had in her room the previous evening, she had told herself that she never wanted to set eyes on the man again. But he had ignored her angry words, unfolding his big body from the dainty bench with ease and tipping his hat to them both. "Mornin', ladies, or I guess I should say *partners*. Pleasant day, isn't it?"

Then he had patiently waited while Emily opened the big double doors. When she stepped inside, he had followed her and had proceeded to go methodically through every room in the place. Then he had tipped his hat again and said merely, "I'll see you ladies later."

And he had seen them later... at least twice, sometimes three times a day. He was infuriatingly proper. He always addressed them both equally. There was never any direct comment to Emily, nor even a look out of place. It was driving her crazy. She would almost prefer a visit from the opera ghost.

"Why doesn't he leave us alone?" she said furiously to Ida Mae out of the corner of her mouth. He looked incredibly handsome today in a navy blue suit that outlined the superb masculine lines of his body. His hair had grown longer than when she had first met him and curled around his white collar.

Ida Mae giggled. "If I had a man that looked like that waiting for me every morning, I wouldn't be complaining."

"He's not waiting for me."

"Well, he's sure not waiting for me."

"He's not waiting for either of us. He's just here to protect his investment."

Ida Mae rolled her eyes. "Sure, and I'm a Barbary pirate."

Emily puffed out her chest. "Don't be foolish, Ida. Mr. Matthews has a lot of money in this venture, and we all just want to be sure nothing goes wrong before Mr. Twain's arrival tomorrow."

"No more ghosts, you mean." Ida Mae shivered.

Emily looked grim. "We haven't had a problem since the sheriff rode out to that lumber camp asking questions. Maybe we've scared him away."

"I hope so. But if it really is a *ghost*, Emily, I don't think they can get scared."

Emily snorted. "Don't be silly. There's no such thing."

Ida Mae's eyes were big and doubtful. She, for one, looked glad to see Austin, and welcomed his presence as they opened the door to the opera house.

"You ladies look lovely this morning," Austin said gallantly. "You make a beautiful summer day pale by comparison."

Emily kept her expression even, but Ida Mae said with a little blush, "Thank you, Mr. Matthews. It certainly is a beautiful day. I do hope this weather holds another week for the wedding."

"Ah, yes. You and Mr. Smedley are planning your nuptials. May I offer my heartfelt good wishes, and also my opinion that Eldo Smedley is a very lucky man?"

Ida Mae's blush deepened. "Thank you," she murmured.

He turned to Emily. "And may I be so bold as to inquire how the plans are proceeding for *your* marriage to Mr...ah ...Kingsman, isn't it?"

Emily scowled. "Fine," she said curtly, then added snidely. "We are to be married a week after Ida Mae. Don't expect an invitation."

"Emily!" Ida Mae looked shocked.

Austin merely shook his head. "Well, now, that's a shame, because I had a wedding gift for the two of you."

"Thanks anyway. We shan't be needing gifts . . . my new husband intends to provide amply for my welfare."

The discussion was cut short when Emily opened the doors and they entered the loge. As usual, Austin left them for a thorough tour of the premises.

"I don't know why you're so mean to him, Emily," Ida Mae whispered furiously. "I feel much better when he's here to check things out."

Emily shrugged. She *did* feel mean, but then, Austin deserved it. It was partly his fault that her mood had gone from bad to worse over the past two weeks. Although, she had to admit, it was not completely his fault. He had advised her against her hasty engagement. Every day she became more certain that marrying Dexter would be a big mistake. But as the wedding date approached, she felt helpless to do anything about it. The plans had been set in motion and they seemed as inexorable as the movement of the planets.

"All clear, ladies," Austin said cheerfully, coming in the front door again after having walked around the outside of the building.

Ida Mae had gone into the theater to start practicing, and she called out, "Emily, did you take our picture from on top of the piano?"

Emily looked puzzled. "What picture?" she called back. She walked into the theater and started down the aisle with Austin close behind.

Ida Mae was standing next to her piano. She lifted the enameled top and looked inside. "The picture of the two of us. You know, the one that street photographer took in Panama City. I've kept it on the piano, but it's not here this morning."

Emily gave an impatient shake of her head. "It probably fell off and someone put it backstage."

Ida Mae looked doubtful. "Why wouldn't they just put it back here?"

"Look, Ida Mae, we'll find it. This is a big building," Emily said brusquely.

Austin's forehead was furrowed. He deliberately hadn't told the women about the reports of lights seen at odd hours of the night inside the opera house. If Ida Mae became any more frightened, he had reasoned, she might refuse to perform, which would leave Emily without one of her mainstays. So he had kept the sightings to himself and made it his business to be here in the morning before they opened the doors, just to be sure. He himself did not believe in ghosts. Yet there was something about the cavernous size of a big theater and the nooks and crannies around the curtain and backstage that gave one an eerie feeling. But he didn't know what a ghost would do with a photograph.

"Let's look around for it," he suggested.

"It will turn up," Emily protested.

"It wouldn't hurt to look, Emily," Ida Mae said gently.

So, in spite of Emily's objections, they made a thorough search of the place. The photograph was nowhere to be found.

"I told you, Emily," Ida Mae wailed. "Any more ghost visits and I won't come here anymore."

Emily answered her friend testily. "Don't be such a goose, Ida. Anyone could have taken that picture.

People are in and out of here all the time. *People,* not ghosts."

Ida Mae looked unconvinced, but bit her lip and didn't say anything. Emily felt a little guilty for being so unsympathetic with her friend's worries. She really would have to do something about her crabby mood, Emily thought remorsefully.

"I think things are safe enough in the daylight, Miss Sprague," Austin said gently. "By tomorrow Mr. Twain will be here, and I'll make it a point to come around myself several times between now and the performance Friday night."

Ida Mae sneezed violently several times and excused herself to go find a fresh hanky back in the office.

"If you had any sense, you'd be frightened, too," Austin said to Emily.

"I'm not about to let any ghost scare me away from all of this." She looked around the theater with pride. "I've worked too hard."

Austin followed her gaze with reluctant admiration. It was true, the theater grew more splendid every day. The wallpaper had come from back East, flocked with gold vines and flowers, giving a regal texture to the walls. On a ship newly in from Russia, Emily had found some Oriental carpeting for the aisles. And she and Ethan Witherspoon, after hours of painstaking experimentation, had managed to link all the side lamps in a network of lighting that could be dimmed and brightened like the finest theaters in Europe. She had a right to be proud of her achievements, Austin concluded.

"Nothing's going to chase us away," Austin said softly. "But that doesn't mean you have to take foolish chances. Are you still riding out alone on Strawberry?"

"I haven't exactly had time," she snapped.

Austin nodded, refusing to get riled. "I know. You've been working very hard. I'm sure Mr. Twain will be amazed at the sophistication of this place. It undoubtedly rivals anything they have in San Francisco."

The praise felt good, and Emily's anger faded. "Maybe he'll write about us when he gets back, and more artists will want to come here."

They exchanged smiles of shared success. Then Austin sobered again. "Will you just promise me you won't ride out alone until we get this thing solved?"

Emily was about to refuse, just to assert her independence, but then decided against it. Austin's help had really been invaluable. She never would have been able to build the opera house in the first place without his backing. "All right." Then, so as not to sound too submissive, she added, "As I said, I probably won't have time, anyway."

Austin gave a satisfied nod. "I'll be back later this morning. If you notice anything else missing or odd, come and get me."

Emily merely nodded and watched him leave, her heart giving a little twist. Why couldn't Austin Matthews be the sawmill owner in town and Dexter the saloon man? she asked herself, and gave a little kick to the back of one of the imported theater seats, denting the toe of her best satin slippers.

Chapter Fourteen

From the moment Mr. Clemens ambled off the ship, Emily knew she would like him. He had longish red hair with a temperament to match, but his blue eyes literally twinkled as he greeted Emily and glanced down the full length of her new print dress. Parmelia had made it for her for the occasion from a dress length she had bought in San Francisco. Emily had wanted to look as cosmopolitan as possible for the renowned humorist, and his approving glance told her that she had succeeded.

Dexter had decided to join her at the dock to meet their visitor. He hadn't felt it entirely proper for his future wife to be receiving a man by herself. He greeted Mr. Clemens with a hearty, man-to-man handshake, but then receded into the background and let Emily give the formal welcome.

Several of the townspeople had come down to the dock. Seattle had never really had a visitor who could be classified as famous, and there was a great deal of interest. The articles and essays of Mark Twain had been widely circulated around town since the announcement of his visit.

Emily herself had been fascinated by his writings. She enjoyed his sense of humor immensely. It was droll and silly sometimes, but every now and then there was a real bite.

She studied him as they walked together to Dexter's phaeton. Mr. Clemens was tall, dressed in a comfortable corduroy suit, and entirely more dignified than one might be led to expect, except for those twinkling eyes that never seemed to be quite still in his head.

They chatted pleasantly on the way back to the hotel. For a relatively young man, Samuel Clemens had done a remarkable number of things. He'd been a journeyman typesetter at the age of twelve, a printer in New York City, a steamboat pilot, a silver miner, a journalist. Finally his printed lectures and tall tales had begun to spread his fame beyond San Francisco.

Emily hoped his reputation was enough to launch her opera house in style. The other brides had gotten into the spirit of things and helped her with handbills and publicity for Mr. Twain's performance. She expected a good turnout. If only their ghost would stay away, everything should go smoothly. She and Ida Mae had never found the missing photograph, which led to the inevitable conclusion that someone or something had indeed taken it. But Emily tried to convince herself that perhaps it had been one of Ethan's workers who just wanted a souvenir to take back to his shanty.

Austin had made so many visits to the opera house that he seemed to live there, but Emily had not spoken with him privately again, and he had resumed his role of the courtly, detached protector.

She put the ghost resolutely out of her mind and turned her attention back to her guest.

"I had no idea Seattle was so developed," Mr. Clemens was saying. "And you, Mr. Kingsman," he said with a nod to Dexter, "you say you're a member of the town council. Impressive. Very impressive."

His manner of speech was such that it was difficult to tell if he was serious, or if a thin blanket of irony lay under his words. Emily had read enough of Mr. Clemens's writings to know that his opinion of most bodies of government was not high. "Boodlery," he called their dealings, his own word for pretentious and conniving political activity. Dexter, however, seemed to have no misgivings as to the sincerity of Mr. Clemens's remark. He turned toward the humorist and gave him a detailed account of the latest doings of the city fathers. Mr. Clemens listened with avid interest, his head cocked to one side.

Emily didn't try to interrupt. She didn't really care if Dexter made a fool of himself or if Mr. Clemens harvested some new nuggets for his latest satire from the proceedings of the Seattle City Council. All she cared about was the performance tomorrow. If they had a full house and everything went well, the reputation of the Seattle Opera House would be established. Then getting more performers would be easy.

They reached the hotel and Emily stayed in the lobby while Dexter walked Mr. Clemens to his room, where he could rest before the reception they were giving for him that evening. It would be a simple affair in the hotel dining room, but it would be a chance for many of the most influential people in town to meet their guest and would create even more interest in tomorrow's performance.

As Emily awaited Dexter's return, she suddenly saw Ida Mae barreling toward her across the lobby. Her face bore implications of disaster.

Emily felt her stomach sink, but she kept her voice calm. "What is it, Ida Mae?"

"The reception is ruined."

"Is it the ghost again?"

Ida Mae looked startled. "Oh, no," she said. "Nothing like that."

Emily let out a breath. "What's the problem?"

"The brides are refusing to come."

"What? They've helped us put all this together. What do you mean?"

"It's that Rose Bartlett again. I swear I could easily put that woman on a boat to China."

Emily smiled at mild-mannered Ida Mae's vehemence. "What's she done?"

"Well, she's gotten together all the girls and told them that if that Flo McNeil is going to be at the reception, decent women shouldn't attend."

Emily almost laughed at the ridiculousness of the statement, but she could see that Ida Mae was serious. "Miss McNeil has come with Austin to almost every concert since we started. Why would they suddenly object now?"

"Rose says a public concert is different, but to attend a private reception would be wrong."

Emily felt her blood begin to boil. If Rose really succeeded in keeping all the brides away, Ida Mae was right, it would ruin the reception, because then most of the men would stay away, too. She had to think. For a moment she entertained the idea of talking to Austin and asking him not to bring Flo, but she rejected the plan immediately. Austin had done more than anyone to make this event happen, and she wasn't going to tell him whom he could or could not bring.

"Where are they?" she asked Ida Mae, her face set.

"They're quilting at Parmelia's house."

"Ida Mae, wait here, and when Dexter comes down, tell him I had something to do. Tell him I'll see him at the reception tonight."

"What are you going to do, Emily?" Ida Mae asked anxiously.

Emily's face was grim. "I'm just going to go have a little talk with our New England friends."

The door to Parmelia's plain log home was wide open, so Emily didn't bother to knock. She stomped up the two steps and marched into the main room, which served as kitchen, dining room and parlor all together. Several of the brides were sitting around a big quilt that was spread over Parmelia's oak table.

"What's this I hear about not coming to the reception tonight?" She spoke bluntly, but made an effort to keep her voice pleasant.

Parmelia looked up at Emily with embarrassment, but Rose Bartlett put down her needle and said loudly, "You can't expect us to socialize with a... fallen woman, Emily."

"Don't be absurd. Flo McNeil is half owner of the Golden Lady. She's a businesswoman, and a lot more successful than most of us will ever be."

Rose's sewing spectacles slipped down her nose and she eyed Emily over them. "Nevertheless, consider the woman's... past. She's not at all proper company for decent women. Why, just look at the way she dresses."

Though some of the brides looked uncomfortable, Emily saw a number of them nodding their heads in agreement. So much for staying pleasant, Emily decided.

She marched around to the head of the table where Rose was sitting. "Listen to me, all of you," she said firmly. She looked first at Rose, then at each one of the women around the table. "We're here today because we had the nerve and the imagination to leave behind old ways and search out a better life for ourselves. We're not New Englanders anymore. We're frontierswomen. Our home is the great new West, where there's still space to grow and breathe and welcome new ideas."

Emily paused for a dramatic moment and looked around at the group. She could see that at least some of the women were impressed by her words. "Out here you might be associating with a lot of people you wouldn't back in New England, but that's the glory of it," she continued. "It's a new land with equal opportunity for everyone—men and women alike. Do you think that back home you would be attending an opera house managed by a woman?"

Most shook their heads. Emily gave a satisfied smile. "Let's leave propriety to the old biddies we left back in Boston. We're western women. We do as we please."

Rose's glasses had slipped almost to the end of her nose, giving her a comical expression. Emily looked at her to give her a chance to say her piece, but for once, she was silent. "I'll expect to see you all at the hotel tonight, then, ladies. You'll enjoy meeting Mr. Clemens. He's quite a charmer."

Then she spun around and hurriedly left the room, before Rose could gather her wits enough to begin a rebuttal.

* * *

"The native beverage in the islands, *awa,* is so terrific that mere whiskey is foolishness compared to it." Mark Twain narrowed his vibrant eyes and looked out at the audience, who sat spellbound in the dim theater. "It turns a man's skin to white fish scales that are so tough a dog might bite him and he would not know it till he read about it in the papers."

From her position backstage, Emily could hear the delighted laughter. She had been too nervous to take a place out in the audience. She wanted to be sure that everything went well—that the new lighting system worked properly, the curtain went up and down on time, and, most particularly, that there were no dirty tricks from the mysterious intruder.

The evening had been a resounding success. Mr. Twain was a genius, and the Seattle audience had never heard the like. He'd been talking for more than two hours and there was not a sign of restlessness in the packed house.

She peeked around the curtain and watched the absorbed faces as Mark Twain ended his story with an account of the visit of two of the members of Sandwich Island royalty to California where they had drunk the Californians into a state of torpidity without being the least affected themselves. The islands' peculiar monarchy had been the target of several of his jibes throughout the evening.

"The population of the islands is but 50,000 souls," he was saying, "but over that handful of people roosts a monarchy with its coattails fringed with as many titled dignitaries as would suffice to run the Russian Empire. It is one of the oddest things in the world to stumble on a man there who has no title. I felt so lonesome, as being about the only unofficial person in Honolulu, that I had to leave the country to find company.''

There was a moment of silence as the account ended, then the first smatter of applause, which quickly grew to a thunder. The speaker acknowledged the response with a droll half smile and a modest tip of his head, then he sauntered off the stage.

She offered Mr. Clemens her hand as he left the stage, and he took it and brought it to his lips. She had already discovered that he had the manners of a southern gentleman, despite being born in Missouri. He had, in fact, fought briefly for the South in the recent conflict, a fact she had fervently hoped would not become public, at least not before the New Englanders had bought their tickets.

She scarcely had time to congratulate Mr. Clemens on his performance before they were engulfed by members of the audience who had crowded backstage for a personal greeting. With good humor, Mr. Clemens had a handshake or a nod for each one. Emily backed away. He seemed to be enjoying himself, and it looked very much as if her job was done.

She made her way through the congested back hall to her office and slipped inside, relishing a moment of solitude. The evening had gone even beyond her expectations. Better than a sellout. At the last minute they had had to devise a special price for standing-room-only tickets. She smiled to herself. Success felt good.

The crowd outside was so noisy it took her a minute to realize that someone was pounding on the office door.

"Miss Emily, are you in there?" The voice sounded urgent and upset.

Her moment of self-congratulation ended abruptly. She pulled open the door. It was Ethan Witherspoon. Wanting to take every precaution, she had again asked him to post his men around the building. "What is it, Ethan?"

"You'd better come round back, ma'am. It looks as if we might have caught your ghost."

Emily followed close behind him through the crowd, using his broad frame as interference. They went out the back door, leaving behind the hot, oppressive air of the packed hall for the cool, fresh evening breeze. There was a group of men a short distance behind the opera house. In the light of the nearly full moon, Emily's eyes picked out Austin's tall form.

"What's happened?" she asked Ethan.

"It's Matthews...he caught Missouri Ike out here stone-cold drunk."

Emily hurried over to the group. Two of Ethan's men were holding up a weaving Ike, while a third was wrapping him around and around with a stout length of twine. Ike appeared to be having trouble focusing his eyes, but after a moment he said groggily, "Why, it's Miss Emily. Evenin', Miss Emily. I came to see the show."

Austin stepped out from the group and took Emily's arm. "You don't have to be out here. No telling what he might say or do. He's drunker than a sailor on seven-day leave."

Emily looked up at him. "So he really is the one, after all?" she asked. Austin's strong hand at her elbow was reassuring.

"It appears so." He pointed to a dirty cotton bag lying on the ground. "I don't know any normal person who walks around carrying dead animals."

Emily eyed the bag with distaste. "What's in it?"

Austin kicked it aside. "A rabbit . . . like the one left here before. Don't worry about it. We'll dispose of it later."

There was something in the way he said the words that made her think he wasn't telling her the whole story. Fighting her repugnance, she reached down and picked up one end of the bag. The limp body of a snowshoe rabbit fell heavily to the ground, followed by a piece of cardboard. Expecting another nasty message, she turned it over with her foot, then backed away with a little cry. It was the photograph of her and Ida Mae. Their smiling images on it had been carefully smeared with zigzagging lines of blood.

Emily looked from the photograph to Ike in horror. He gave her a lopsided grin and said again, slurring the words, "I came to sheee your show." He looked more silly than dangerous.

Austin pulled at her arm. "Here comes the sheriff, Emily. We'll let him handle things from here. Come on, I'll take you inside."

With a last glance at the bloody picture, Emily allowed herself to be led into the opera house. "It's hard to imagine what would make a person do something like that," she said, sounding dazed.

"The human mind . . . it's a strange thing. Maybe some day they'll be able to figure it all out and do something to help crazy people like Ike."

Emily shook her head. She remembered how Ike had taken such pains to clean himself up for their meeting together. She hoped it hadn't been her fault that he had become so deranged.

They pushed their way back into her office. The crowd around Mr. Clemens was as enthusiastic as before. It appeared that few people had noticed anything amiss.

Austin closed the door behind them. "Why don't you sit down a spell?" he asked gently. "It's been quite a night for you... a triumph. Congratulations."

Emily smiled wanly and walked around her desk to do as he suggested. Her previous exhilaration had disappeared at the sight of Missouri Ike being trussed up like a holiday turkey. "They said it was you who caught him... not Ethan's men."

Austin shrugged. "I was just checking things out."

"So you've rescued me once again, Austin Matthews."

Austin smiled ruefully. "It's become a habit, I guess."

"Well, maybe this will be the last time."

Their eyes met for a long moment. Emily felt a lump rise in her throat. Rescue me one final time, Austin, she thought to herself. Come and pick me up and take me away with you forever and ever, and never let me go.

The door opened and Dexter burst in. "Emily, I've just heard. Are you all right?"

The lump dissolved. "I'm fine, Dexter. Nothing even happened this time. They caught the culprit before he could do anything."

Dexter seemed incensed. "I know... Missouri Ike, that dirty bushwhacker. I suppose they can't hang him for trying to scare people, but I promise you, Emily, I'll see they toss the low-down filth in jail and throw away the key."

Emily looked up at Austin. His face was unreadable. "I'm sure the law will take the proper course, Dexter," she said in a low voice.

Dexter walked around to her chair and bent to kiss her cheek. "I'm so glad this is all over with. Now maybe you can concentrate on our wedding." He straightened and looked across the room at Austin. "What are you doing here, Matthews?"

Austin smiled pleasantly. "I'm your future bride's business partner, remember?"

Dexter scowled. "Yes, well, that's a situation that will have to be cleared up one of these days. But we don't have to discuss it tonight. I think I should be taking Emily back to the hotel."

Austin nodded in agreement. Emily looked small seated in her big office chair. Her face was pale and her green eyes lacked their normal luster.

"I should be with Mr. Clemens," she said. "He probably could use help getting away from that crowd of admirers."

"I'll deal with it," Austin said firmly. "You go on back to your room. You can see Mr. Clemens in the morning."

With the two men in rare accord, Emily gave in and let Dexter escort her home. At the door to her room, he stopped and grasped both her elbows. "I don't know what I would have done if that madman had harmed you," he said, his voice husky with emotion.

"Somehow I just don't picture Ike as dangerous," Emily replied thoughtfully. "Perhaps he just wanted to get attention by scaring us all."

Dexter shook his head. "The things he did were demented. I'm just glad that you're safe." He drew her up against him and bent to kiss her, a more thoroughly passionate kiss than he had ever attempted with her before. Emily tried her best to respond, but, to her utter frustration, found herself thinking of Austin. By comparison, Dexter's kiss was inexpert. But it did not leave her entirely unmoved.

"Emily, I don't know if I can wait another week," he said. His eyes seemed to have lost their color. They looked like ice.

"I think we'd better say good-night, Dexter."

He took a step back. "Of course, I'm sorry. I hope I didn't...offend you."

Emily shook her head. She felt guilty and miserable. She had just been kissed by a perfectly honorable man who cared about her and treated her like a lady. And all she could think about were the two long, erotic nights she had spent with a wickedly handsome scoundrel who switched women more often than he did his socks.

Ida Mae had spent the entire day with a slab of bacon draped around her neck. It was the latest suggestion from a dentist who had arrived in town to set up one of his Painless Parker Tooth Parlors. It was a desperate measure, but she was determined to rid herself of her sniffles before her wedding ceremony.

"All of these things are remedies for colds, Ida Mae, and you do *not* have a cold," Emily told her friend for the dozenth time.

"Then what is the matter with me?" Ida Mae wailed.

"It all started when we were crossing Panama. Have you been doing anything different since then?"

Ida Mae shook her head glumly.

"How about eating anything different?"

"No. It's no use, Emily. I'm afraid I'll have to go through life dripping like an old bucket."

"Well, Eldo likes you, anyway," Emily said comfortingly. "I've never seen a more excited bridegroom."

Ida Mae giggled. "Last night he poured the whole salt dish into his coffee before he realized what he was doing."

Emily laughed. "You see? He doesn't care about a few sniffles." She took the last few papers out of Ida Mae's hair and began carefully forming tendrils all around the back of her head. "When he sees how beautiful you are in your wedding dress, he's going to plumb forget his own name."

Ida Mae sighed. "It's too bad we have to have such a small ceremony. I feel as if this might be the one time in my life when I'll be truly beautiful."

"Dexter and I will be there to see you . . . and so will Eldo. He's the important one. I just wish he weren't so sensitive about Mr. Briggs's feelings. I guess I think that if Mr. Briggs is silly enough to still be upset about the two of us getting married, then that's his problem."

"Well, it just shows that Eldo is a very sensitive person."

Ida Mae smiled dreamily. "Yes, he is. Kind and sensitive . . . and he's a good kisser, too."

"Ida!"

"Well, he is." Ida Mae blushed beet red.

They finished with her hair and were ready to put on her dress, which was a real store-bought dress from New York City. It had been passed along for the occasion by Agnes Cramer, who had gotten it from Lucy Hartwick, who had gotten it from Parmelia. It was light blue with white-and-yellow daisies appliquéd down the front, and it made Ida Mae look like a spring bouquet.

Emily had not yet decided what she was going to wear for her own wedding, which was just a week away. She had been strangely dispirited since the arrest of Missouri Ike and the departure of Mr. Clemens.

Logically, she should be happy and excited. The appearance of Mr. Clemens had been a success. She could now properly aspire to bring even more famous performers to Seattle—perhaps Lotta Crabtree or even the famous acting company of Joseph Jefferson and Laura Keene.

The opera ghost was safely tucked away in Sheriff Cutler's jail, sleeping through the second day of his massive hangover. In his few lucid moments, he had vehemently denied having anything to do with the incidents at the opera house, and claimed he had never seen the bag with the dead rabbit and the photo. But the evidence seemed irrefutable.

To top off her good fortune, in one week she would be married to the most eligible bachelor in Seattle. There was absolutely no reason for her to be down-hearted.

"Are you still angry with me for inviting your Mr. Matthews to the wedding?" Ida Mae asked.

Emily lifted her head with a jerk. It was eerie the way Ida Mae read her thoughts sometimes. "He's not *my* Mr. Matthews," she answered testily.

Ida Mae looked at her sympathetically. "Your partner, Mr. Matthews, then."

"*Our* partner."

"Whatever. He's been so good to us, protecting us and all, you know. I just felt it would be terribly impolite not to ask him."

"I couldn't care less whether Austin is there or not," Emily said airily. "I was just worried about Dexter's feelings on the matter."

"Well, Mr. Matthews is *our* business partner. I can't see how Dexter should have anything to do with it."

Emily shrugged. "It doesn't matter. You've already invited him and that's that."

Ida Mae gave a relieved smile. "Good. Now, I'll put on my Esencia and then you can help me with my dress." She reached for the thick glass jar that contained the special perfumed cream that she had bought from the same itinerant photographer in Panama who had taken their picture.

Personally, Emily thought it smelled disagreeably sweet. "Why do you always wear that stuff?" she asked.

Ida Mae blushed again. "It's supposed to make you irresistible to men. And, Emily, it works. Just think, back in Lowell, I never had even one single beau. Here, I no sooner stepped off the boat than I had men fighting over me."

Emily hid a smile. "The men in Lowell were blind fools, Ida. Why, just look at how lovely you are today. You don't need any native love cream." She refrained from pointing out that with a ratio of ten men to every woman, being female was just about the only qualification for matrimony in Seattle these days.

"Do you really think so?" Ida Mae leaned over and looked at herself carefully in the cheval glass. "I think I'd better put it on just in case. I've worn it faithfully every day, and I wouldn't want Eldo to suddenly change his mind at the last minute." She dipped her finger in the cream and brought it toward her face. Just as she was about to smear it along her right cheek, she stopped and gave a great sneeze that blew the cream all over the mirror. "Oh, now look what I've done!"

Emily's eyes widened. "Ida Mae, that's it!"

"What's it?" Ida Mae had taken a hanky and was wiping the mirror.

"Your sneezing, your sniffles. It's that stupid cream."

"Don't be silly. How could a cream make you sneeze?"

"I don't know, but I'll bet you anything that if you don't wear your Esencia today, you'll enjoy a sniffle-free honeymoon."

Ida Mae looked doubtful. "And you think Eldo will like me, anyway?"

"I'm sure of it." She snatched the cream from Ida Mae's hands and threw it in the wastebasket. "There . . . so much for exotic creams."

Ida Mae took a couple of thoughtful sniffs. "You know, my nose always did itch when I put that stuff on."

"All right, we've solved your problem. Now let's get you dressed for your wedding."

As Ida Mae hummed a tune of happiness, Emily pulled the flowery dress on over her friend's head.

It's true, Emily reflected glumly. All our problems have been solved, even Ida Mae's "cold." The opera house ghost has been caught, and we've made a life for ourselves out West even better than we had ever imagined. And so, she asked herself as she and Ida Mae started downstairs, why is it that I'm unhappy?

* * *

Though Eldo had wanted to keep the wedding small, in the end at least half the contingent of brides was in attendance, most with their own new husbands firmly in tow. To Emily's relief, the size of the group made it possible for her to avoid any close contact with Austin. She had nodded to him from across the room when she entered to stand next to Ida Mae, but that was the extent of it.

The ceremony was mercifully short. Ida Mae and Eldo both beamed through the entire length of it. When the minister pronounced them man and wife, Eldo gave a kind of whoop, grabbed Ida Mae's arm and almost danced her out of the church. It was *not* like any wedding Emily had seen back in Lowell.

Dexter had gallantly offered his phaeton to transport the couple from the church to the Empire Room, where the reception was to take place.

"Do you want to ride with us?" he asked her hurriedly as the bridal pair disappeared out the church's front doors.

"No, this is their moment. You go on and drive them to the party. I'll just walk over with everyone else and meet you there."

Dexter looked uncertain for a moment, then gave her a hasty peck on the cheek and took off toward the front of the church at a fast lope.

Eldo's whoop had broken the solemnity of the church setting, and the wedding guests filed out amid much laughter and calling back and forth. Almost everyone there was a newlywed, and the men tossed ribald comments back and forth that had the women laughing and blushing at the same time.

Emily watched them leave, wishing she could share in some of the gaiety. She turned, startled, at the feel of a hand on her back.

"They certainly looked happy, didn't they?" Austin's voice made her heart skip a beat.

"Yes, they did . . . they are. They're very lucky."

"I've always believed that people make their own luck." He was looking at her intently.

"I agree," she said.

"Which is why you'll be tying the knot with the very wealthy Mr. Kingsman next week?"

His scrutiny made her uncomfortable. "If you'll excuse me, I need to be getting on over to the wedding party," she said stiffly.

They were alone now in the dim church. It was a plain building with no adornments other than a simple wooden altar and cross in the front. The only light came from four small side windows. Emily made a move to go past Austin up the center aisle.

"You didn't answer my question," he said, blocking her path and grasping her arms with an unyielding grip. His hands felt warm against the silk of her dress.

Emily's heart doubled its beat. "Let me go," she protested.

"No," he said softly.

Chapter Fifteen

"What do you want from me?"

"Are you going to marry Kingsman?"

"Yes!"

She could feel the touch of his lips before they actually reached her mouth. His arms went around her and she was crushed up against him, her body welcoming the pressure in spite of herself. His kiss was devastating and seemed to drain her of all the tension that had built up in the past few days. Within seconds it provoked a response. Her breasts hardened against him. Her tongue and lips mated frantically with his.

Austin found his own response equally overpowering. He hadn't intended to kiss her, hadn't even intended to talk with her. He had come to the wedding today in deference to Ida Mae and Eldo, but he had intended to stay as far away from Emily as possible. Then he had seen her, standing in the front of the church, a shaft of light outlining the ripe curves of her figure. And he had seen the animation in her green eyes and the spirit in her smile as she watched her friend's happiness. And he had known, without question, that he had to get near her, if only for a moment.

Then the thought of her standing in front of that same altar and looking at Kingsman the way Ida Mae had looked at Smedley today made something snap inside him. He felt an overpowering combination of angry lust and fierce possessiveness. He *needed* her—her body, her mind, her soul—as he had never needed another woman in his life.

He poured his need into his kiss, relieving one tension and setting up another. He lifted her slightly, allowing different parts of their bodies to rub together in passionate harmony.

Suddenly he realized that Emily was pulling away, pushing against his chest with delicate hands that made not the least impression on his grip of her. He raised his head and looked down into her eyes, which were no longer closed in passion. They were blazing with anger. He let her go.

"How dare you," she said furiously. "We're in a church!"

Austin was having a hard time slowing down his raging senses. He took a long, full breath. "Let's go somewhere else, then," he said, his voice still husky.

Emily had taken a full step back. "I'm not going anywhere with you. I'm engaged to Dexter. In one more week I'll be a married woman."

"There's no way," Austin said slowly, "that you can kiss me like that, and be in love with another man."

Emily bit her lip. "Dexter and I are a perfect match. Everyone says so. We'll have a wonderful future together... if you'll just *stay away from me.*"

Her voice was shaky and pleading. Austin's heart tightened in his chest. She was right. It was exactly what he had told himself time and again over the past few days. She would have a good life with Kingsman, and the decent thing for him to do was to leave her alone.

He dropped his arms and looked down at the floor. "I'm sorry. If you're sure that this is what you want, I won't bother you anymore."

Emily felt again the feeling she had had over the past few days—as if she couldn't get enough air. He was no more than two feet from her, his broad chest blocking the light from the back windows. "That's what I want," she said in a choked whisper.

He lifted his eyes and looked straight into hers for a long moment. Then he nodded, turned on his heel and was gone.

The party was already in full swing by the time Emily arrived. She had walked slowly and taken the long route to give herself time to recover. She would have preferred to go directly back to her room, but she couldn't disappoint Ida Mae. Dexter came up to her the minute she arrived.

"Where have you been? I was just about to go back to the church looking for you."

"I'm sorry. I stayed at the church for a while saying a little prayer for Ida Mae's happiness." She hoped the good Lord would forgive such an irreverent lie, but at this point, she didn't really care much one way or the other.

Dexter looked a little surprised at her sudden piety. "Well, you're here now, so let's start celebrating. We can see what it feels like as kind of a rehearsal for next week," he said with a wink.

Emily managed a wan smile and meekly took his arm as he led the way to the punch table. Eldo was standing next to it, surrounded by several other recent grooms. "Where's Ida Mae?" Emily asked.

Eldo twisted his smile into a grimace. "Ah, shucks, Miss Emily. I'm such a danged fool sometimes, and now I've got her all upset."

"Upset?" Emily was taken by surprise. Ida Mae had looked the picture of happiness at the wedding ceremony.

Eldo adjusted the starched collar of his brand new shirt. "I was so excited when Rev. Hardy said 'husband and wife' that I forgot the part about kissin' the bride."

Emily smiled. "Surely, Eldo, you remedied the error as soon as she reminded you."

"That's just the problem. She didn't tell me what was wrong. We got into Dexter's carriage that was decked out in flowers, all elegant as you please, and she wouldn't say a word till we got here to the restaurant. Then she said somethin' about how's I didn't kiss her and she was going to go back to her room and get some kind of cream so I would think she was beautiful again."

Emily shook her head. "Poor Ida Mae, I'd better go look for her."

"I swear, Miss Emily, if I'd thought she was any more beautiful, we'd've never made it over here to the party."

Emily reached over and patted his arm. "I know. Don't worry about it, Eldo. I'll bring her back."

With a short explanation to Dexter, she left the restaurant and went to the hotel in search of Ida Mae. She had a certain sympathy with Ida Mae's obsession with her beauty cream. After all, Emily herself felt more confident when she had her faithful almond paste to

cover up her freckles. But she had to convince her
friend that Eldo's love had nothing to do with any silly
cream. For one thing, what would she do when she ran
out...go back to Panama? And for another, it was
insanity to go through life making yourself sniffle and
sneeze just for the sake of beauty.

She had her speech nicely rehearsed by the time she
reached her room. But when she opened the door, the
room was empty. She walked across the room and saw
that the cream was still in the wastebasket where Emily herself had thrown it before the ceremony. Ida Mae
had evidently not been here. Surely she wouldn't have
been so upset that she ran off somewhere, Emily
thought. But she began to feel worry gnawing at the pit
of her stomach, similar to the feelings she had had
when the opera house ghost was still at large.

Perhaps Ida Mae had changed her mind and gone
back to the party. Emily half ran down the long hotel
stairs and across the street toward the restaurant. The
closer she came, the more she became afraid that
something had gone terribly wrong. By the time she
reached the reception, she was out of breath and agi-
tated.

She went directly to Eldo. "Has Ida Mae come back?
Have you seen her?" she gasped.

Eldo froze, his punch glass halfway to his mouth.
"What's wrong?" His normally florid face went pale
and his sideburns twitched.

"She's not at the hotel. I don't think she ever went
back there."

Dexter walked over to put an arm around Emily's
shoulders. "My dear, what's the matter? You need to
calm yourself."

Emily turned to him. Dexter would be the best person to take charge. Poor Eldo looked as if he were about to crumble into pieces. "Ida Mae's missing. We don't know what's happened to her."

Dexter gave Eldo a friendly shove. "What did you do to the poor girl, Smedley?" he asked with a smile. "Don't you know these are delicately bred New Englanders? You have to go easy on 'em."

Eldo shook his head vehemently. "I didn't do anything, honest."

Dexter turned back to Emily. "She probably just needed a little time to herself. Some women are that way, you know. They take these things hard."

Emily had caught her breath enough to feel anger building at Dexter's nonchalance. What did he know about women, anyway? Ida Mae might have some insecurities, just like everyone else, but she wasn't about to miss her own wedding party.

"Something must have happened to her," she said firmly. "Maybe she's been kidnapped."

"By another one of your ghosts, I suppose." Dexter meant his comment to be funny, but to Emily it sounded like sheer male arrogance.

"Well, there *was* a 'ghost.'"

"Yes, a poor old drunk trying to get some attention. And he's now safely out of the way enjoying the hospitality of Sheriff Cutler."

"Are we sure he's still in jail?" Emily asked, looking around at the group that was beginning to gather. Several heads nodded.

"Well, we need to send out a search party...or something," she said urgently.

Dexter leaned over and dropped a kiss on the top of her head. "She'll be back, Emily. Just give the girl some time to herself."

Again a number of male heads in the group surrounding her nodded their agreement. Emily looked at Eldo, whose white face had turned to a kind of gray. "Well, *I* am going to go look for her," she snapped.

Dexter smiled indulgently. "Why don't you try down by the millpond? She probably wanted to take a little air. And tell her she'd better get back here in a hurry or the food will all be gone."

Ida Mae had simply vanished. Emily had gone back to the hotel and searched the restaurant, the lobby and their room again. She'd thought about trying in some of the other rooms, but all the brides who still lived at the hotel had been at the wedding ceremony, so Ida Mae wouldn't be visiting any of them. She'd checked over at the opera house, then walked all the way around the millpond, as Dexter had suggested, and down the path to the cemetery, calling Ida Mae's name along the way. There was just no sign of her.

She couldn't have ridden out of town. Ida Mae had refused all Emily's offers to teach her to ride horseback. But just so that she hadn't missed any possibilities, Emily walked back to the hotel livery.

"Homer, have you seen Miss Sprague today?" she asked the stable boy.

His eyes shot open as they always did when Emily came around. "Here in the stables, you mean? She don't usually come around here."

"I know, but I can't seem to find her."

"Well, I did see her a bit ago over to the hotel."

"When?"

"A bit ago. She was talkin' to the tanner. You know... Mr. Briggs."

Emily suddenly felt cold all over. Briggs! He had not been at the wedding, of course. According to Ida Mae, he'd been so hostile that Eldo had said he hardly recognized him as the same man who had been his friend for years.

All at once she thought of the dead rabbits. Briggs owned a tannery. Missouri Ike had claimed that he had never seen that bag before that night. Maybe he had been telling the truth. She felt sick to her stomach.

"Thank you," she said hurriedly to a bewildered Homer, then dashed off down the street. She could go back to the party and demand that some of the men go with her to the tannery shop, but that would waste precious time. If it had actually been Briggs who had done those sick things at the opera house, Ida Mae could be in real danger. She shuddered as she remembered the photograph of the two of them smeared with blood. Then she started to run.

Austin came banging through the swinging doors of the Golden Lady and took off his hat, sailing it across the room to land skittering on the polished bar. "Flo!" he hollered.

Jasper and Dixie were behind the bar and looked up in surprise. "Where's Flo?" he asked them angrily. The noise in the room ceased as customers stopped talking to look at the commanding figure of the saloon's owner.

"What's the problem, Austin?" Jasper asked calmly.

Belatedly, Austin realized that he was causing a commotion. He walked across to the bar and lowered his voice. "Nothing, really. I just wanted to talk to Flo."

Jasper's moustache bobbed once. "She's upstairs," he said.

Austin mounted the stairs two at a time. He felt as if there was a devil inside him. He wanted to hit someone ... or get drunk ... or ... Flo would help him cool his head, he told himself. If she couldn't accomplish anything with his head, she could at least help him cool the rest of his body.

He entered her room without bothering to knock. She was seated at her dressing table. Her automatic smile at his entry changed to a frown when she saw his expression. She gave him a wry smile. "Do you want to talk about it?" she said.

Austin flung himself onto her bed, his arms over his head. "No, I don't want to talk."

"Oh." She turned back to her mirror. "What *do* you want, then?"

"Do you have anything to drink up here?" He rolled over and leaned up on one elbow to look at her.

"No. Besides, you've been drinking too much lately."

"Too much for what?"

"For your own good, you big lug." She turned and looked at him, her eyes sympathetic. "Now, come on, why don't you tell Mama Flo all about it?"

"I told you," Austin growled, "I don't feel like talking."

"Then maybe you'd better go on downstairs and look for that drink," Flo said, losing her patience.

They glowered at each other for a moment, then Austin said, "Why don't you come on over here?"

Flo eyed him suspiciously. "Why?"

He grinned nastily. "C'mon over and I'll show you."

"I don't think so," Flo said slowly.

Austin swung his long legs over the side of the bed and sat up. "What d'ya mean? Why not?"

"Because I don't trust your intentions."

"Intentions, hell. They're the same as they've always been."

"No, Austin, lovey," she said softly. "They're not."

"C'mon, Flo," Austin said with a groan. "Don't get complicated on me. I need you."

She shook her red head slowly back and forth. "It's not me you need."

"You'll do," he said flatly.

Flo winced. Cruelty was not usual to Austin's nature. "Look, my friend, a couple of months ago, if you'd snapped your fingers, I'd have come running, but things have changed."

"Changed? What are you talking about?"

Flo looked off into empty space. "I've been doing some har-r-rd thinking lately about what I want to do with the rest of my life."

Austin's eyes widened. "Is it Jasper?"

For the first time since he met her, Flo blushed. "I've accepted his proposal."

Austin was dumbfounded. "Of *marriage?*"

Flo laughed. "Well, there's not much more he could propose at this point."

"But I thought you said...weren't you the one who said that people like us didn't get married?"

Flo stood and walked over to sit next to him on the bed. "Yeah, well, I'd sung that tune so long that I'd begun to believe it myself, but you know what was the real crux of the matter? I was afraid."

Austin reached out and tweaked one of her red curls. "You've never been afraid of anything in your life, you stubborn Scot."

Flo nodded seriously. "Yes, I was. Afraid of getting hurt, afraid of risking it all and losing. The same things you're afraid of, Austin Matthews."

Austin was silent for several moments. "Are you sure this is what you want?" he asked.

"Of course I'm not sure. Who's ever sure in this life? But it feels right. And then..." She blushed again, a bright red that clashed with her hair, and cleared her throat. "And then that Jasper can be pretty persuasive."

Austin grinned. "The old goat. I ought to fire him."

"I'd just hire him back. We're partners, remember?"

The tension was gone and they sat side by side comfortably, immersed in their own thoughts. "So when is the momentous occasion?" Austin said finally.

"We haven't set the date yet. But Jasper says the sooner the better."

Austin shook his head. "It appears that every damn soul in Seattle is getting married."

"It's something to think about," Flo said with a sideways look.

Once again Austin brushed away her insinuations. "So I guess this means I'm out of luck tonight?" he asked with another engaging grin.

"Unless you want Jasper polishing up that new Colt revolver of his."

Austin laughed. "It is definitely not my lucky day." Then he grew serious. "I'm real happy for you both. I mean it, Flo."

She leaned over and kissed his cheek. "I know you do. And I'll tell you, even though that little rascal has somehow gotten hold of my heart, it did give me some pangs to turn down your offer a few minutes ago."

"I can make it again," Austin teased.

Flo gave him a little push. "Go on, get out of here, before I regret my decision."

Austin stood. "What changed your mind?" he asked.

She looked puzzled.

"About not being the marrying kind."

"I guess I'm getting smart in my old age." She looked down at the carpet for a minute. "Seriously, I woke up one day and said to myself, 'If this man can give me everything I want, why should I keep hopping from one bed to the next?'"

Austin nodded. "You made a good choice. Jasper's crazy about you. He'll worship you till the day he dies."

"You know," Flo said, "you might not be able to understand this, but it wasn't really a choice. It was just *there* . . . like the sun in the morning."

Austin looked at Flo's serene expression. She had a kind of glow about her that he had never seen before. "I think I can understand it, Flo," he said with a bittersweet smile. "In fact, I understand it all too well."

Flo stood and put her arms around him. "Well, I've made my move. Maybe it's time for you to make one for yourself."

He pulled her against him and kissed her full on the lips. "That lucky bastard Jasper had better take darn good care of you . . . or he'll answer to me."

Flo's eyes grew moist. "Go on, then," she said with an affectionate push against his chest. "Get out of here."

With a sigh of regret she watched as his broad frame disappeared through the narrow doorway. "Lordamercy, but the lad is bonny," she said to herself under her breath. "Jasper, my love, you'll never know what I'm givin' up for ye."

The tannery was only three blocks from the hotel on Washington Street. As Emily ran along, the entire area appeared to be deserted. The stores were all shuttered for the night and there were no horses tied to the hitching rails.

The tannery was in the middle of the block. Like the other buildings, it was shuttered and dark. Emily slowed to a walk as she approached. Perhaps Briggs had taken Ida Mae to the little house he had built for himself at the edge of town.

Suddenly, she felt frightened and uncertain. Dusk was gathering, and it felt cooler. What would she do if she found them? With disgust, she realized that she hadn't been using her head. It would be foolish for her to confront Briggs by herself. She would have to go back over to the restaurant and get some help.

She had turned to retrace her steps when she heard a sharp cry. Her stomach plunged and the hair at the back of her neck tingled. It had been a woman's voice, and it had come from the tannery.

Without further thought, she raced up to the door that said in neat block letters, Tannery. Skinning, Cleaning and Curing. The blood pounded in Emily's ears. She tried the latch, and the door opened noiselessly.

She entered with tense caution, then recoiled in horror as she almost stepped on the severed head of a deer that was lying on the floor just inside the door. A purple tongue protruded from its mouth and its eyes were open and glassy. One glance around the dim room showed that it was full of dead animals in various states of processing. There was a strong odor of chemicals and rotten meat.

Dear Lord, she thought, where is Ida Mae? She picked her way across the room, carefully avoiding the animal carcasses. A dingy curtain blocked the room off from another in the back, and as she approached it she heard voices. It was Ida Mae and Briggs.

"I'll make you happy, my darling, I swear I will," Briggs was saying. His voice sounded higher than normal, out of control. Emily edged closer, bumping against a table in the darkness. At the other end a bowl wobbled, then fell to the ground with an echoing crash.

Instantly the curtain was flung aside and Briggs stood in the doorway. His hair stuck out in clumps from behind his ears, and there were dark circles under his eyes. In his right hand he held a derringer. His smile froze Emily in her tracks.

"Ah, Miss Kendall, how nice of you to come." He looked at her oddly, as if he were watching a point above her shoulder. With dreadful clarity, Emily understood that, whatever Mr. Briggs may have been before, he was now a deranged man.

"Thank you," she said carefully, her eyes darting to the gun in his hand. "I'm looking for Ida Mae. Is she here?"

"Of course. Where else would she be?" He gave a little laugh that sounded almost like the quacking of a duck. "Ida Mae and I belong together, you know. I tried to get you to make her see that when I came to see you at the hotel that day. And when you were out riding. But you ran away from me." A vague frown crossed his face. "You ran away from me," he accused her again.

Emily tried to keep her voice steady. "I didn't know it was you, Mr. Briggs. I thought it was someone who wanted to rob me."

The frown disappeared. "It doesn't matter. Ida Mae's mine now."

His eyes glittered insanely. Emily grasped the table next to her for support and fought to speak calmly. "May I see her?"

Briggs turned to look over his shoulder into the room behind him. "She's *mine* now."

Emily swallowed hard. She hadn't heard any further sound from the back room. "Ida Mae!" she called out.

At her shout, Briggs jumped toward her and clamped his arms around her. His grip was like a band of iron around her upper arms. He dragged her with him through the curtain and into the back. Ida Mae was lying lifelessly on a long bench.

"What have you done to her?" Emily cried, and with a desperate wrench, pulled herself free of him. She ran across the room and sank to her knees beside Ida Mae. With utter relief, she could see the gentle rise and fall of her friend's chest. She was alive.

"She doesn't want me," Briggs growled. His voice had once again changed entirely. It was raspy and harsh.

"Mr. Briggs," Emily pleaded, "you've got to stop this. Let us go. Ida Mae was very fond of you, but she had to make a choice—"

Before she could finish Briggs whipped a length of rope from a shelf and roughly started winding it around her. He still held the derringer. It pointed crazily around the room as he coiled the rope, and Emily was terrified that it would go off at any minute.

"You fancy pants eastern ladies think you can come here and lead us on, then stomp all over us, but I'll show you . . . I'll just show everybody." His face was twisted and ugly.

"Please, listen to me." She tried to reason with him once more, but he jerked on one end of the rope, which sent her careering against a wooden cabinet.

"Shut up!" he croaked. "You're coming with me." Pushing her in front of him, he opened the back door to the little alleyway behind the row of shops.

"Where are we going? What about Ida Mae?"

He pushed the cold steel barrel of the derringer painfully into the tender area just under her ear. "One more word and I will blow your head off," he said softly.

In total silence he led her along through deserted back streets until they came to the rear door of the opera house. "Open it," he commanded.

Emily fished the keys from the deep pocket of her skirt and did as he requested. Inside, the back hall was in near total darkness, but Briggs didn't seem to care. He pulled her into the nearest dressing room, then pushed her to the floor. Kneeling beside her, he tied the length of rope around her lower legs and ankles, leaving her trussed like a branded calf. Then he was gone, only to appear in a few minutes carrying a still-unconscious Ida Mae. Without ceremony, he dropped her to the floor beside Emily.

Emily's eyes had grown accustomed to the dark, and she could see that he was no longer holding the pistol, so she ventured to reason with him once more. "Mr. Briggs, why don't we just talk about this. I'm sure something could be worked out...."

His voice grew high again and there was that cackling laugh. "We'll just let the opera ghost take care of you two," he shrieked.

With that, he left the room. The way he had her tied, Emily could only barely wiggle her fingertips. There was no way she could reach the knots that tied her legs. "Ida Mae!" she called in a loud whisper. "You've got to wake up."

There was no response from the dark mass on the floor.

Then, to Emily's horror, she realized the room was filling with the odor of kerosene. Briggs intended to set fire to the place, burning them alive. In desperation she pulled at the ropes around her, but they didn't budge. She stretched herself over to give Ida Mae a nudge with her foot and called her friend's name again. There was no response.

Why hadn't she gone for help before she went to the tannery? she berated herself. Why hadn't she swallowed her pride and found Austin? She would give anything to see him here right now.

It was too dark to see the smoke, but she could smell it, and she could hear the first crackles of the fire. She couldn't believe this was happening to her...that all her high hopes and plans for the future were doomed to end in a blazing inferno set by a madman.

Her eyes smarted and she began to cough. She tried to avoid taking deep breaths, but in just a few seconds, her lungs felt as if they were burning.

"Ida Mae, help me!" she cried desperately. And then, finally, just before the smoke overtook her, she gave one last scream.

"Austin!"

Chapter Sixteen

Austin hesitated, then pulled on the stout iron handle that opened the door to the saloon safe. This was without a doubt the craziest thing he had ever done in his life, he told himself, as he counted out the bills one by one. It didn't make the least bit of sense for a saloon owner and a proper New England lady to hitch up. But as he had listened to Flo talking about finding the one man who could make her happy, he had come to the inescapable conclusion. He had to have Emily, and that was that.

He put the three hundred dollars in his pocket and set off toward the wedding reception with a grim face. It wouldn't be easy. He'd backed away from Emily so many times that he wasn't at all sure that now she would take him. And he'd have Kingsman to contend with. And maybe even Mercer, since he hadn't been among the original bridegrooms. Though he suspected that Asa would be happy enough to see another three hundred dollars coming into his enterprise. Despite the limited success of the first mission, he was already planning another bride-hunting foray back East.

When Austin reached the restaurant, he found several of the men already tipsy from the wedding punch.

He had to shoulder his way through to where Dexter and Eldo were still stationed by the refreshment table. The two of them, at least, appeared to be still sober.

"Where's Emily?" he asked without preamble.

Kingsman and Smedley exchanged glances. "We don't know," Eldo said finally. He wrung his hands and licked his lips nervously.

"What do you mean, you don't know?" Austin asked indignantly.

Dexter stepped in front of Austin and said with authority, "What business is it of yours, anyway, Matthews?"

Austin ignored him and kept his eyes on Smedley. "What's the matter, Eldo? Where is she?"

"Ida Mae took off, Austin, and Emily went to fetch her. But it's been a mighty long time, now, and I don't know where they could've got to."

Austin felt a chill run through his limbs. "You let them go off by themselves ... in the dark?" His voice was low with fury. "Didn't either of you stop to think that we've had a lunatic running around town?"

"Missouri Ike is behind bars," Dexter said. "He's no longer a problem."

Austin fixed his rival with an icy stare. "Ike says he had nothing to do with the incidents at the opera house. And until he's been proven guilty, we can't be sure we have the right man."

Dexter shrugged. "If you ask me, it's some kind of 'woman thing.' They'll be back here any minute."

Austin shook his head in disbelief. "I'm heading over to the opera house. Smedley, you go get the sheriff and tell him that for once he'd better put some grease under his skidders and start looking for those women."

Without another word, he took off, fear propelling him into a dead run. He'd had some questions about the arrest of Missouri Ike since the night he caught him, and now his doubts were blossoming into a certainty. There was no way that Emily and Ida Mae would simply disappear from the wedding party, unless something dire had happened to them.

He could see the flames licking the black sky from half a block away. His heart hammered heavily in both ears, and he raced until he felt as if his chest would burst open. There was no sign of anyone around the opera house. The front door was engulfed in fire. Dear God, don't let it be too late, he prayed silently.

He sprinted around the back. The door was open, and the blackness inside showed that the blaze had not yet reached this area. Just as he cleared the three back stairs in a giant leap, he heard a voice screaming his name. With unutterable relief, he realized that the voice belonged to Emily.

Once inside, the heat roared at him like a fully stoked forge. It was totally black, but he made his way through instinct and terror in the direction of the sound he had heard. It had come from the middle dressing room. The door was shut. He didn't even attempt to find the handle, but instead sent it splintering open with a strong kick. "Emily!" he called, choking on the thick smoke.

There was no reply. He began to grope straight along the floor. Just a few feet from the door, he found her. She was bound from head to toe with stout rope, but she was breathing. For just a moment he hugged her to him, then he picked her up in his arms and made his way unerringly out of the building.

Dexter and Smedley were waiting outside with several of the other men who had been at the reception. Lanterns had been brought, and some of the men were attempting to set up a bucket brigade from the mill-pond.

Dexter ran up and reached for Emily. Austin began to refuse to give her up, but changed his mind when he saw Eldo behind Dexter, his face white and terrified. "Ida Mae," the hapless bridegroom wailed as great tears rolled down his cheek.

Austin dumped Emily's inert form into Dexter's arms. "I'm going back for her," he yelled.

Once more he made his way through the smoky blackness, the fire sounding curiously like the roaring of water all around him. The heat was getting too intense to stand. Fortunately, he found her immediately. He stumbled with her out of the building, the smoke starting to sear his lungs and blur his eyes.

By now most of the people in town had gathered in a ring around the outside of the building. Several people came to help him with Ida Mae. Coughing and unsteady, Austin relinquished her gratefully and looked around for Emily. She was on the ground, still apparently unconscious, and Dexter was holding her in his arms.

Austin took a moment to take some deep breaths of fresh air. His throat burned all the way down to his stomach. He took a step back and looked up at the opera house. The flames had reached the roof.

"What in the world happened here?" Ethan Witherspoon came to stand next to Austin. He had been the organizer of the bucket brigade, but one by one the participants were giving up. Their bucketfuls of water were having as much effect as a sulphur match in a maelstrom.

Austin shook his head in answer to Ethan's question. Suddenly there was a moan from Ida Mae. "It was Briggs," she said groggily. "I think he's still inside."

Ethan and Austin looked at each other. Briggs, the tanner. Briggs, who had so uncharitably made the life of his best friend and Ida Mae miserable over the past while. Austin had always disliked the man, but he never would have suspected him of all this. Nevertheless, he was a human being, and if someone didn't get him out of there, he'd burn to death.

"It's too intense to go back in," Ethan said finally.

"We can't just let him die," Austin insisted, his voice husky from the smoke.

"But he set the fire in the first place," Ethan argued. "And anyway, we wouldn't know where to start looking for him inside there."

Austin looked back over at Emily. Dexter had lifted her to his lap and was bathing her face with a towel. "I'm going in," Austin said, and before anyone could stop him, he jumped to the top of the stairs and disappeared into the burning building.

He headed back toward the dressing room where he had found the two women, but suddenly, above the roar of the fire, he could hear a maniacal laugh. It seemed to come from the area of the stage. He felt his way along the wall until he reached the curtained door that led backstage. Pulling it aside, he could see the theater itself, brightly illuminated with dancing flames of brilliant colors. The laughter continued, giving Austin a chill in the midst of the raging heat.

He strained his stinging eyes to see through the smoke. Suddenly there was a flash of brightness, and a glowing red ceiling beam came crashing toward him.

Austin awoke with a jerk, and the sudden movement of his head made lights swim in the back of his eyes. He sank down into the pillow with a groan. A wave of nausea hit his stomach, then subsided, and slowly he opened his eyes once more.

He was in his own bed in his room at the Golden Lady. He focused on the shaving stand across the room. It was tilted at a crazy angle, then slowly became upright as he straightened his head. Gradually the room started making sense.

He lifted his hand to his head. There was a bandage wrapped around it, and his left temple hurt when he rubbed against it.

The last thing he remembered was the beam falling toward him. It must have hit him with a good-enough wallop to knock him senseless. He looked out the window. It was daylight. He'd been out all night.

He tried once more to raise his head, but the dizziness and the nausea started again immediately. He'd just lie still a couple more minutes, he decided, and then go and find out what had happened, see if everyone was all right.

The door to the room opened and Flo's bright red head peeked around the corner. "About time you woke up," she said with a brusque voice that masked the emotion underneath. She pushed the door open and entered the room.

"Is it morning?" Austin asked, surprised at first to hear his own voice functioning normally.

"It's afternoon. You've been out like a wet camp-fire for more than twelve hours."

"How'd I get here?"

"Ethan Witherspoon and two of his men dragged you out of there before the whole blazing building fell in, you blasted idiot."

Austin gave a weak grin. "It's nice to know you care."

"The very idea of going back into that thing to rescue a crazy man," she said indignantly.

"Did they get Briggs out?" Austin asked, sobering.

Flo shook her head gravely. "Poor crazy fool."

"What about Emily?" Austin's stomach tightened with tension.

"She's fine... she and the Sprague girl, both. Just a little shook up. They went through some pretty harrowing moments."

"She was unconscious...."

Flo nodded. "Kingsman took her back to his place and got the doc right away. He said it was just the smoke. She'll be fine."

Austin's head throbbed at the mention of the mill owner's name. Of course, Emily was with Dexter, he told himself. Where else would she be? She certainly wouldn't have come back to the Golden Lady with him. That wouldn't be proper for Miss Emily Kendall. He wondered if she'd even thought to ask about his condition after he'd saved her life. But he wasn't going to bring it up with Flo. Last night he'd been ready to forget all his resolutions and embark upon a future he had never before imagined for himself. But maybe that piece of wood had knocked enough sense into him so that now he would know to stay where he belonged.

He reached into the pocket of his vest. The three hundred dollars were still there. And Emily was with Kingsman. He should be relieved, he told himself.

"So how're you feeling?" Flo asked gently. She walked over to the bed and laid a cool hand on his forehead.

"I've had clearer heads after an all-night bender," he said with a wince.

"The doc says you'll live."

"The doc was here?"

"Yup. Your Miss Kendall insisted on it."

"Emily?"

"Did that knock on the head affect your hearing or something?" Flo asked testily.

Austin blinked and tried to make some sense out of Flo's statement. "So Emily sent the doc over from Kingsman's?"

"Nope. She *brought* the doc over from Kingsman's."

Austin sat up, ignoring the throb in his head. "She was here?"

Flo gave an exaggerated sigh. "Just hang on, lover boy. The doc says you're not to move around too fast for a while. I made your girlfriend go lie down a few minutes ago. She was up all night sitting alongside you."

Flo turned and was out the door, leaving Austin looking after her in disbelief. He couldn't tell if it was the blow to his head, but his world had suddenly seemed to turn on its axis.

In a minute the door opened and Emily entered. Austin's mouth dropped open. She was wearing one of Dixie's dresses, a gaudy, bright orange silk that just barely covered the tips of her full breasts.

She walked slowly toward the bed, a half smile on her face. Her hair was down around her shoulders, glowing gold in the afternoon sun. The sleepless night had shadowed the delicate lines of her cheeks. Her green eyes looked enormous. Austin tried to speak, but discovered that his mouth had gone completely dry.

"How are you feeling?" she asked in a low voice. She stopped a couple of feet from the bed.

He swallowed. "I'm fine . . . just a little dizzy. What about you?"

Emily smiled. "I'm alive. Thanks to you."

"Pleased to be of service, ma'am," he said, trying to make his voice light.

She took a step closer and her smile died. "It looks like this time you made a bad investment, partner. The Seattle Opera House is no more."

Her chin went up in that stubborn expression Austin had come to know, but he could read the pain behind her statement. His eyes filled with sympathy. "We'll rebuild," he said staunchly.

She blinked several times and gave a stiff nod. "I was hoping you'd say that."

They both smiled. "And is our other partner all right?" Austin asked.

"Ida Mae's doing fine. Of course, it was a horrible thing for her . . . and on her wedding night. Eldo is beside himself over Briggs, but he's grateful that Ida Mae wasn't hurt."

Austin shook his head. "The mind is a funny thing. Maybe someday they'll find out why a person could get so obsessed like that."

Emily shivered. "My skin crawls when I remember. It was horrible in his shop . . . all those dead animals."

"It's over with now, Emily," he said gently, reaching out a hand to her. "Briggs is dead, and the new opera house we're going to build will be free of ghosts of any kind."

Emily took his hand and let him draw her against the bed.

"They said you came looking for me last night," she said.

"Ah . . . yeah."

She waited a moment for him to continue, then, at his silence, finally asked. "So, what did you want with me?"

Austin shifted on the bed and the three hundred dollars crinkled in his pocket. To his ears it sounded as loud as a steam locomotive. "I wanted to talk with you."

"What about?"

Austin pulled himself further up against the headboard of the bed. He didn't like speaking from below her. It put him at a disadvantage.

He changed the subject. "What in tarnation are you doing here, Emily?" he asked angrily. "I thought Kingsman was taking care of you. And why are you wearing that . . ." He gestured toward the general area where the dancehall dress was showing some of her best attributes.

Emily looked down at herself. "Don't you like it?" she asked innocently.

"You look . . ." Austin sputtered, "You look cold."

Emily laughed and plopped down on the bed next to him. "Dexter and I have reached a sort of understanding."

Austin's head banged against the headboard as he backed away from her. "An understanding?"

"Yes. He's agreed not to put up any further opposition to my attempts to develop an opera house for Seattle."

Austin's body stiffened and his reply was cold. "Good for him."

"And I've agreed not to saddle him with a wife who would never settle down enough to make him happy." She smiled and edged closer to him on the bed.

"You're not going to marry him?"

She shook her head. "And as for my attire," she continued with an impish grin, "it's a very kind loan from Dixie. After the wedding I was going to move back into the opera house. I'd already taken all my clothes over there. They're all gone—every last dress."

She looked down at her dress and then back at Austin. Her smile was sheer seduction. He tried to keep his eyes from the creamy expanse of white skin scattered with freckles. "Couldn't you get something from Ida Mae? Something more..."

"Proper?" Emily supplied. She turned her face into a frown and spoke in a deep voice. "'Proper is a relative term, Miss Kendall. You're not in Massachusetts anymore.'"

Austin colored. "I just meant—"

Emily eased closer to him on the bed. Her dress rustled and smelled of perfume. Her neck looked incredibly white against the bright orange silk. "What was it you wanted to talk with me about last night, Austin?" Emily asked again, her voice low and husky.

A wave of dizziness struck Austin's head and continued right on down through the rest of him. One of her hands was on his leg. The other took his hand and placed it gently on her chest, just where the orange dress skirted the bounds of decency. Almost without realizing it, he slipped his hand under the silk to find the perfect smoothness of her breast.

Silk against wool, they came together. In the plain light of day the orange dress was slipped down to Emily's waist while Austin lavished her breasts with greedy caresses.

Then he pulled himself up to find her mouth. "I thought I would go crazy when I realized you were in the fire," he said brokenly.

Emily blinked away the stinging of her tears. "When they told me you were hurt and unconscious, I felt as if someone had stepped on my heart."

"Well, I'm just fine now," he reassured her, and sought to prove it with a kiss that started gently, but soon had them seeking each other with impatient insistence. Too needy to wait for further disrobing, they formed a curious tangle of bodies and clothes.

Emily found his hardness inside his trousers, while he pushed aside yards of petticoat to focus his skillful manipulations on her aching core. They joined quickly, with a kind of desperate harmony that peaked with shattering force.

Austin dropped his head back on the pillow in utterly satisfied exhaustion. Emily pulled up the front of her dress and tucked her face into his shoulder, embarrassed by her own boldness.

It was several minutes before either spoke. "The fire didn't finish me off, so you decided that you'd do it yourself?" Austin asked teasingly.

Emily raised her head. Her cheeks were flushed from the afterglow of their climax. "That was amazing. I'm not sure if I know exactly what happened," she said with the combination of frankness and naiveté that had first captured Austin's heart.

He chuckled and tipped her chin up so that he could look into her eyes. "Do you want to run through it again?"

Emily gave a little puff. "I thought you were supposed to be resting."

Austin gestured to his own prone form. "I am resting. I haven't been out of bed."

Slowly regaining her senses, Emily shook her head in reproof. "No, really. Let me get up. I shouldn't be here like this with you."

He pulled her on top of him and moved sinuously underneath her. "And I intend to stay in bed all afternoon," he said with a wicked smile.

He looked devilish and sexy and thoroughly healthy. Emily couldn't help smiling back. She gave up her struggle to leave and let her body harden again at the feel of him moving against her. She settled back against him, her silken dress sliding smoothly against the fine wool of his trousers and vest. At her movements, there was a rustling of paper, and Austin reached guiltily toward the inside pocket of his vest.

Emily pulled away. "What is it?"

Austin withdrew his hand. "Nothing," he said quickly. Then, more reflectively, he changed his story. "Well, go ahead and look if you must."

Emily reached her small hand inside his vest and pulled out the wad of bills. "It's just money," she said, losing interest.

Austin smiled. "Count it."

Emily looked puzzled. "Why?"

"Just count it."

Before she had reached the three-hundred-dollar total, Emily had guessed the purpose of the cash. It wasn't the most romantic proposal, she supposed, but she was too happy to quibble. Still, she wanted to hear the words. "There must be, oh, nearly three hundred dollars here," she said nonchalantly.

"Pretty near," Austin replied, his smile growing broader.

"A man could buy a lot of things with three hundred dollars."

Austin's hands were again running up and down her back. "I imagine so," he said.

"Did you have any special plans for it?"

"Oh, I don't know." The orange dress was once again down around her waist.

Emily was tired of the game. She pounded hard on his chest. "Austin Matthews!" she complained.

Suddenly the dress was completely unfastened and was being stripped from her entirely. "I thought I might buy myself a woman," he said softly.

Emily pulled away and eyed him indignantly. "I've been told that the going rate in your establishment is *three* dollars, not three hundred."

Austin took a deep breath. "All right. Not a woman. I thought I might buy myself a *bride*."

"Now that," said Emily as she sank back down into his arms, "sounds more like it."

Epilogue

Dear Joseph Junior, Donald and Steven

You boys must be getting so big by now! Do you even remember your Aunt Em who went West searching for adventure? Your mama will show you a photograph of me when she reads you this letter. It was taken on my wedding day. You may recognize Ida Mae Sprague, who is now Ida Mae Smedley. And the other pretty ladies in the picture are new friends of mine. Their dresses are certainly different from those the ladies wear back in Lowell, aren't they? I'm writing to you, my dear nephews, to tell you that soon you will have a new little cousin out here in Washington Territory. Though you are very far away, perhaps one day when you grow up, you will cross the country and see this wonderful new land for yourselves . . .

Emily looked back in surprise as two arms wrapped themselves gently around her bulging middle.

"I thought I told you to stay back at the house and take a nap," Austin said in a low voice.

"As soon as Ethan finishes with the side stage curtains." Her long lashes batted at him coaxingly.

Austin spun her around in his arms and bent to kiss her, lifting her against himself as best he could with the encumbrance of her oversized stomach. His kiss was every bit as passionate as the first time they had made love. He gave a little groan as he pulled away. "It's not going to be much longer now, is it?"

Emily's face was flushed. "I'm hoping the baby will hold off until after the Flaherty Family Singers arrive."

Austin gave a sigh of impatience. "Next week?"

Emily nodded. "They arrive on Wednesday."

"Emily, my love, you're going to have to let me handle this concert. Ida Mae can help me out." Austin gestured toward the front of her dress. "It's just not proper—"

Emily lifted an eyebrow, and Austin changed his words. "It's too much for you right now."

"I want to be here, Austin. We've worked too hard getting the new opera house ready. Besides, Mr. O'Brien, Mr. O'Donnell and Mr. O'Leary have been hanging around all week, because they heard that a family of seven singing Irish colleens was due in any day. Someone needs to keep them under control. This time around, I'm determined that *nothing* is going to spoil the performance."

Austin gave a good-natured smile. "I'd stake you against three fightin' Irishmen any day, Speckles Kendall Matthews."

"So you'll let me keep working awhile longer?"

Austin took a deep breath. "My son is going to be the first baby in Seattle ever born on a stage," he said dryly.

"Or daughter," Emily agreed pleasantly.

Austin took a step backward and eyed Emily with mock alarm. "Daughter! You think I could put up with *two* of you?"

"You'll have little choice," Emily said without sympathy. "We're your family. We belong to you."

Austin moved to take her in his arms again and bent for a thoroughly possessive kiss. "Yes, you are, my love," he murmured. "And don't you ever forget it."

* * * * *

Author's Note

The arrival of the shipload of "Mercer's Belles" in 1866 was a delightful chapter in the history of Washington Territory. Though the trip itself is well documented, it can only be imagined what chaos must have ensued when these forty-six New England-bred ladies stepped off the boat in the wild and woolly frontier town of Seattle.

The method Asa Mercer used to pacify the nearly three hundred prospective bridegrooms when they discovered that only forty-six women had arrived is lost to the ages. But the ingenious and enterprising Mercer stayed on to become a respected member of the community, and even managed to marry one of the brides himself!

Samuel Clemens's fame was just beginning to build during his San Francisco years. Using the pseudonym Mark Twain, his tales of the mining camps and his accounts of his trip to the Hawaiian Islands, which were then called the Sandwich Islands, made him an extremely popular lecturer, though he preferred the term "storyteller." At about the time of this story, he was sent by his newspaper to Europe, from where he would write *Innocents Abroad* and go on to world-wide fame.

There is no record of a visit to Seattle, but I would like to think that if the remarkable Mr. Clemens had known of the tenacious efforts of Emily Kendall to establish herself and her opera house in that frontier town, he would have been happy to make an appearance.

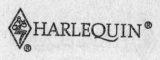

THE VENGEFUL GROOM
Sara Wood

Legend has it that those married in Eternity's chapel are destined for a lifetime of happiness. But happiness isn't what Giovanni wants from marriage—it's revenge!

Ten years ago, Tina's testimony sent Gio to prison—for a crime he didn't commit. *Now* he's back in Eternity and looking for a bride. *Now* Tina is about to learn just how ruthless and disturbingly sensual Gio's brand of vengeance can be.

THE VENGEFUL GROOM, available in October from Harlequin Presents, is the fifth book in Harlequin's new cross-line series, **WEDDINGS, INC.** Be sure to look for the sixth book, **EDGE OF ETERNITY,** by Jasmine Cresswell (Harlequin Intrigue #298), coming in November.

HARLEQUIN®

Georgina Devon

brings the past alive with

Untamed Heart

One of the most sensual Regencies ever published by Harlequin.

Lord Alaistair St. Simon has inadvertently caused the death of the young Baron Stone. Seeking to make amends, he offers his protection to the baron's sister, Liza. Unfortunately, Liza is not the grateful bride he was expecting.

St. Simon's good intentions set off a story of revenge, betrayal and consuming desire.

Don't miss it!

Coming in October 1994,
wherever Harlequin books are sold.

DESTINY'S WOMEN
Trilogy

The DESTINY'S WOMEN TRILOGY by Merline Lovelace is sexy historical romance at its best! The plots thicken and the temperatures rise with each page of her books. A fresh new voice in historical romance, Merline has already begun to lure readers with her exciting, bold storytelling. In ALENA, #220, May 1994, Roman Britain exploded with passion. In SWEET SONG OF LOVE, #230, July 1994, love blossomed amid the rich pageantry of the Middle Ages.

Now, in September, look for SIREN'S CALL, #236, the final book in the DESTINY'S WOMEN TRILOGY. Set in Ancient Greece, passion and betrayal collide when a dashing Athenian sea captain finds his life turned upside down by the stubborn Spartan woman he carries off.

Available wherever Harlequin books are sold.

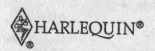

Fifty red-blooded, white-hot, true-blue hunks
from every State in the Union!

Look for MEN MADE IN AMERICA! Written by some of
our most popular authors, these stories feature fifty of
the strongest, sexiest men, each from a different state in
the union!

Two titles available every month at your favorite
retail outlet.

In September, look for:

WINTER LADY by Janet Joyce (Minnesota)
AFTER THE STORM by Rebecca Flanders (Mississippi)

In October, look for:

CHOICES by Annette Broadrick (Missouri)
PART OF THE BARGAIN by Linda Lael Miller (Montana)

You won't be able to resist MEN MADE IN AMERICA!

1994 MISTLETOE MARRIAGES
HISTORICAL CHRISTMAS STORIES

With a twinkle of lights and a flurry of snowflakes, Harlequin Historicals presents *Mistletoe Marriages,* a collection of four of the most magical stories by your favorite historical authors. The perfect way to celebrate the season!

Brimming with romance and good cheer, these heartwarming stories will be available in November wherever Harlequin books are sold.

RENDEZVOUS by Elaine Barbieri
THE WOLF AND THE LAMB by Kathleen Eagle
CHRISTMAS IN THE VALLEY by Margaret Moore
KEEPING CHRISTMAS by Patricia Gardner Evans

Add a touch of romance to your holiday with *Mistletoe Marriages* Christmas Stories!

HARLEQUIN®

MMXS94